Essex Poison

THE COUNTY GUIDES

Ian Sansom

W F HOWES LTD

This large print edition published in 2018 by
W F Howes Ltd
Unit 5, St George's House, Rearsby Business Park,
Gaddesby Lane, Rearsby, Leicester LE7 4YH

1 3 5 7 9 10 8 6 4 2

First published in the United Kingdom in 2017
by 4th Estate

A CIP catalogue record for this book is available
from the British Library

ISBN 978 1 51008 963 1

Typeset by Palimpsest Book Production Limited,
Falkirk, Stirlingshire

Printed and bound by
T   ̇
Printforce   lands

To Trinity

I come not from Heaven but from Essex.

WILLIAM MORRIS,
A Dream of John Ball (1888)

CHAPTER 1

LONDON, UNDERGROUND

Berrak the Turk was busy smoking narghile and reading the newspaper while simultaneously dispensing hot sweet mint tea from the tarnished silver urn perched on the edge of the counter. He was dressed as always in a wrinkled white shirt and was seated on the long, low lumpy leather sofa that served as his office and command centre, old newspapers and his dictionary piled beside him, an enamel bowl of sugar cubes and bright green mint leaves close to hand. The wall behind him was exposed brick, painted a mottled pale blue, presumably intended to resemble a clear summer day. But the wall oozed and trickled silently with damp, making it look rather more like a mourning sky in autumn. The dusty bookcase beside the desk was piled high with worn and ragged towels and beneath the hiss and glare of the crooked gas chandelier hung a stained board marked with prices: the prices never changed and bore no resemblance to what you paid. The gramophone was playing a scratchy '78 of classical classics, the same record that was always playing, ever since I had been coming; there was no other record. Rachmaninoff's Prelude in C-sharp minor; even I knew that the second movement of Mozart's Piano Concerto No. 20 was about to follow. I wondered if Berrak ever grew tired of it. He showed no signs of doing so.

'*Selam! Selam*! Mr Sefton, you are back. You have returned! *Nasilisiniz*? We haven't seen you for so long.'

I had been away with Morley and Miriam in Westmorland, where things, it must be admitted, had not gone entirely to plan. For every good memory from those years there is always something else, something that can't be avoided or denied: some death or disaster, some terrible discovery or disappointment. I'd learned in Spain that dread and despair are constant companions to adventure and during my time with Morley, for all its good, it often felt as though I were somehow being buried alive in yet more bad memories and that there was no escape. I had to do everything and anything to help me breathe.

'Mr Sefton!' continued Berrak. 'It is very good to see you. Very very good.' He shook me warmly by the hand. At least Berrak never changed. 'My uncle was asking about you.' He offered me tea. 'Smoke?' I declined both the tea and the smoke. 'Uncle will be pleased.'

Berrak's uncle was not his actual uncle. He may well have had a dozen actual uncles back home in Turkey but his English uncle was a Mr Klein, the owner of the Russian Turkish Baths and

Berrak's employer. I had met Klein on a number of occasions. We'd got on well. He was an educated man – neither Russian nor Turkish nor indeed English but from Poland, via Hackney – tiny, barely feet five tall, and fascinated by literature and by art, and with almost as many opinions as he had business interests. Klein made and sold his own rouges and fragrances ('Klein's Perspiration-Proof Make-Up'), he made and sold wigs (formed of real human hair), he ran a chain of haberdashers and hairdressers (patronised by the stars of British cinema), he rented properties and owned part shares in cinemas (including the beautiful old Capitol cinema in Winchmore Hill), he sold furs and jewellery, and he had the baths. He was a businessman in the very broadest sense. When I had first returned from Spain he had been kind enough to offer me work in the import and export branch of one of the businesses based down at St Katharine Docks, but I had been unable to take him up on the offer – not being in a fit state at the time to do anything but patronise his baths and go drinking. Sometimes I wondered what my life might have become if I had thrown in my lot with Mr Klein rather than with Morley. Things might have worked out better – or maybe not. Different, certainly.

'It is very delighted to see you, Mr Sefton,' said Berrak. He was paid to make people feel welcome, of course, but, nonetheless, he was good at his job. 'We are all very glad to see you! I will tell

Mr Klein you were here. Immediately, hereupon and in a jiffy.'

I had known Berrak for two or three years. I knew nothing about him except that he was a keen student of the English language and was always eager to try out the new words that he learned from his dictionary and from the newspapers.

'Some people came here asking for you.'

'When?'

'Today. Yesterday. The foretimes.'

'Did they say who they were?'

'They said they were your friends.'

'I see. What did they look like?'

Berrak shrugged his shoulders. The narghile didn't only contain tobacco.

'Was it a man and a woman?'

Berrak shrugged again. He could be intolerably vague, as well as unconditionally welcoming; perhaps the two things were related. He was in many ways the perfect doorman and receptionist, though one wouldn't want to have relied on him as a witness. I paid my money and he handed me a greasy metal token and a threadbare towel that had perhaps once been royal blue but which was now a very definite shade of grey.

I went to Klein's Russian Turkish Baths not to get clean – there were plenty of places in London you could go to get clean. (Probably the best baths in those days were on Grange Road in Bermondsey, a palace in marble and stone, but they were always crowded with women doing their washing and

4

children in the swimming baths.) I went to Klein's, and to the old Ironmonger Row Baths, and one or two other places in Soho that offered other services, for the same reason in those years that I went to bars and to pubs, and to bottle parties: to escape.

The effect of entering Klein's was profound and instantaneous. You walked down the corridor away from the reception and into a world that was warmer, hazier and altogether more pleasant than that which you left behind – the effect of heat and damp, of low lights and lowered voices. A few Moorish-style lanterns on the wall lit the way to the changing room.

I undressed and showered: you always showered before bathing. The rusty spigots that served as showerheads spat out a trickle of warm water that ran into a gutter that circled the room like a castle moat, and which was always almost-but-not-quite full to overflowing with a foaming tide of suds. Berrak probably needed to spend less time smoking narghile and more time slopping out, but then again this was all a part of the charm of the place. Klein's was neither a true Turkish hamam nor a Russian banya: it was a step down and away from the city into the secret and endless comforts of the River Lethe and the waters of forgetfulness. Some people said that the water was diverted from the River Fleet itself. It was London, underground.

Leaving the changing room, I walked down more

slippery stone steps and through and along another corridor, inhaling the rich, thick damp vapour as I went. Pipes overhead hummed and belched and rattled with steam. It was as though the building were alive, an actual being, welcoming you and embracing you. I felt my shoulders relaxing and my chest expanding with every breath. I had spent the evening gambling and drinking – gin, cheap white wine, and whatever else I could get hold of. I was feeling pretty tight.

The corridor led to a tiny pool not much larger than a water tank, which you climbed up and into via stepladders. There was nothing down here – ten, twenty feet beneath High Holborn – but darkness and the sound of running water. Set around the pool was a series of steam rooms of varying heat, set aside for various activities. Mixed bathing was permitted at Klein's, but I never once saw a woman there. It was a place for men to be men – and to forget to be men.

I had paid Berrak for the masseur, a tough little Lascar who everyone called Darjeeling, though of course that can't possibly have been his name. I'm rather ashamed now to admit that I never bothered to ask him what he was really called. He had permanent quarters established in one of the cooler steam rooms. I knocked, stepped in and handed him my token. As was his custom he immediately set to work without a single word.

The Darjeeling Room, as everyone called it, always smelled the same: of sweat, cheese and tobacco. It was a place where time stood still and where Darjeeling practised the ancient arts that he may have learned in India, or in the navy, or perhaps indeed from a book like *Morley's Scientific Massage: Principles and Techniques* (1922), in which Morley recommends the vigorous application of talcum, vaseline and lanolin, not only for the purposes of improving muscle tone and relieving pain, but also in order to 'align the body's organs and to release the natural flow of human energy'. Darjeeling was not much interested in alignment and releasing human energy. He worked as if you were a horse or some show dog presented for grooming. He used a hard horsehair brush, which he worked in small circular motions all over the body to remove the top layer of dirt, before hosing you down and getting to work with his fingers, elbows and – occasionally – his entire fist. The experience was painful, but there was no doubt that it was also a pleasure, an honour even to be worked upon by a man with such skills. In the privacy of Klein's, Darjeeling became your mother, your lover, your persecutor, comforter and friend.

Duly pummelled, exhausted and exhilarated, I thanked him – you left tips upstairs with Berrak – and worked my way weakly and slowly through the other rooms to the Russian Room, the hottest steam room known to everyone as the Oven. Between Darjeeling and the Oven there were three rooms: the Smoke Room, the Silent Room and the Golden Ring. The Smoke Room contained a red-hot wood-burning stove: the experience resembled that of being caught in a clearing in the smouldering remains of a forest fire. In the Silent Room one simply gazed at glowing hot rocks kept boiling in a pit, while in the Golden Ring men congregated for the privilege of *schmeissing*, a practice I have never encountered elsewhere, where complete strangers rubbed and scrubbed at one another with a hard raffia brush until the skin turned red and golden. I was not a great *schmeisser*; my one and only experience had involved a man, not a regular, who'd started pawing at me. (This sort of carry-on, though not unheard of, was generally frowned upon at Klein's, though to make my point and to throw off my *schmeisser* I'd had to grab him roughly by the throat, pinch his nostrils and tell him that I wasn't going to let go until he stopped. He stopped.) In Klein's it was my preference to act as an observer rather than as a participant. Unfortunately, that night in the Oven, I became the object of unwelcome attention.

CHAPTER 2

IN THE OVEN

A group of well-basted regulars stood around the furnace in the centre of the room, as though gathered for warmth. They were – naturally – entirely naked, their towels slung over their shoulders. I recognised some but not all of them. There was Willy Mann, who owned a couple of restaurants up around Fitzrovia and who also ran a number of Klein's businesses on his behalf. John Jacobs, who I knew was an art dealer of some kind, though of exactly what kind was never made entirely clear. And a tiresome American, Ned Price, who was some sort of journalist and who had arrived in London from Paris a couple of years earlier and who never tired of reminding us that London was not Paris, as if we didn't already know. There were also three or four others who from the neck down looked almost feminine, rather Rubenesque – what Klein would have called *zaftig* – but who from the neck up looked like they had been hit repeatedly by Jim Corbett, John L. Sullivan and Joe Louis, slowly and repeatedly, and in relay. In suits they'd have looked menacing. In the flesh, and through the haze of the Oven, they were grotesque. (In an article, 'Getting Ugly', published in the popular magazine *Photoplay* in 1932, Morley writes about the work of the actor Lon Chaney, one of his great heroes, 'The Man of a Thousand Faces', who dared to play grotesques, and also about Boris Karloff and his relationship with the Hollywood make-up artist Jack Pierce, who was responsible for Karloff's incredible make-up in *Frankenstein*. Morley loved monsters. 'We should always remember,' he writes, 'that physical defects are not necessarily signs of moral deformity.' Not necessarily. But Morley had never been to Klein's.)

'Well well,' said Willy Mann, who spotted me as I entered. Willy was a humourless individual with the manners of a second-rate maître d', who liked to think he knew a little bit of everything about everyone. 'If it's not the famous Stephen Sefton. Are we not honoured?'

The others turned to stare, and it was difficult not to stare back. It takes a moment to adjust to speaking to half a dozen naked men.

'Where have you been, Sefton?' asked Ned Price, ever the journalist.

'I've been travelling,' I said, which was true. The stone floor was hot beneath my feet.

'Somewhere nice, I hope?' said John Jacobs.

Devon and Westmorland – and Norfolk – were pleasant enough places. But I wouldn't exactly have described our experiences there as 'nice': the Appleby crash had been national news; events in Devon had caused a minor scandal; Norfolk was a mess.

Willy Mann took me by the arm and leaned close towards me, lowering his voice.

'How are you fixed at the moment, young man?' Willy was only a few years older than me – not even thirty – but he referred to everyone as 'young man'. He thought it made him sound avuncular and authoritative.

'Fixed?' I asked. He could easily have meant a number of things.

'For work?' he clarified.

'I'm fine, thank you, Willy.'

'You're in gainful employment?'

'You could say that.' My work with Morley was certainly employment – of a kind. But gainful? In what sense it was gainful I wasn't at all sure. Certainly I was paid; it got me out of London; but apart from Miriam it was sometimes difficult to see the benefits; indeed, because of Miriam it was sometimes difficult to see the benefits.

'I'm guessing you could always do with a little something on the side?' said Willy. 'Am I right, or am I right?'

The Oven was beginning to work its effects on me. I usually lay down on one of the benches to prevent myself becoming dizzy. My head was beginning to feel cloudy.

'Mr Klein has some business he needs taking

care of,' continued Willy. 'And he needs someone
. . . presentable to take care of it. A fresh face. A
front man. Someone . . . educated. Someone . . .
like you, Sefton.'

'And what's the business that needs doing?' I
asked, trying hard to focus on Willy's face.

'You'd have to talk to Mr Klein, if you were
interested.'

'What sort of thing is it?'

'I can't go into details, I'm afraid. It's to do with
a little land deal up around Becontree.'

'Becontree?'

'Out in Essex, where they're building the big
estates.'

'No thanks, Willy,' I said. 'I don't want to go to
Essex.'

'What have you got against Essex?'

'Nothing. I just . . .' I couldn't even picture Essex
in my mind. East of London? South of London?
Essex was just another county. I'd had enough of
other counties. If I could, I'd have stayed right
here, in the Oven.

'Well, anyway. The offer's there. You let me know
if you change your mind.'

'I will, Willy, thanks. I . . .'

As I spoke I felt my legs buckling and I began
to fall sideways: one of the grotesque men caught
me by the arm.

'Oh God, get him out,' said Willy Mann.

'Not used to the heat any more, Sefton?' said
Ned Price.

12

'Good to see you, wouldn't want to be you!' said John Jacobs, as the door to the Oven slammed behind me and I found myself abandoned, flat on my back in the cool of the pool room.

I somehow pulled myself up onto the stepladder and went up and up and then head first into the pool, all the way down to the bottom. I could feel the burn in my chest and the thrill of light-headedness as the cool water began reviving and cleansing me. I sat at the bottom of the pool for as long as I could before I thought my lungs might explode. Coming gasping to the surface felt like being born again. I felt free. I could breathe once more.

Half an hour later, entirely refreshed and dressed, I said goodbye to Berrak and stepped back out onto London's streets. Klein's had worked its magic. My mind was clear.

No sooner did the big scarred metal door of Klein's bang conclusively shut but two men instantly approached and fell into step behind me.

'What date is it, Mickey?' asked a voice.

'The eleventh, the twelfth?'

'The thirteenth I thought, isn't it? October the thirteenth?'

'The thirteenth, well, well. Unlucky for some, eh, Sefton?'

It was my old friends Mickey Gleason and the Scot MacDonald.

'There's someone who'd like to see you,' said MacDonald.

'Very much,' said Mickey. 'You've been missed, Sefton.'

CHAPTER 3

THE RENDEZVOUS

Smoke rings slowly spooled and unspooled around Delaney's smooth fat brilliantined Irish head as he sat by the window overlooking the Windmill Theatre, which extended its chest out over Great Windmill Street and bellowed in neon, 'CONTINUOUS PERFORMANCE', 'REVUDEVILLE', 'THE ONLY NON-STOP SHOW IN THE WEST END'.

As usual, Delaney wore a suit the colour of whipped cream and a large diamond ring that might more properly have graced the fingers of some shrivelled, pale-skinned dowager duchess. He was a plush Miss Havisham: the two of them would have got on well. He sat perfectly still. He didn't move, except to touch his cigar to his lips, slowly and leisurely, as though silently blessing it: Delaney was the sort of man who had time to kill; he was the sort of man with cigars silently to bless. He was a man with wide margins, broad horizons and narrow sympathies. A man who knew the power of being still.

Traffic sounded outside, though it was by now perhaps three or four o'clock in the morning –

long past the witching hour. If you are awake and you are in Soho and it's three o'clock in the morning it's probably safe to assume that you're looking for trouble, or that trouble has already come to find you. The sky was as black as your hat, or the devil's arse – depending on what kind of company you keep. But it was also orange and flashing red from the Windmill. It was set-lighting from hell.

We had been talking for some time. I had been trying to explain to Delaney what had happened to a package of his that I had accidentally-on-purpose picked up at one of his clubs, and why I'd had to make a quick exit without paying my gambling debts. It was a complicated conversation, made all the more complicated by the fact that I was accompanied by my old International Brigade chums, Mickey and MacDonald, who were flanking me like guards, standing heavily at my shoulder as if I were on trial, while Delaney, in contrast, was sitting opposite me, accompanied by an attractive brunette, perched happily on his lap, perhaps twenty years his junior, perfectly proportioned, and dressed in nothing but a corset underneath her silk robe. Her eyes were half shut, out of pleasure or boredom or something else it was difficult to tell, though I was pretty sure that if Delaney had stroked her any more she'd be purring.

The odds were definitely against me.

The room, like many of Delaney's clubs, was all

red plush and cheap-opulent upholstery. Gas-lit, potted palms, reproduction art in gilt frames, and with a day-bed big enough to accommodate at least three blondes. Thick-set filing cabinets sat obediently under the windows, and an inconveniently large desk boasted nothing on it but a telephone. It was a room, like Delaney, that suggested big business and low life. This was Soho and this was exactly the sort of place and the sort of carry-on that had made Delaney such a success in Soho.

'You are a normal healthy young man, Mr Sefton, are you not?' asked Delaney. 'A normal red-blooded young man?'

'Yes.' I had the strong feeling this was going to be a trick question.

'It must be difficult for you then, to have to be explaining yourself in the presence of our innocent young friend Grace here.' Grace wriggled innocently in his lap.

'Yes,' I agreed.

'Difficult for you both.'

'It's OK, Mr Delaney,' said Grace, in a voice like Betty Boop's.

'Run along, Grace,' said Delaney, and innocent young Grace got up and ran along. She glanced at me as she walked out and I thought perhaps I saw some hint of fellow feeling, but I may have been mistaken. It's easy to misread the glance of a half-dressed, half-bored, half-drugged beautiful woman. Much of Delaney's business was based on exactly such misunderstandings.

17

Delaney allowed more smoke to gather around him before he spoke.

'Are you a religious man, Mr Sefton?'

My guess was that 'yes' was probably the right answer. To say 'no' might have led to serious problems. 'Yes', as always, opened up possibilities. It kept my options open.

'Yes,' I said.

'Catholic or Protestant?'

I was neither, but I knew that Delaney was from Kerry and I was banking on the average Kerryman being of the Catholic persuasion.

'Catholic,' I said. Wise gamble.

'Good. So. I am myself a devout Roman Catholic.' I could feel Gleason and MacDonald behind me nodding in approval at this announcement, as if Delaney had revealed that he were in fact the Holy Father, or indeed the Son of God himself. 'You'll doubtless agree with me then that theft is a sin. A grievous sin.' More grievous a sin, I was given to presume, than his own activities as the owner of illegal drinking clubs, brothels, and as a wholesaler, distributor and retailer of drugs, drink and women.

I nodded.

'The only question then is how you might go about putting things right between us, Mr Sefton. What's upsetting is not only that you stole from me but that you stole that which I might willingly have given.' Or sold, he might more properly have said. As well as his clubs, Delaney controlled a

18

large part of many of the other businesses that kept Soho so . . . lively. 'Now,' he continued, 'we could of course go to law over the matter.' He laughed to himself at the thought of this clearly ludicrous suggestion. Going to law with a complaint about my own modest misdemeanour would only lead to questions about his own vast empire of sin. We would not be going to law over the matter. 'Fortunately for you I'm not a man who believes in punishment, Mr Sefton. I believe rather in making amends, in restitution. In making good.' He took up his cigar from the ashtray and applied it delicately to his lips, producing a few more pale rings of smoke. The tip glowed like the neon signs outside. 'I like to think of myself not so much as a businessman, more as a problem solver.' Again, Gleason and MacDonald nodded vigorously at this generous self-assessment. 'And the good news is, I think I have a solution to our little problem.' I feared as much. *Beware big men in fancy suits offering simple solutions*: this was not, I think, one of Morley's maxims, one of his proverbs or wise sayings, though it might have been. The closest I can find in *Unconsidered Trifles* (1934) is from Horace, *faenum habet in cornu, longe fuge*, 'stay away from the bull, he has hay on his horns'. What can I say? Delaney had a lot of hay on his horns.

In Spain I had gone 'absent' once for a few days, having been unable to reconcile what was happening all around me with what I thought was going to be happening in a true people's republic.

19

When I was caught trying to board a ship in Barcelona I was immediately sentenced to a week's work in the Brigade's disciplinary battalion. No one ever mentions the disciplinary battalion: no one spoke about it then; no one speaks about it now. We were billeted separately from others and forced, unarmed and ill-equipped, out into no-man's-land at night, to dig trenches and erect barbed-wire fences, out among the vermin and machine-gun fire, on reduced rations and subject to ridicule and abuse. There were twelve of us on the Monday. By Friday, only ten of us remained, two men having been shot dead beside me. The crack of rifle fire overhead had reduced us to crawling in the mud among the rats to go about our work. One week's disciplinary work.

I had a pretty good idea of how men like Delaney solved problems. They got rid of them. They used their disciplinary battalions.

'My friends here tell me that you acted bravely in Spain,' said Delaney. I glanced round at Gleason and MacDonald, who stood staring straight ahead. Acting bravely in Spain meant killing people before they killed you. It wasn't exactly chivalric. It was a matter of survival. 'Brave. Educated. Intelligent. When I look at you, Sefton, what I see is not what other people might see: a common thief, a cheat, a liar, a bitter and confused young man who has lost his way and wasted every opportunity in his life.' As a summing-up you wouldn't necessarily have wanted it on your gravestone but it wasn't

20

entirely inaccurate. 'No. No. When I look at you, Sefton, what I see is leadership potential.' What I saw was trouble. 'Men like you can be very useful in my line of business. So.' Delaney quietly and leisurely cleared his throat. 'I'd like to offer you an opportunity,' he said. I had a bad feeling I knew what was coming: in my experience, opportunity always comes with a cost, and often at a serious inconvenience to the opportunee. 'If you were to come and work for me, Mr Sefton, I think we'd probably be able to write off your gambling debts.' He stroked his chin. 'And in time I think we'd also be able to overlook the unfortunate incident concerning the theft of goods. Though it might take us a while of course to really learn to trust one another. What do you think?'

Well. That was two job offers in one evening: first from Willy Mann on behalf of Mr Klein, and now from Delaney on behalf of Delaney. I had a feeling that Delaney's offer was going to be harder to refuse. (On this theme – let us call it the Perennial Problem of Saying No – even Morley admits to a number of difficulties and confusions. In *Morley's Tried and Tested Temptations: Thinking About God, the Devil, Sin and Salvation* (1931), for example, he provides a very troubling and troubled little gloss on Matthew 4:8–9: 'Again, the devil taketh him up into an exceeding high mountain, and sheweth him all the kingdoms of the world, and the glory of them; And saith unto him, All these things will I give thee, if thou wilt fall down

21

and worship me.' Writes Morley: 'All of us will have been subject at some time to the temptation of intellectual pride. Intellectual pride is spiritually most damaging, an affliction of perhaps the most damaged among us, a sin that represents not only a defect of the will but which also betrays and betokens the deep scars of emotional wounds.' Anyway.) Nonetheless.

'That's a very kind offer,' I said. 'But I'm afraid I'm going to have to turn you down, Mr Delaney.'

'Oh dear,' said Delaney. 'Oh dear, oh dear, oh dear.' I had the feeling he was not a man who was used to being turned down. 'I'm not a man who is used to being turned down,' he said.

'It's just, I'm currently working for someone else,' I explained.

'I see. And who is this . . . "someone else" you're working for?' asked Delaney. 'Anyone I know?'

'A writer,' I said.

Delaney laughed – loudly, uproariously, as if I were Frank Randle on stage at the height of the summer season in Blackpool.

'A writer? Very good. And he pays you money? Or he pays you in stationery supplies?'

He wasn't far off.

Gleason and MacDonald sniggered beside me.

'I work for Swanton Morley,' I said, expecting some sort of recognition. Morley wasn't exactly unknown. He was at the time, and had been for many years, England's best known and best loved journalist, editor and publisher.

'Never heard of him,' said Delaney. 'Boys?'

I could hear Gleason and MacDonald vigorously shake their heads.

'Swanton Morley. He writes for the newspapers. Writes books. He's very . . . popular.' The word died on my lips.

'Well, if you don't mind my saying so,' Delaney said with a grin, 'he's clearly not *that* popular, Mr Sefton, is he?' Delaney reminded me of someone in the way he spoke – the chimpish bravado – but I couldn't for the life of me remember who it was.

'Maybe not,' I agreed. 'You've never read one of Morley's books?' Everyone had read at least one of Morley's books.

'I am proud to say, sir, that I have never read *any* book.'

'Never?'

'I'm sure I may have read *parts* of books. But the average man does not read whole books, Mr Sefton. In this day and age I think you'll find that the average man looks elsewhere for his entertainment. Which of course is where I come in . . .'

'Of course.'

'. . . as an entertainment provider. And I think I probably have a pretty good understanding of what is "popular". A much better understanding, I dare say, than either you or your "writer".'

'I'm sure.'

Delaney glanced over towards the flashing neon of the Windmill Theatre.

'In my position, Mr Sefton, in my line of work, you might say that I am blessed *every day* with a profound insight into the workings of the average human mind.' He rolled his cigar between forefinger and thumb, savouring it – and there it was again, that reminder of someone else, that performance, that knowing nod and wink of the king or the jester. 'And I'm afraid it is not always a pretty sight. You work full-time for your writer?'

'I do.'

'And you obviously enjoy your work?'

'Yes.'

'Well, that's good, that's very good.' Delaney rubbed a cigary finger along his protuberant bottom lip. 'Yes, good. Because I want you to be clear, Mr Sefton, that I am offering you what is a once-in-a-lifetime opportunity to join us in what we might call the new entertainment economy.'

'I understand that.'

'And yet you seem to be telling me that you're not interested, is that correct? Just so we're clear, you understand?'

'Yes. That's right.'

'You're not interested?'

'I'm afraid not.'

'You're absolutely sure now?'

I hesitated. 'Yes.'

'Well,' said Delaney, sighing deeply. 'That is unfortunate, Mr Sefton. Very unfortunate.'

'Yes,' I agreed. I was disappointed myself.

'Mmm. Well, as I say, it is a shame, because if

you're really not in a position to accept the offer it would mean that you and I still have a little bit of a problem to resolve, wouldn't it?' He rolled the tip of his cigar around the edge of the ashtray.

And in that moment I realised who Delaney reminded me of: he reminded me of Morley. They had a different repertoire of gestures and lines, of course, but it was a repertoire of gestures and lines nonetheless, a kind of performance, a top-of-the-bill performance in both cases, a captivating performance, a performance almost entirely uninhibited by petty concerns about the audience, which is ultimately what made it a great performance, a carefree performance closely resembling and mimicking the expression of the natural self, but a performance nonetheless. I always felt that I would never know Morley, in the same way I hoped I would never really know Delaney – perhaps because they would never truly know themselves. They were actors, being themselves. Which made them both utterly unlike average people, who are too busy living their lives to be bothered much with acting – and which is of course what made both Morley and Delaney so fascinated by the average and the everyday. They were not average and everyday, neither of them, and never could be.

'I'm afraid I am at something of a loss then, Mr Sefton. I have offered you a solution to the problem, which you have refused. Perhaps you should tell me what *you* think we should do?'

'I could just pay you back,' I said.

'Really?' Delaney gave a sinister little laugh. 'Well, if I had known you were simply going to *pay me back* then there'd have been no need for this long discussion, would there? This *rig*-marole.' He rolled the 'r' of the rigmarole. 'A cheque is acceptable, but I would prefer cash. You might be so kind as to visit my cashier downstairs on the way out. I'm assuming you have the money with you now?'

'I was wondering actually if we could arrange some sort of . . . payment plan?'

'A payment plan?'

'A schedule of repayments,' I said.

Gleason and MacDonald sniggered again.

'Well, I suppose it's not an unreasonable request,' said Delaney. Gleason and MacDonald immediately stopped sniggering. 'How about if I give you to the end of the month to pay me in full?'

'I was hoping actually that you might be able to extend the period of repayment a little longer,' I said. The end of the month gave me about two weeks. I was thinking more like two years – maybe until 1939. Or 1940. By then things might have calmed down. I might have straightened myself out.

'Longer?' said Delaney. 'You want longer?' Delaney examined the tip of his cigar. 'Oh dear. I am disappointed, Mr Sefton. You see, that just shows a lack of . . . ambition, don't you think?

'I—'

'Also I don't know if you're familiar with traditional banking practices, but I'm afraid it's really not common practice for the *borrower* to determine the terms of repayment. It is the *lender*, rather, who holds all the cards, as it were.'

'Of course,' I said.

'Good. So we're agreed then that you'll be paying me back at the end of the month, payment in full, in cash. Plus the small matter of compensation for the stolen goods, of course; shall we say we'll double the amount and round it up to, what, one hundred pounds?'

'One hundred pounds?'

For me, and indeed for almost anyone except for the very wealthy and the very lucky, one hundred pounds in 1937 was an unimaginable amount. For me, working for Morley, it was almost a year's wages.

'That's a deal then,' said Delaney. 'Gentlemen, would you show Mr Sefton the door?'

Gleason and MacDonald hauled me out of my chair and began to escort me – drag me, rather – to the door.

'Oh, Mr Sefton, just before you go.'

Gleason and MacDonald paused and turned me around just as we had reached the top of the stairs. I could see Delaney smiling, framed in the doorway like a painting of some all-powerful potentate: hand-grained features, black-enamelled hair, ivory teeth, the very image of the inscrutable and implacable.

'I wonder,' he said, 'I'd be interested to know: have you perhaps heard rumours about my methods for calling in debts? In those *very very* rare cases where people are not able or unwilling to make their payments?'

'Yes, I have,' I said.

'Well' – he chuckled – 'the rumours, you will be delighted to hear, Mr Sefton, are not *entirely* true. Isn't that right, boys?' Gleason and MacDonald wholeheartedly agreed that not all the rumours were entirely true. 'Not at all. Not at all at all at all. Just be careful going down the stairs now.'

The Windmill Theatre sign winked red at me, I stepped forward, Mickey Gleason pushed, and I began to fall.

CHAPTER 4

THE MUSIC WRITERS' MUTUAL PUBLISHING CO.

Nothing was broken. That was the main thing. I was sure nothing was broken. I had managed to put out a hand to prevent myself from going head first but I had rolled and skidded and smashed my way down and was at the bottom of the stairs when I heard my Brigader friends rushing towards me. I'd curled into a foetal position to protect myself from the inevitable beating. I pressed myself into the cracked linoleum and waited for the first blow. Instead I felt a hand reach down to pull me up.

'Sorry about this, mate, no hard feelings, eh?' said Gleason.

'Sure,' I said, relieved, beginning to stand.

Which is when MacDonald took a well-aimed kick that knocked me back against the door.

'Just pay up, you swine,' said MacDonald, or words to that effect, with his characteristic Glaswegian charm. The rest of what he said, and exactly what he said is, alas, unrepeatable. Suffice it to say, I was left in no doubt that it would be in my best interests to pay my debt to Delaney without delay or hesitation.

When they finally pushed me out the door back onto Windmill Street – 'See you in two weeks with your hundred pounds!' called MacDonald with one final thump, as I staggered back – I noticed a tiny brass plaque indicating the name of Delaney's offices, which I had never noticed before. The Rendezvous. Indeed it was.

I was breathing hard – panic and pain, a bad combination. I checked my ribs. I needed somewhere to rest. Somewhere to gather my thoughts and tend my wounds. Somewhere safe.

Some of the places I stayed in London in between assignments with Morley during our time together: Berwick Street, Dean Street, Greek Street, Wardour Street, in 'hotels', basements, flophouses and grand apartments, in mews, rows, streets, yards, courts, drives, circuses, both inside and out in the cold. There is nowhere, however, that I can particularly recommend: there is nowhere that remains the same. Time and money, tourism and sheer merchant greed have swallowed up the Soho that I knew and loved.

My most reliable stopover during those years, the place I dragged myself to when all seemed lost and there was nowhere else to go, was the offices of the Music Writers' Mutual Publishing Company, on the fourth floor of 14 Denmark Street – long since disappeared but fondly remembered.

During my time at college – when I wasn't

drinking or suffering the after-effects of drinking – I had somehow become involved with the college Music Society. I was in a Gilbert and Sullivan and a couple of end-of-term concerts, and was a stalwart of the – often rather rowdy – revues, which is where I first met Ronald 'Easy' Pease, of the Pease family brewers of Batley. Ronald was studying music. He was a multi-instrumentalist who played the violin, the viola, the oboe, the flute, the French horn, the organ, the piano and – most proficiently and competently of all – the fool. Ron was a prankster, the sort of person who liked to enter a room and immediately set about causing mischief. He even looked like a puppy, with masses of dark unruly curls and big soulful eyes. He also had charm and money, which meant that he managed to escape rustication on a number of occasions for various incidents of drunkenness, vandalism, nudity and – after one memorable night out – for 'fouling' on the doorstep of the Master's Lodge. (It probably helped that Ron's father and grandfather had both attended the college before him and that the generously endowed Pease Building was an important addition to the college estate.)

After college, Ron had attempted for a while to pursue a conventional career as an orchestral musician, but because he was an independent-minded sort of a fellow, and because he was of considerable independent means, conventions could pretty much be disregarded and after a couple of years of professional musicianship, and a couple more of entirely reckless behaviour, he eventually settled into the unlikely profession of musical arranger and lyricist, a profession that guaranteed only an irregular income but which he supplemented by happily working as an agent for the old pawnbroker on Denmark Street who specialised in musical instruments. This brought him into contact with exactly the kind of people he most liked and admired: artists, jazz musicians, reprobates and thieves. Ron's 'career' was indeed almost as precarious and unpredictable as my own, the only difference being that he could afford for a career to be precarious and unpredictable, since he was one day destined to inherit a fine house in Chelsea, a place in the country, an estate in Scotland and at least one-third of a brewery. He was utterly unreliable, incapable of taking anything even half seriously, and a very good friend, but most importantly, he was the sole proprietor of the Music Writers' Mutual Publishing Company, and had kindly provided me with a key to his office on the fourth floor of 14 Denmark Street, which meant I had a place in Soho where I could occasionally sleep when necessity demanded.

Necessity now most definitely demanded.

It was fast approaching dawn. Denmark Street was deserted. I let myself into the building and went through the lobby towards the stairs. Ron's lease prohibited using the office for anything but commercial purposes but if you paid your rent and didn't cause too much trouble you could get away with almost anything. There were plenty of people in the building who were getting away with almost anything. You'd often find musicians sleeping in the lobby, and pimps, and the sort of people who come out at night and then mysteriously disappear during the day, or when their bills are due. The first floor was always the busiest: on the first floor there were a couple of rooms used by prostitutes, so there'd be people in and out – as it were – at all times. Ron used to go mad because the prostitutes would hang their underwear in the shared bathroom and make a terrible mess. (I was there in fact the night that Ron decided enough was enough and started throwing their underwear down into the street, tossing silk panties and brassieres onto passing pedestrians: you scored points if you managed to land a pair of knickers on an unsuspecting bowler. I was also there the night that Ron decided his office was too small, and since the office next door was empty we just broke right through, making a big hole in the wall: for a while we called ourselves the Hole in the Wall Gang, until we realised it wasn't funny. The building was falling apart, even without our jolly japes. We were young, carefree and hellbent on destruction.)

The lobby was empty. Not even the girls were working. I was glad no one was around. I wasn't in the mood for conversation. Many years later, during the course of our travels, Morley, Miriam and I had to contend with the sad case of a sweet-shop owner who had apparently fallen down her stairs and broken her neck. I had been lucky in my single-flight fall from Delaney's office – at worst I had maybe sprained an ankle – but I was bruised all over from my little chat with MacDonald and felt like I'd been mauled by whatever creature it is who is the most proficient at mauling: some lean, mean-featured pitiless Scots sort of creature, no doubt. I dragged myself up the stairs, let myself into Ron's office and wearily settled myself into an armchair, clearing away piles of unanswered post and musical scores. Sleep came instantly.

CHAPTER 5

A TOPOGRAPHICAL CREMESCHNITTE

I was woken what seemed like only moments later by the sound of a piano playing and the unmistakable smoky-sweet stench of Russian tea. I wasn't sure if I was dreaming or if Ron had arrived early at the office. Knowing Ron, this seemed highly unlikely; and sure enough, when I half opened my eyes I saw that it was in fact Morley, Morley with his moustache and his grin, Morley seated at Ron's piano, singing and strumming a song in a minor key.

> Once I built a railroad, I made it run
> Made it race against time
> Once I built a railroad, now it's done.
> Brother, can you spare a dime?
> Once I built a tower up to the sun
> Brick and rivet and lime
> Once I built a tower, now it's done
> Brother, can you spare a dime?

'Ah, Sefton, good morning!' He raised his cup of tea towards me in greeting.

I was about to reply when there came a horrible sharp dinning in my right ear: I wondered for a second if I had perhaps burst an eardrum after my fall down the stairs. I hadn't: it was just Miriam, with a trumpet to her lips, attempting some sort of reveille.

'How did you find me?' I managed to ask them, through my confusion.

'Really, Sefton. It doesn't exactly take a Miss Marple to track your movements,' said Miriam. She laid down the trumpet and was about to pick up a trombone.

'I've got a bit of a headache, actually,' I said.

'I'm not surprised. You look dreadful. What on earth's happened to you? Have you been in another fight?' I saw that her eyes had alighted upon the xylophone in the corner.

'Please,' I said. 'I really do have a—'

'Well, if you will insist on drinking and carousing, Sefton, what on earth do you expect?'

'A most singular method of enjoying oneself, if you don't mind my saying so,' added Morley. 'Not at all good for one. The old ivory dome.' He tapped a finger to his head. 'One has to take care of it, you know. I was at Madison Square Garden when Max Baer beat Primo Carnera – goodness me, that was a fight. Couldn't you take up chess instead? Do you know Max Euwe?'

'I can't say I do,' I said.

'World champion? Defeated Alekhine?'

'I must have missed that,' I said.

'Good dose of Eno's Fruit Salts will see you right,' said Morley.

'Mmm,' I agreed.

'Or this,' said Miriam, and she thrust her left wrist under my nose. 'Have a sniff. It's Schiaparelli's Shocking. My new scent. Given to me by an admirer. Do you like it?'

I took a quick sniff. It smelled like all other perfume.

'Well?' said Miriam.

'Very nice,' I said, finally beginning to gain full consciousness.

Miriam and Morley certainly had a way of waking a man up in the morning.

Morley was opposite, at the piano, looking as spruce and as chipper as ever: bow tie, light tweeds, dazzling brogues. Miriam was doing her best to lounge on Ron Pease's office chair – and her best was more than good enough. She somehow looked at this unearthly hour as she always looked: as though she had just finished a photo-shoot, perhaps for *Vogue* magazine, or some publicity stills for MGM. Her eye make-up was fashionably smudged, her white dress and matching jacket exquisite. She was also sporting some sort of barbaric necklace that looked as though it might recently have been wrenched from the neck of an aboriginal tribesperson, and then set with diamonds, the sort of necklace that one sometimes sees in the window of Asprey – the sort of necklace that might cost at least one hundred pounds or more.

I put the thought immediately from my mind.

'Who let you in?' I asked.

'Well, it's a surprisingly busy little building, isn't it?' said Morley. 'A charming young lady from the first floor escorted us up. I think she said her name was Desiree?'

'I think you'll find her name is probably *not* Desiree,' said Miriam, looking knowingly at me.

'Sorry?' said Morley.

'"That one may smile, and smile, and be a villain – At least I am sure it may be so in Denmark."'

'*Hamlet*?' said Morley. 'I can't see the relevance, my dear.'

'Denmark. Street,' said Miriam.

'Anyway,' I said.

'Yes, quite,' said Morley. 'Anyway. No time to lose, eh, Sefton? Another book to write.'

'Sorry, did we finish the last one?'

'Yes, *we* did,' said Miriam.

'Westmorland,' said Morley. 'Almost finished.'

'In your absence,' said Miriam.

'Few tweaks, few i's to dot and some t's to cross, but we should have it done by the end of next week, Miriam, shouldn't we?'

'I would have thought so, Father, yes.'

'So, ready for the printers and into the shops by the end of October, I would have thought. *Excelsior*!'

'Right,' I said.

Morley was publishing books almost faster than I could read them. I'd been in his employ since early September, working on *The County Guides*, and we'd already covered Norfolk, Devon and Westmorland. I'd travelled more widely in England within a month than I had in the previous twenty-six years of my pre-Morley existence.

'You'll be thrilled to hear, Sefton, that our next county is Essex,' said Miriam.

'Essex?'

'That's right,' said Morley. 'When you think of Essex, Sefton, what do you think of?'

'When I think of Essex.' When I think of Essex? It was not a place I had ever given a first – let alone a second – thought to. 'When I think of Essex I think of . . .' I thought of Willy Mann asking if I'd like to work for Mr Klein on some project.

'Oysters!' said Morley. 'Correct! And cockles, sprats, whitebait, flounder, dab, plaice, sole, eels, halibut, turbot, brill—'

'Yes, Father, we get the picture.'

'Lobster, haddock, whiting, herring, pike, perch, chub—'

'Yes, Father.'

'Gudgeon, roach, tench—'

'Father!'

'Winkles. But above all the *Ostreaedulis*! The English native!'

'Sorry? The English native . . .?'

'Oyster, Sefton! It is our privilege, sir, to have been invited as guests of honour to the annual Oyster Feast in Colchester!'

'Very good,' I said.

'Colchester, ancient capital of England.

Camulodunum – the fortress of Camulos! A place arguably more important historically than London itself. Home to the mighty Coel and his daughter Helena, not to mention the mighty Boadicea.'

'And tell him, Father.'

'Tell him what, Miriam?'

'Father's terribly excited, Sefton, because one of the fellow guests at the Oyster Feast is going to be—'

'Oh yes!' cried Morley. 'The aviatrix!'

'The who?' I asked.

'The aviatrix!' repeated Morley.

'By which he means the famous female aviator Amy Johnson.'

'Really?'

'Apparently, according to Father.'

'Well, I very much look forward to—'

There came the sound of bells ringing outside. St-Giles-in-the-Fields. This was one of the disadvantages of staying at 14 Denmark Street: the close proximity to Christian bell-ringing, which could play havoc with a hangover, though frankly Morley and Miriam more than matched the din. At the last stroke of the bell, Morley checked all his watches: the luminous wristwatch, the non-luminous wristwatch and his pocket-watch. He doubtless had an egg-timer concealed somewhere about his person, but there was no need to consult it on this occasion.

'Not bad,' he said. 'Not bad. I'd better push on, though, chaps. I'll see you there this evening?'

40

'Father is travelling up by train,' said Miriam. 'We're going to take the car. Now, I do expect to see you there on time, Father.'

'Yes, of course.'

'There's an exhibition at the Royal Albert Hall,' explained Miriam. 'Father's very keen to go.'

'Ah,' I said.

'By the Ford Motor Company,' said Morley.

'At the Royal Albert Hall?' I said.

'That's right!'

'You're not allowed to buy any more motorcars, though, Father. Understand?'

'Yes, of course,' said Morley.

'We have quite enough already.'

'Yes, yes.'

'If you were going to buy another we'd have to sell one.'

Morley was an absolute car fiend. He was an autoholic. To my knowledge he never parted with a car, any more than he ever parted with a book, or a typewriter.

'You're just looking, remember?'

'Yes, yes,' said Morley. 'I thought it was worth a visit,' he explained to me. 'Because we're going to Essex. I tried to persuade Miriam that we should visit the Ford Works at Dagenham but she wasn't keen.'

'I thought Father going to an exhibition would be just as good. Don't you agree, Sefton?'

'Yes,' I agreed. I probably had as little desire as Miriam to visit a motor vehicle manufacturer – probably less.

41

'They're bringing all the men and machines from Dagenham anyway,' said Morley. 'So it'll be as if we were actually witnessing them constructing an actual vehicle in an actual factory!'

'In the Albert Hall?' I said. 'Really?'

'Yes, yes. Quite remarkable, isn't it? Way of the future, Sefton. Arts, crafts and manufacturing joining together to usher in the Age of the Automated Arts. I wonder if we might organise some sort of society, actually . . . The AAA. Sort of an RSA for the twentieth century. What do you think, Miriam?'

'I think we need to concentrate on the task in hand, Father.'

'Yes, yes, of course. Very good. So, I have taken the liberty of drawing up a little list here of places in Essex for you two to visit on the way to Colchester, for the purposes of research for the book.'

He handed me a complicated diagram that looked as though it were a sort of geological map.

'One needs to think of Essex, Sefton, as like a series of layers.'

'Ah,' I said.

'Like a cake?' said Miriam.

'Precisely like a cake, Miriam,' said Morley. 'A sort of topographical *cremeschnitte*, in five parts: the coast, the marshes, the farms, the villages, and the towns dominated by London.'

'OK,' I said.

'Our account of Essex will begin here, on the

very bottom layer of the cake, as it were. In Becontree.'

'Becontree?' asked Miriam. 'Must we?'

'In years to come, Miriam, mark my words, Becontree will be regarded as one of the great wonders of the world. New housing for tens of thousands of workers? Quite extraordinary. Like something created by the pharaohs. It was a market garden at one time, of course. Now a sort of city planted on the Nile delta! A testament to the spirit of our age!'

'Becontree?'

'Fit for heroes, Miriam, remember. Fit for heroes! Think of yourselves as the companions of Columbus, setting forth to a New World, discovering the future!'

'Becontree though?' repeated Miriam.

'Yes!' insisted Morley, rather tetchily. 'Now, some photographs of the Dagenham Borough Council building, Sefton, if you wouldn't mind? Quite a thing, I'm given to understand. Early Saxon settlement, Dagenham.'

'Really?'

'Yes, Daecca's home, I think.'

'Right.'

'I remember it as a village, of course.'

'Very good.'

'So, some sort of atmospheric shots of the great boulevards and avenues, if you would.'

'The great boulevards of Becontree?' said Miriam.

'If you would, Sefton,' said Morley, ignoring Miriam.

'Certainly, Mr Morley.'

'And on from the delights of Becontree, Father?'

'Well, I thought we'd make a sort of clockwise journey, up from Becontree, to Romford, Brentwood, Chipping Ongar, Dunmow – Maid Marian laid to rest at Dunmow Priory, I believe. Some nice shots of Dunmow, Sefton. You know the story of the Dunmow Flitch of course?'

I must admit I had momentarily forgotten the story of the Dunmow Flitch.

'A flitch of ham awarded to a married couple who can live without quarrelling for a year and a day.'

'Ha!' cried Miriam.

'And then across to Colchester and back round via Manningtree – the Witchfinder General was from Manning-tree, I believe. Full of witches, Essex.'

Miriam raised a finger and pointed at me. 'Don't you dare say a word, Sefton.'

'I wasn't going to,' I protested.

'Thank you, children. And then on to Clacton, Southend, etcetera, etcetera, further details to be confirmed. If we have time I'd very much like to call in on Margery and Dorothy, if Dorothy's at home in Witham. She's a bit of a gad-about. Margery's bound to be there at Tolleshunt D'Arcy. We could hardly visit Essex without calling on the county's two greatest living writers.'

'Margery Allingham, Father?'

'Yes.'

'Oh no.'

'What? Why? What's wrong with Margery?'

'She's just a little . . . strange, Father, isn't she?'

'Margery?'

'Yes.'

'But she's a writer, Miriam. And a very fine one at that.'

'That's no excuse, Father.'

'Have you read Margery, Sefton?' asked Morley.

'No, I can't say I have, Mr Morley.'

'No? Goodness me, man. *Sweet Danger* is in my opinion one of the great detective books of this century!'

'Really?'

'Absolutely. You should read it immediately! I rate her rather more highly than Agatha, actually.' Morley glanced around him, lowered his voice, and put a finger to his lips. 'But don't tell Agatha I told you.'

'You have my word, Mr Morley.'

'Dorothy's fine though,' said Miriam. 'I don't mind visiting Dorothy. She's a hoot.'

'The divine Miss Sayers,' said Morley. 'Now, she *is* a little strange, Miriam.'

'I rather like her,' said Miriam.

'Well, of course you would, my dear: the most likeable thing about Dorothy is that she doesn't care whether you like her or not.'

'Exactly,' said Miriam.

'Anyway, social calls permitting, I think a couple of days should do it, shouldn't it, for Essex?'

A couple of days chasing around Essex: another utterly lunatic enterprise, of course, just like all the others. But I had no reason to stay in London and every reason to get away. It would give me time to work out how to find a hundred pounds.

'Great,' I said.

'What time is your train out of Liverpool Street later, Father?' asked Miriam. 'There's a special train hired, for those invited to the Oyster Feast, Sefton.'

'Really?'

'Yes,' said Morley. 'Same every year, apparently. Tradition. Very good of them. And quite appropriate – in a sense Essex begins and ends at Liverpool Street Station, don't you think?'

'Indeed it does, Father,' said Miriam. 'Indeed it does. The rot sets in almost as soon as one leaves the station. Before, in fact. It's a perfectly horrid place.'

'I quite agree with you about Liverpool Street Station, my dear, but I think you'll find you're entirely wrong about Essex. Entirely lacking in the great beauty of Devon, of course, or indeed the wildness of Westmorland, or the sheer splendour of Norfolk, but it does make the most of what little it's got.'

'Hardly a recommendation, Father.'

'Anyway,' said Morley. 'Must run!'

'The time, Father, of the arrival of your train?'

'I'll send you a telegram,' said Morley.

'To where?' said Miriam. 'We'll be in the Lagonda. And you'll be on the train.'

'Ah,' said Morley. 'Good point. You know, one day someone needs to invent some kind of mobile communication device. A sort of pocket telegram machine.'

'I'm not sure it'd catch on, Father.'

'Perhaps not,' said Morley.

'It would just involve people telling each other they were on board trains.'

'Ha!' said Morley. With which he got up from the piano stool and dashed for the door. 'Good luck then, you two. Until we meet again in Essex!'

'Very good,' said Miriam. 'Goodbye, Father.'

'No slacking,' he called from the corridor.

'No shilly-shallying,' replied Miriam loudly.

'No funking,' I mumbled.

'Although . . .' said Miriam, turning towards me, and adopting her lounge position on the chair. 'While the cat's away the mice shall play, eh, Sefton?'

I needed a cup of coffee and a pick-me-up.

And a hundred pounds.

CHAPTER 6

THE BOULEVARDS OF BECONTREE

Denmark Street is ideally situated in Soho, if for no other reason that it marks a kind of boundary and thus provides a perfect and speedy exit onto High Holborn and all roads east. I managed to persuade Miriam that I was in urgent need of a hearty breakfast, and this hearty breakfast once duly procured – in a neat little café opposite Foyle's run by a family of natty Italians, with whom Miriam insisted on practising both her rudimentary Italian and her highly advanced arts of flirtation – we were soon heading off in the Lagonda across London.

London in 1937 was of course entirely different to the London of today, which has seen so many changes that have rendered many parts of it almost unrecognisable. If one aspect, one characteristic remains the same, however, it is this: for all its ugly wounds and gashes, and for all its hasty rebuilds and reconfigurations, east London remains the undisputed territory of the poor. Morley had a curious map on the wall of his study back in St George's which showed an aerial view of the city marked prominently with all its churches, as

48

though the Church Triumphant were massing and converging and sailing up the Thames towards Parliament, spires aloft like mainsails. To set out in the opposite direction, to move away from the centre, to go east, has always been to go against this flow of the great and the good and the godly, away from money and power, away from Christopher Wren, and out into unpredictable territory of Hawksmoor's baroque, and crumbling Georgian terraces, and the squat fat brick and concrete mansion blocks that were then already replacing the old Victorian terraces. To go east was and is – and shall surely forever remain – to venture into the wild.

'Dreadful,' said Miriam as she gunned the Lagonda out along the Commercial Road and on into Poplar. 'Can you imagine actually living here?'

'I rather like it, actually,' I said, as we proceeded at alarming speed onto the East India Dock Road and caught full sight of the great wharves of London's docks, with their vast cranes towering above and behind like some giant backstage machinery for scene-shifting and which made the east London streets seem like a stage set where at any moment absolutely anything and everything might happen: tragedy, comedy, history, farce; the East London Palace Theatre of Varieties. It felt thrillingly alive, a place where things were being made rather than merely consumed, a place where lives were actually being lived and not simply performed, where a cat might look at a king, where a fool and his money might soon be parted, and where a little of what you fancy does you good. There were young children swinging high and wide around the lampposts, and mothers young and old were pushing prams, and people were going about their daily business, street sellers with barrels of herrings and bagels, and butchers and bakers and fishmongers, their goods spilling out onto the streets, a cornucopia of bread and fishes and strings of sausages, and men unloading vans, and news-stands, and cars and bikes and horses and carts: it was a kind of people's paradise . . .

'Oh come on, Sefton, don't attempt your old communist nonsense with me. You'd rather live here, or in a nice flat in Kensington?'

'To be honest I'd rather be living entirely elsewhere,' I said.

'Don't be ridiculous,' said Miriam. 'Everywhere is elsewhere, isn't it? Otherwise nowhere is anywhere.' She had certainly inherited her father's eccentric logic. 'But anyway' – the subject had strayed away from Miriam's favourite subject, Miriam, for long enough – 'I have great news.'

'Who's the lucky man this time?'

'Not that sort of news, silly.'

'What then?'

'I've been offered a column in a new magazine for women.'

'Congratulations,' I said. 'What's it called?'

'The magazine? *Woman*, silly,' said Miriam, 'obviously,' and, 'Get out of the way, you little beast!' she screamed, as we swerved in order to avoid a child no more than four or five years old, and dressed all in white, as though in an advert for Omo, who had run into the street chasing a ball, chased by a rather grubbier-looking older girl who fortunately swept up the young one in her arms before she made irreparable and very messy contact with the Lagonda. 'Damned children! Aren't they supposed to be in school?'

'How much are they paying you?'

'Paying me?' said Miriam. 'I have no idea, Sefton. I didn't ask about payment.'

Which was really the great difference between us. Miriam was someone who never asked, or had to ask about payment: I was someone who was only ever really interested in payment. I wondered if she might be paid as much as a hundred pounds.

'And what are you going to write about?'

'My silly, empty way of life, what do you think?' She flashed me a sarcastic smile.

'Seriously though,' I said.

'Seriously though, Sefton, I am going to tell the truth about the lives of young women today.'

'I'm sure people will be absolutely fascinated,' I said.

'I'm sure they will, actually,' she replied. 'I think it's about time that women spoke out about their *real* lives, rather than pretending all the time to be second-rate men.'

'I'd hardly describe you as someone pretending to be a second-rate man, Miriam,' I said. 'You're more like a . . .' I was going to say another species, but decided to hold my tongue.

'Superior man?' said Miriam.

'Yes,' I said.

'Sui generis?'

'Exactly,' I agreed.

'Good. Well, at least we're agreed on one thing. Now do be a darling and light me a cigarette and remind me of the route, would you?' (She was at this time, as far as I recall, happy to accept any cigarette from anyone: this was before she took up smoking exclusively De Reszke Minors, with their famous 'Red Tips for Red Lips', with whom she had some kind of advertising arrangement, connected to her column in *Woman*. Frankly, in the early years, if you'd offered her a pipe filled to the brim with good old-fashioned stinky Balkan Sobranie she'd have smoked it.)

We were now following the A13 out of London and into Essex: through Canning Town, with the views of Bow Creek and the Beckton Gas Works, and then on and up past Barking where finally you get to see the famous Becontree estate looming on the horizon. If you've ever been you'll know that there is a kind of perpetual grey fog hanging over the place: all those houses and all those people, all that coal and wood being burned to keep them warm and alive, as though Becontree itself were an actual being, a slumbering beast, curled up and breathing out its slumbering beastly fumes into the unforgiving Essex sky.

From a distance the Becontree estate at first gives the appearance of a frontier town in Westerns – one half expects on arrival to find the old clapboard bordello ringing with the cries of good-time girls and grizzled crap-shooters, the saloon doors banging open as you stride in and order a whiskey and the conversation suddenly dies and you realise you're in the wrong place at the wrong time, and the sheriff's office is under siege, and the gunslinger is in his buckskin shirt, squinting through the sun's glare, riding onto Main Street to confront the bad guys in the big black hats – just as in the novels of Zane Grey, another of those writers beloved by Morley whose work seemed to me almost entirely without worth. (Morley's great paean to the Western is of course *Home on the Range: Life in the Wild West* (1933), a book perhaps more wildly inaccurate even than any of his others, but which contains an intriguing account of his meeting with Buffalo Bill himself, when the old cowboy had been touring Europe during the early years of the century. Buffalo Bill, according to Morley, was much more than a showman. 'Few men have done as much for our understanding of the lives of the American Indian,' according to Morley. 'Buffalo Bill's Wild West was a circus with a purpose.') But in reality Becontree was no Deadwood. It was no Dodge City, no Tombstone, Arizona. Borderland Essex in the late 1930s was like no other place at no other time. It was a place situated somewhere between the present and the future, stranded in a now that never was and could never be – a place entirely between the wars.

As we made our way down Becontree Avenue I was struck first of all not by the buildings but by the extraordinary sight of what seemed like never-ending rows of privet hedges leading off in every direction, all short and trimmed at regulation waist height and which made it look as though the actual buildings of Becontree were some kind of a weird garden planted in behind the hedges, almost as an afterthought, square, overgrown red brick flowers and shrubs. The Becontree hedges, perhaps more than anything else, sum up that dream of another England that Morley so admired and cherished, a perfect, planted petit-bourgeois green and pleasant land.

'Ghastly,' said Miriam.

It was certainly strange – like a brightened, whitened East End, as though having been boil-washed and run through the mangle. There were tramways and cheap cars and uniform shopfronts all with identical awnings. There were long monotonous rows of houses, each with a handkerchief patch of garden out front, all equivalent in size and shape, except for those few homes set further back from the road around miniature greens, and odd corner sites that had young trees planted, and fresh, ugly churches. It all looked terribly clean and also rather Dutch; something to do with the pitch of the roofs, perhaps, and also the fact that everywhere one looked there were men and women on bicycles, furiously pedalling, as if the life of the nation itself depended on the men and women of Essex getting to work on time. And yet somehow, for all it looked longingly towards Europe for its architectural inspiration, it also seemed inevitably and undeniably American: the wide streets clearly built not for boulevardiers and bicycles but for cars and trucks and lorries, and the low-rise buildings not the stuff of the Low Countries but rather of the New World, the only ornament and interest the advertising hoardings that glued the streets together with Parkinson's Biscuits, Eno's Fruit Salts, Lavvo and Pumphrey's Lemon Curd. We pulled over beneath a sign for Bile Beans, in a spot designated by another sign for 'PARKING', in front of a shop called Clifford's, at the corner of Becontree Avenue and Valence Avenue. A convoy of lorries piled high with sand and gravel came thundering past, spraying fine dust and diesel fumes in their wake.

'What on earth *is* this place?' asked Miriam.

'This,' I said, 'is the modern world. I'll maybe get a few photographs,' I said, 'and then we can be on our way.'

'Well, if this is the modern world, Sefton,' said Miriam, 'I want no part of it.' Which of course is what made Miriam so thoroughly modern.

As I was carefully framing a shot for Morley, featuring the dusty boulevards of Becontree, and while Miriam sat smiling regally at the passers-by ogling both her and the Lagonda – not an everyday sight in south Essex, either of them – a man came sauntering proprietorially along the pavement towards us. His hat was pulled down tight on his head, his hands deep in the pockets of his double-breasted overcoat, and he had the kind of bullying walk that suggested he was prepared to pick a fight with anyone, at any time, and preferably now. It was Willy Mann, Mr Klein's business agent and fixer. The last time I'd seen him was just the night before, when he was all shiny and naked in the Turkish baths: now, thank goodness, he was cooled off and dressed, though no less menacing.

'Well, well,' said Willy. He was the very definition of shifty, with a habit of moving and shrugging inside his clothes, as though avoiding a punch, or calculating his next blow. 'Sefton, again.' He nodded towards my cuts and bruises. 'Trouble?'

'Hello, Willy,' I said. 'Sorry, I didn't recognise you with your clothes on.'

'A joke, presumably?'

'Don't encourage him,' said Miriam, lighting a cigarette.

'Hello, hello,' said Willy, removing his hat and going to shake Miriam's hand. 'You're not with him, surely, a fine young lady like yourself?'

Fortunately Miriam was accustomed to compliments from men far more accomplished than Willy and was more than ready with a put-down.

'"With him" in the strict sense of being accompanied by him, sir, yes.' She paused and took a long thoughtful drag on her cigarette, effectively establishing her dominance over the conversation, over the cigarette, and of course over Willy. 'But certainly not "with him" in the broader sense of having, possessing and thus, crudely and colloquially speaking, being in a relationship "with him", if that's what you're asking, certainly not, no.' She took another long draw on her cigarette and raised an eyebrow at Willy. 'So it rather depends in what sense you were using the term, doesn't it?'

'Goodness me. Lively one,' said Willy to me. 'Not her who roughed you up, was it?'

'I haven't laid a finger on him,' said Miriam.

'More's the pity, eh?' said Willy, nudging me.

Miriam gave a furious little growl at this and flashed her ruby-red fingernails at Willy, cigarette aloft, one of her more alarming gestures, suggesting a panther – or some blonde equivalent thereof – about to pounce. 'I suppose you'd better introduce me to your witty little friend here, Sefton,' she said wearily to me. 'Since you are "with" me, though only in the strict and obvious sense.'

'Yes, of course,' I said. 'This is Willy Mann, Miriam. Willy, this is Miriam Morley.'

'*Very* pleased to make your acquaintance,' said Willy, with, I thought, rather too much feeling in his 'very': Miriam tended to have an instant mesmerising effect on men. I recall there being one or two chaps in fact who proposed marriage within an hour of meeting her. I hoped Willy wasn't going to embarrass himself.

'And where do you boys know each other from?' asked Miriam.

'Sefton and I—'

'Have a lot of mutual friends,' I interrupted.

'I didn't know you had any friends,' said Miriam, blowing smoke, as she liked to, as though in an aside.

'Sefton always likes to play his cards close to his chest,' said Willy. 'I didn't have you down as a man to be driving a Lagonda, for example.'

'I think you'll note that *I'm* driving the Lagonda, actually,' said Miriam, from the driver's seat. 'Sefton is my passenger.'

'Indeed,' said Willy. 'All the more remarkable, Sefton.'

'Anyway,' I said, 'what are you doing up around these parts, Willy?'

'I might have asked you the same thing, old chap. Not your usual stomping ground, is it?'

'Not exactly,' said Miriam, on my behalf. 'But here we are. And why are you here, Willy?'

'Mr Klein has business interests up here,' said Willy.

'Ah, yes,' I said, vaguely remembering what Willy had explained to me the night before.

'And who is this Mr Klein when he's at home?' asked Miriam.

'He's a businessman,' said Willy. 'Good friend of ours.'

'And what would be Mr Klein's business in Becontree, of all places, if you don't mind my asking?' Miriam was cursed with her father's curiosity.

'Do you have half an hour?' asked Willy.

'No,' I said.

'It rather depends,' said Miriam.

'I thought perhaps I might show you something,' said Willy.

'Did you now?' said Miriam. 'And I wonder what that might be?'

She had a habit sometimes, I noticed, when she was talking to men, of moving her cigarette between her fingers very slightly and very carefully. She was doing it now – a subtle and expressive gesture.

'You'll have to trust me to find out,' said Willy.

'Hmm. What do you think, Sefton? Should we trust Willy here to show us something? Or should we not?' And she again moved the cigarette ever so slightly between her fingers. She had us both in the palm of her hand.

CHAPTER 7

THIS IS ENGLAND

As so often, with so many people, and so many things, what Willy actually had to show us was something of an anticlimax. What he had to show us was a building site on Klein's new development on the edge of Becontree. He was shouting facts and figures at us, vainly trying to impress Miriam, as lorries went thundering past.

'You see, apart from the construction,' he yelled, 'there's all the haulage and the materials themselves. So in the average house you've got perhaps forty thousand bricks, plus your lime and sand and cement, and then there's your plaster and roofing tiles, fireplaces and what have you. Which is about a hundred and fifty tonnes worth per house, which has all got to be hauled to site somehow – plus your excavations. So you're looking at quite a job.'

'And quite a profit,' said Miriam.

'Exactly,' said Willy.

'So Mr Klein builds the houses, he provides the materials, and he provides the means by which the materials are transported? Is that right?' said Miriam.

'That's right.'

'Quite a business model.'

'I didn't know he was into haulage as well,' I said.

'Indeed he is, Sefton,' said Willy, as a lorry nudged its way slowly through the building site towards us.

'Quite the all-rounder, your Mr Klein,' said Miriam.

'You could say that. He was rather hoping in fact that Sefton here might be able to assist us with one or two of our current projects.'

'Sefton!?' Miriam laughed.

'Yes.'

'Assisting your Mr Klein?'

'Yes.'

'Has he met him?'

'Thank you for that vote of encouragement, Miriam,' I said.

'Well anyway, he's too late, isn't he, your chap,' said Miriam. 'Sefton's already in steady employment – working for me.'

'And I'm sure you work him pretty hard,' said Willy.

'You have no idea,' said Miriam.

I wondered how much Mr Klein might be paying.

The lorry was now reversing its way perilously close to the Lagonda.

'There we are,' said Willy. 'That's what I like to see. Another lorryload down from the quarries.'

And as if on cue, the lorry upended its vast load of sand, close enough to the Lagonda to coat it in a fine pale yellow mist.

'Little bit close for comfort,' said Willy. 'Sorry about that.'

'Lovely lorry,' said Miriam, taking no notice of Willy: she never really cared about the things that other people cared about. I thought for a moment she'd said 'lovely lolly'.

'A Thornycroft Trusty,' she continued. 'The lorry.'

'How on earth do you . . .' began Willy. 'This is quite a girl you have here, Sefton.'

Miriam was quite a girl, but she certainly wouldn't thank Willy for telling her so.

'Father's a great admirer of Thornycrofts,' she said. 'He has a little Handy that he runs on the estate.'

'Really?' I said.

'Who's your father?' asked Willy. 'Not that it's any of my business.'

'Swanton Morley,' said Miriam. 'Not that it's any of your business.'

'The People's Professor?'

'The very man.'

'Good stock then,' said Willy, as if appraising a prize cow. 'I am impressed by your choice, Sefton.'

'Might I refer you to my earlier answer about being "with" Sefton only in the strict sense of being accompanied by him, sir. He has no more

62

"chosen" me than he has chosen the weather. I am an entirely separate entity.'

'An entirely separate and unpredictable entity,' I added.

'Thank you, Sefton,' said Miriam. 'I'll take that as a compliment.'

'Anyway,' said Willy, interrupting Miriam's teasing, 'this is the finished article.' He pointed to a large plain, pebble-dashed building to our left. It looked rather . . . municipal.

'It's certainly spacious,' said Miriam.

'It's maisonettes, actually,' said Willy.

'Oh,' said Miriam. 'I thought you meant the whole building.'

'No, no! That's a dozen flats there, miss,' said Willy.

'How continental,' said Miriam.

'They're very well appointed inside,' said Willy.

'I'm sure they are.'

'Perhaps we'll make a house call, shall we?' said Willy. 'See it for ourselves? Come on.'

'We should really be getting on, Willy,' I said.

'Nonsense,' said Miriam. 'Bit of colour for the book, eh, Sefton? Some photographs? Also, some material for my new column.'

'You're not a journalist, are you?' asked Willy, suddenly alarmed.

'No, no, silly!' said Miriam. 'I just write about my life for a woman's magazine.'

'Talents that know no end,' said Willy, who was clearly smitten, as so many before and after were smitten.

We picked our way amid piles of sand and gravel and pallets containing bricks and long white wooden A-frames and beams and trusses and Willy rapped officiously on the door of one of the ground-floor maisonettes in the pebble-dashed building. A climbing rose had been rather forlornly planted by the door, nailed and tied with string to some sort of frame made from scavenged wood.

A woman answered almost immediately, wearing a pinny and a sharp expression. Willy explained that he was a representative of the firm that was building the maisonettes and wanted to show some visitors round.

'Good!' said the woman.

'Excellent,' said Willy.

'I've been waiting for you.'

'So,' continued Willy, walking straight past her into the narrow hallway, indicating for us to follow. There was just room for the four of us to stand shoulder to shoulder.

'I've written to you three times,' said the woman. 'And I've spoken to your foreman goodness knows how many. Where have you been?'

'As you can see,' said Willy, opening a narrow door to a tiny bathroom to the right. 'All the houses come with indoor sanitary facilities.'

'Well, well,' said Miriam. 'How marvellous.'

'It doesn't flush,' said the woman. 'It's not worked for months. We're having to slop it out.'

'Oh dear,' said Miriam.

'Have you brought your tools?' continued the woman. 'Are you going to fix it now?'

'I'm sorry,' said Willy. 'I represent the builders rather than the landlords, madam, I'm afraid,' said Willy. 'I thought I explained.'

'We need this fixed,' said the woman.

'And I'm sure it will be fixed,' said Willy. 'If you don't mind?' He leaned past the woman and tapped a wall. 'Solid brick construction throughout, as you can hear.' The wall gave a hollow echo in response. 'Homes for heroes!'

'It's all partition,' said the woman. 'No insulation. Walls are like paper. Look, the other problem is this damp in the bedroom. There's mushrooms growing in here!' She started to walk into the room leading directly off the hall, but Willy turned right instead and we followed into what was the one and only reception room, just big enough for a tiny square table on a rag rug on the lino floor, and an old iron fold-up bed concertinaed under the window. 'And a fireplace in every room,' continued Willy, gesturing towards the tiny brown-tiled hearth.

'Gives no heat,' said the woman. 'We all have to sleep in here together in the winter, for the warmth.'

'You've got electric lights, I see,' said Miriam, gesturing at the bare bulb dangling over the table.

'Doesn't work half the time.'

'Kitchen,' said Willy, gesturing towards a room leading off the reception room, which accommodated a Baby Belling, a sink, a few shelves, and nothing else.

'Kitchenette,' said the woman.

'A few chromium fittings and it'd be the equal of anything on Park Lane!' said Willy.

'What's he talking about?' said the woman.

'And so concludes our tour,' said Willy, beating a hasty retreat to the front door.

The woman grabbed at Miriam's arm as we caught up with Willy in the hall. 'You're not thinking of renting one of these, are you?' she asked her.

'No,' said Miriam.

'Good. Because my advice is don't. These places are worse than the tenements.'

'Surely not,' said Miriam.

'Teething troubles,' said Willy. 'Only to be expected. Rome wasn't built in a day, eh?'

'We've been here a year,' said the woman.

'Well, thank you, madam, for showing us round,' said Willy.

'Yes,' said Miriam. 'It's really been an education.'

'Bit of a whistlestop, I'm afraid,' said Willy, striding away from the building as fast as he could, and lighting a cigarette. 'But gives you an idea, I hope.' He stood at a distance and admired the building. 'What do you think?'

'Absolutely ghastly,' said Miriam. She was never shy of stating her opinions.

'Can I offer you a cigarette?' Willy asked Miriam.

'I have my own, thank you.' Which she did not.

'It's not for the likes of you, of course,' said Willy, his eyes fixed on Miriam. I'd seen it before: men often became drawn into argument with Miriam, mistaking the argument for a kind of flirtation. I often made the same mistake myself.

'Not for the likes of anyone, I wouldn't have thought,' said Miriam.

'People need houses,' said Willy.

'People need homes more than they need houses,' said Miriam, 'and I'm afraid I find it difficult to see how your buildings could ever be regarded as homes.'

'Matter of taste, perhaps?' said Willy.

'Nothing to do with taste,' said Miriam. 'And everything to do with quality – and intention.'

Willy took another couple of quick, excited drags on his cigarette and then ground it out underfoot. 'With all due respect, miss, I hardly think you're an expert in housing.'

'With all due respect, sir, I hardly think you and your Mr Klein are experts either, on the evidence of these buildings.'

Willy laughed.

'Hardly a laughing matter, is it?' said Miriam. 'Jerry-building? I'm sure there must be rules and regulations about this sort of thing, aren't there?'

'There are indeed, miss. And we know exactly what we're doing, thank you.'

'Yes,' said Miriam. 'I'm sure you know exactly what you're doing. That's hardly reassuring though, is it? Have you by chance visited the Karl-Marx-Hof municipal buildings in Vienna?'

'I can't say I have,' said Willy.

'Well, I have. Father and I visited, for some article he was writing. And I have to say, I thought they were a fine example of how to provide housing for the masses.'

'I don't know how they do things in Vienna, miss. But this is England.'

'And might we English not expect housing of a similar standard to the Austrian?' said Miriam.

'Anyway,' said Willy, realising that he wasn't going to get anywhere with Miriam, but playing a final gambit. 'Perhaps I can take you for dinner sometime and we could discuss it further?'

'I don't think so,' said Miriam. 'I doubt we'd have anything to talk about beyond your blatant buccaneering, sir. We should really get on, shouldn't we, Sefton?'

'Yes,' I agreed.

Willy looked crushed – and determined. I'd seen the look before. There was not a man who didn't think he was a match for Miriam, and who wasn't.

'Well, just remember Mr Klein's offer, Sefton,' he said to me. 'Give it some thought, won't you?'

'I certainly will, Willy,' I said.

'He certainly won't, Willy,' said Miriam.

I was glad to get out of Becontree.

CHAPTER 8

THE DAGENHAM GIRL PIPERS

I can only describe the scene that we eventually came upon in Colchester as 'strange'. (Morley, I should say, did not like the word 'strange'. He regarded it as lacking in specificity, 'a terrible failing in a word' – see *Morley's Vocabulary Builder: Words to Use and Words to Avoid* (1932) – as if it were somehow its own fault.)

Morley's ambitious itinerary for our trip up through Essex suggested that after Becontree we were supposed to visit Epping Forest ('Poor John Clare!' read his scribbled notes. 'Mad as a hatter!'), Romford's famous brewery, Tiptree for the jam, the villages around Saffron Walden ('Cromwell's head-quarters – the heart of Radical Essex!'), the Marconi works in Chelmsford ('Inventive Essex!'), before finally heading to Colchester for the Oyster Feast. But after our tour with Willy Mann of the jerry-built houses of Becontree we were forced to cut short our peregrinations and to press on directly to Colchester to make it in time for the Oyster Feast. Miriam, needless to say, drove like a maniac. I shan't even attempt to describe the Essex countryside: it all looked perfectly pleasantly blurred.

And it got blurrier. The Lagonda had started juddering and had picked up a distinct knocking sound somewhere just past Ongar.

'What's that?' asked Miriam, above the sound of the roar of the engine.

'I'm not sure,' I said. 'We should stop and get it looked at.'

'It's probably fine,' said Miriam. 'It'll stop in a minute.'

It didn't stop in a minute. Or indeed in five or in ten minutes.

'I really think we ought to stop, Miriam.'

'We are not stopping,' said Miriam.

'I think we should.'

'You can think what you like, Sefton. I am not going to miss the Oyster Feast for the sake of some pathetic grumbling engine, thank you,' said Miriam.

'You may not have a choice, Miriam,' I said.

'Well you see, that's the difference between us, isn't it?' said Miriam, looking at me pityingly, with one of her hard-edged sideways stares. 'You don't seem to understand that there is always a choice, Sefton. And this,' she continued, stamping her foot violently on the accelerator, causing the car to jolt forward, 'is my choice.'

Essex was jerked out of my vision. The Lagonda kept making its unhappy sounds and Miriam kept on thrashing it mercilessly. I made one last attempt to intervene.

'The Lagonda is a very finely balanced car,'

I shouted, somewhere around the Rodings. 'If you don't treat it right you're going to end up doing it serious damage.'

'And I Am a Very Finely Balanced Woman, Sefton,' yelled Miriam back at me. 'And exactly the same applies.'

Controlling the Lagonda with sheer willpower, and not inconsiderable strength, she pushed it to the very limits, tearing through the roads of Essex towards Colchester, slow into corners, fast out, continually over-revving – a terrible habit of hers – until somehow we all arrived in one piece. Just. The car smelled of misery and burned fuel. It would clearly require some serious mechanical care and attention, but Miriam didn't care. She was triumphant: she'd taught the machine obedience; she'd shown it who was boss.

'See,' she said. 'I told you it'd be fine. Come on then. Let's not hang around, now we're here. We have oysters to eat!'

We had parked some distance away from the centre of the town, there being roadworks every-where; it seemed like every street was being dug up at once. Despite her admonitions to me, Miriam spent a long time carefully reapplying her make-up in the car and then changing into evening wear – a scarlet gown with green evening coat and long black gloves – which was no mean feat, even on the accommodating and well-appointed back seat of the Lagonda, the outfit requiring much energetic wriggling and a helping hand with the zip.

(With my eyes shut tight, I should say – which was also no mean feat.)

We then left the poor vehicle and trudged up a steep hill amid a crowd of men, women and children who were most definitely not dressed in evening wear but who were all busy consuming roasted chestnuts and cramming themselves into the streets around Colchester's magnificent Town Hall, a vast and bewildering building that had all the appearance of a stout English yeoman's version of a Venetian palazzo. 'A fine example of Victorian baroque,' according to Morley in *Essex*. 'Built between 1898 and 1902 for the princely sum of £55,000, making it one of the most expensive public buildings in England, Colchester's Town Hall contains many offices, grand public rooms, the magnificent mayor's parlour and of course the famous Moot Hall, the whole thing topped off with a huge and ornate tower that is in effect a giant gauntlet thrown down to the town's upstart rival, Chelmsford.'

Morley was a great fan of Colchester's rather strange and aggressive architecture, controversially describing the town in *The County Guides* not as 'picturesque' but rather as 'picaresque', a 'town that seems to invite adventure'. As well as the Town Hall, and the presence of so many Roman ruins, and the barracks – all of which contributed to the town's peculiar air of menace – there was also the presence of Jumbo, the vast building in the centre of the town, which dominates the

72

skyline much as the Empire State Building dominates New York, or the Eiffel Tower Paris, the only difference being that Jumbo is not a world-famous tourist attraction or a state-of-the-art office building but an enormous, ugly, red brick water tower. Built in the late 1800s, the building apparently received its nickname from a local clergyman, whose rectory fell beneath its enormous shadow. 'If not exactly one of the seven modern wonders of the world,' writes Morley of Jumbo in *The County Guides*, 'then it is most certainly one of the seven modern wonders of Essex.' He did not specify the other six.

Dusk was falling and Jumbo was brooding as Miriam and I came to a halt before the Town Hall. We could go no further: the crowd was too dense. Above the sound of mass roasted-chestnut munching came a low moaning sound in the distance; Miriam raised one of her expressive eyebrows at me and asked if I knew what it was.

'I think I know what it is,' remarked some wag standing next to us in the crowd. 'I hear it once a week, regular as clockwork, on a Saturday night when I get home from the pub. That's the good old sound of an Essex girl, if you know what I mean, miss.'

Miriam, thank goodness, did not respond in kind to this crude provocation and fortunately the moan soon became a drone and eventually a definable tune: it was in fact the sound of the Dagenham Girl Pipers.

The Dagenham Girl Pipers. According to Morley in *The County Guides: Essex*, nothing sums up the odd, eccentric spirit of the county more clearly than the Dagenham Girl Pipers. For anyone who has never been lucky enough to see the actual kilted Cockney sparrows in full fig and full flow all I can say is that their name is an entirely complete and proper summary. They are from Dagenham, they are girls, and they are pipers – facts and states that in and of themselves are of course unremarkable, but as Morley always liked to say, there is nothing new under the sun, except in combination. Formed in 1930 by Reverend Joseph Waddington Graves – 'lovely man,' according to Morley, who had interviewed him for some newspaper or other, 'Canadian, absolute loon' – the Dagenham Girl Pipers initially consisted of just a dozen keen young girls from his Sunday School but within a few short years they had become a fully professional touring troupe who skirled their way round Europe in their distinctive Royal Stewart tartan.

The crowd burst into applause as the girls appeared at the bottom of the road in their fabulous costumes – kilts, tartan socks, black velvet jackets and tam o' shanters – bellowing on their bagpipes, a vision guaranteed both to haunt and delight even the hardiest and hardest-hearted onlooker, perhaps even a Scot, and all illuminated by the town's remarkable bright modern street lighting, which made it look as though the girls were performing on a West End stage, rather than a tarmacked Essex street in early autumn.

'Those lassies certainly know how to blow,' remarked the wag standing by us, as we all watched the girls, utterly entranced, as they marched up to the Town Hall, promptly stopped blowing, laid down their pipes, and launched into a complex choreographed reel and sword dance.

'Don't they just,' said Miriam. 'And they know how to move. A winning combination, I would say.'

If anything, the evening then got even stranger. Following the Dagenham Girl Pipers came a procession of school-children wearing papier mâché shell heads, a troop of Lancers from the local barracks on their horses, the band of the 1st Royal Munster Fusiliers banging out 'The Men of Merry England', and a long solemn line of dignitaries, including Morley, who didn't spot us waving and shouting frantically in the crowd. This motley crew paraded up to the doors of the Town Hall and disappeared inside.

'Now what?' asked Miriam.

'Now they all go and get drunk on our money!' said the man standing next to us.

'Well, we'd better go and join them, hadn't we, Sefton?'

CHAPTER 9

THE ROLE OF PAGEANTRY

Forcing our way through the crowd, we eventually made it to the doors of the Town Hall, which would not have disgraced the Florence Baptistery. (Indeed, it is 'Essex's answer to the *Porte del Paradiso*', according to Morley in *Essex*.) Miriam's name was included on the guest list for the Oyster Feast with Morley, but alas my name was not and so I was invited – politely but firmly – to leave the building.

'He's with me,' protested Miriam, linking her arm with mine in a gesture of pleading affection.

'But he's not on my list,' said the man guarding the door, who was dressed in cheap, ill-fitting beadle-style ceremonial robes, which made him look like a cut-price lord mayor.

'That may be,' said Miriam. 'But I'm sure you'll agree that I cannot possibly be held responsible for any errors on *your* list. *He's* with *me*.' And she began dragging me towards the door.

''Fraid not, miss,' said the man, who stood before the door with arms wide. 'If he's not on the list he's not getting in.'

'Well, really!' said Miriam. 'If that's the attitude

you're going to take I'll speak to your superior, if you don't mind, and we'll see what he has to say about it.'

The beadle duly called over another man, dressed in slightly less cheap and better fitting ceremonial robes, who also insisted that I would not be gaining entry to the Oyster Feast, since I was not on the list, and who furthermore suggested, after what can only be described as a heated exchange, that if Miriam continued to protest and cause trouble she might prefer to leave with me and not attend the Oyster Feast herself. I was all ready to leave but Miriam suddenly had a brainwave, grabbed at my arm, hissed at the men, and dragged me away from the door and began fishing around in her handbag.

'Honestly!' she kept exclaiming, as she dug around in the bag. 'The sheer cheek of them!' Anyone with the temerity to refuse or challenge Miriam's will or whims – right or wrong – was liable to be accused of sheer cheek. It was one of her favourite terms of disparagement – along with 'the brass neck on them!' and 'the bodger on their bonce!' – which was ironic, since she was the only person I knew to be actually in possession of sheer cheek, a brass neck and indeed a bodger on her bonce, whatever that was. Her handbag contained, I can confidently state, since she handed the entire contents to me, opera glasses, a corkscrew, matches, a cigarette case, several lipsticks, volume one of George Bernard Shaw's blue Pelican *The Intelligent*

77

Woman's Guide to Socialism and Capitalism, and her brand-new press card, which had apparently been issued to her by *Woman* magazine, in recognition of her recent appointment as a columnist.

'*Perfetto*!' she proclaimed, triumphant; she often slipped into Italian when excited, usually at the most inappropriate moment. Reclaiming the other items, she left me holding the press card and tugged me a few yards away from the entrance to the Town Hall.

'That should get you in,' she whispered.

I looked at the press card and pointed out that it seemed to be issued in her name.

'Well of course it's issued in my name, silly. It's my press card.'

'Which means I can't use it,' I said, pointing out the obvious.

'Oh, don't be so blasted feeble, Sefton. Just put your thumb over my name and you'll be fine. The one and only time I'll be under your thumb, mind!' she said, throwing back her head and marching straight over to the entrance and proceeding inside with a little backward wave of her hand. 'Make the most of it! See you inside!'

During my years with Morley I became a rather accomplished and convincing liar – it requires sheer cheek, a brass neck and a bodger on the bonce – and I did indeed manage to make my way into the Town Hall that evening, thumb firmly over Miriam's name, the beadles far too occupied to prevent me, and then up the stairs to the Moot

Hall, where the Oyster Feast was due to take place. Members of the press were allowed to mill around outside the doors, obstructing the waiters who were busy hurrying in and out.

From my occasional glimpses inside, and from what Morley explained to me later, what appeared to happen was this.

As every schoolboy knows, every year the Essex oyster fishery is declared open by Colchester's mayor. The oystermen present the mayor with their produce and the mayor then invites important guests to the Moot Hall for the Oyster Feast, a grand civic occasion that also acts as a useful advertisement for the local oyster industry. Though it is perhaps now hard to believe, the kind of brouhaha that these days surrounds a film premiere was then guaranteed the Oyster Feast. The mayor that year was a local businessman – 'a classic chamber of commerce sort of chap', according to Morley – named Arthur Marden, a local quarry owner, who was a rather witty-looking fellow with thinning ginger hair, freckles, and an endearing amused expression on his face. The guests at the grand civic reception included Mr Ormsby-Gore, Secretary of State for the Colonies, Sir Holman Gregory K.C. and indeed the aviatrix, Amy Johnson – about whom much more later.

The Oyster Feast is an event of great pageantry but – according to Morley, at least – of no great antiquity, dating back only to the late nineteenth century. What it lacks in age it more than makes up for in enthusiasm. ('Reminds me rather of the theatre-state of Bali,' Morley remarked to me later that evening. 'Ever been?' I had – of course – never been to Bali. 'Rather impressive,' according to Morley. 'And also indicative, all forms of ritual amounting to much more than mere drapery and dramatics, don't you think, Sefton?' I agreed, since that was all that was required. 'Pageantry plays an altogether more substantial role in our personal and political affairs than we care to admit, does it not? In the kitchen. In the boardroom. In the bedroom.' I suppose it does.)

The Moot Hall itself looks rather like a cross between a gaudy hotel ballroom and some crazy baroque Italian church. There are colonnades, a big barrel-vaulted ceiling, lots of stained glass, an organ, and also lots of massive and rather second-rate-looking oil paintings. In addition, on that evening the Hall was decked throughout with roses, the scent powerful enough to mask the strong competing smells of women's perfume and rather musty macho civic pride. 'It's all very Essex, isn't it?' remarked Miriam. By the time I got my first peek into the Hall all the guests and dignitaries were already seated, impatiently jangling and glittering in their chains of office and fine jewellery.

As we journalists stood at the door – or the journalists and me, I should perhaps say, my credentials being not my own and belonging entirely to Miriam and *Woman* magazine – a little man came striding past us and into the Hall, all done up in white tie, white gloves, a blue coat with brass buttons, and carrying a threatening-looking gold mace.

'Who's he?' I asked the journalist beside me.

'The White Rabbit,' I was told.

'Seriously though?'

'That's Len Starling, the Town Sergeant.'

I thought Mr Starling the Town Sergeant had a rather sad and courageous sort of a face as he marched through the Hall and set the mace before the mayor's throne, which sat at the far end on a raised dais. The mayor – Arthur Marden – sat in his robes looking endearingly amused, weighed down with the considerable medallions of his office and the mace now before him. He did his best to nod solemnly through his permanent smile, in response to which Mr Starling bowed, turned and marched swiftly out of the Hall, only to enter again moments later carrying a vast silver platter bearing oysters, which he proceeded to parade slowly to Mayor Marden, who this time stood solemnly to receive it, smiled, chose an oyster from the platter and noisily slurped it down. And so the feast began.

Amid all the oyster-slurping there were interminable speeches in praise of the brilliance and the renown of the function, and the brilliance and the renown of the guests, and the brilliance and the renown – and the famed hospitality – of the mayor, jovial Arthur Marden. These speeches were followed by equally interminable toasts to the

81

king, the royal family, the armed services, the clergy, the Houses of Parliament, the town and trade of Colchester, the oyster fishery, to health, happiness, education, the arts, the sciences, women, society . . . and so I slipped outside quickly to smoke.

Down the side and round the back of the Colchester Town Hall is rather dark and dingy, the opposite of the inside, but one is granted a magnificent view of what I later learned is the town's Dutch Quarter, so named not because it looks particularly Dutch – though it does look rather pleasant and quaint – but after the Flemish weavers who settled in the area during the reign of Elizabeth I. A small group of men who may well have been Flemish weavers – but who were in fact mostly kitchen staff, waiters and who did not look particularly pleasant or quaint – stood by the open kitchen door, smoking and talking in conspiratorial fashion. I approached innocently enough and asked if I might cadge a cigarette. I was not met with what one would call the warmest of Essex welcomes.

'Who the fuck do you think you are?' asked one of the kitchen staff, cigarette clamped between his teeth. He had a mean face, like a small dead bird, caught with a worm in its beak.

'And who the fuck do you think you are?' I responded. It was the only sensible reply.

'You're not from round here,' he said, immediately squaring up to me.

'You're right about that,' I said. 'Congratulations.' Stupid but not blind.

'I fight anyone who's not from round here,' said the man.

Anyone who's ever been in the wrong place at the wrong time, who has ever stepped inside the wrong pub or onto the wrong street on the wrong side of town will know how easy it is to find oneself unexpectedly in just such a situation and that it's most certainly not a good situation to find oneself in. I reckoned I maybe had a chance of taking the man on in a fight, but I stood much less chance when faced with him and half a dozen of his companions, who were now gathering all around me. Fortunately I was saved by the actions of one brave man, who stood the others down.

'Come on, leave him,' he told them. 'He only asked for a smoke.' This gallant fellow then shook a cigarette from its packet, offered it to me, and lit a match for me to light it. In the tiny flare of the match, and in the light cast from the open kitchen door, it struck me that the man bore a passing resemblance to a young Cary Grant, if Cary Grant had been a lightweight boxer, who had also trained as a priest: he had movie-star-cum-mauler-cum-monastic features, debonair yet also rough and incorruptible, hair perfectly parted, a confident chin, a truly good-looking young fellow, though perhaps with something lacking about him, something contrite and sorrowful.

'I fight anyone who's not from round here,' insisted the other man. 'He's not from here, I'm going to fight him.'

'Shut up,' said my Cary Grant lookalike.

'Do you know who I am?' said the other man.

'I'm afraid I have no idea,' I said.

'I'm one of the Cowley Brothers,' he said.

'Uh-huh,' I said.

'I said leave it, Joe,' repeated the Cary Grant lookalike. 'Don't be stupid.'

'You better watch who you're calling stupid!' said the man who was one of the Cowley Brothers, and who was clearly keen to take on anyone who wasn't from here.

'Come on,' said my new friend, ignoring the Cowley brother, as if he were less than an irritant. 'Come inside.' And so I followed him into the Town Hall kitchens.

Safely inside the kitchens, which were a proverbial hive of feast-related activity, my saviour introduced himself as Billy Ball. 'Everyone calls me Bouncing,' he said. 'For obvious reasons.' He was indeed an energetic sort of fellow. 'Don't take any notice of Joe. The Cowleys are all crazy. They'd fight their own shadow.'

He explained that he was one of the senior waiting staff at the Oyster Feast. 'And what are you doing here?' he asked, not in a challenging way but in an entirely friendly fashion.

I said I was a journalist, which wasn't actually true, but which was the pretext on which I had gained entry to the Town Hall and which therefore seemed like a prudent answer. I also said that I was writing a book about Essex, which had the

84

more obvious merit of being true, and in the grand scheme of things I thought that the small lie and the bigger truth probably balanced each other out. Billy Ball not only took my explanation at face value, he was impressed – which of course made me feel rather embarrassed at my rather tricky moral equivalencing.

'I've never met a journalist before,' he said. He wasn't meeting one now, but I thought it better for him to persist in this misapprehension rather than my having to go back outside and explain myself to the Cowley brother. I suggested that I was intending to write something about behind the scenes at the Oyster Feast. He was delighted.

'Here, I'll show you how the lads prepare the oysters,' he said.

'No need,' I said.

'No no,' said Billy. 'Come on.'

There were three men working away at a long table in the middle of the kitchen, furiously shucking and laying oysters onto silver platters. Crates and baskets of fresh oysters were arriving at an alarming pace.

'Mind if we join you?' asked Billy.

'Be our guest,' said one of the men, without looking up.

'Many hands,' said another.

'Make light work,' said the third.

'He's a journalist,' said Billy, nodding towards me.

'Is he?' said the third man.

'Writing about the Oyster Feast,' said Billy proudly.

'Tell your readers it's a waste of money,' said the first man.

'Shush,' said Billy. 'Take no notice of him.' He grabbed an oyster from a basket set in the middle of the table. 'Here we are then,' he said. 'We give them a quick scrub, just for appearance sake.' Scrub he duly did. 'And then we take one of these.' He picked up from the table a vicious-looking short pointed knife.

'Not a butter knife, mind,' said one of the men at the table.

'Or a screwdriver,' said another.

'Definitely not a screwdriver,' said the third man.

'A proper Essex oyster knife,' said the first man.

'And then we do this,' said Billy.

'Careful, Billy,' said the first man.

'I'm being careful,' said Billy. Holding the oyster shell firmly in one hand, he inserted the knife at the hinge point between the upper and lower shells of the oyster, then began rotating it slightly, first one way then the other.

'You've got to be careful,' said the first man.

'Or you'll have your ruddy fingers off,' said the other.

'As Charlie here can show you!' said the first man.

The third man standing at the table held up his left hand, grinning, displaying just three and a half fingers.

'The knives are sharp,' said the first man.

'And strong,' said the second.

'You could gut a man,' said the third, 'with an oyster knife.'

'Oh,' I said.

'Anyway,' continued Billy, 'once you're in, you move the knife across here – as close as possible to the upper shell so you that you sever the muscle that holds them together, without scrambling the meat.'

'You don't want to scramble the meat,' said the first man.

'That's right,' agreed the second man.

'Never,' agreed the third.

'There we are!' announced Billy – and with that the two parts of the oyster shell came apart and there was the oyster, creamy white, the colour of bacon fat, glistening on the lower shell. 'Look at that. Beautiful. Nice and firm, isn't she?'

'Just as nature intended,' said the first man.

'Not bad for an amateur,' said the second man.

'Takes a few goes,' said the third man.

'But you soon learn how,' said the first.

'Like undoing a brassiere,' said the second.

'Right,' I said.

'Look,' said Billy, 'that little muscle there, that's what keeps it shut.'

I studied the tiny white oyster muscle as Billy carefully transferred the oyster to a tray of ice, to join another half-dozen or so.

'Oysters should always be served on the round,'

explained Billy. 'The lower shell. Never on the flat, the upper shell.'

'And why's that?'

'You want to keep as much liquor as possible, don't you?'

'It's all about the liquor,' said the first man.

'Is it?' I asked.

'That's what makes 'em special,' said the second man.

'Essex oysters,' the three men said together. 'Essex water.'

'Right,' I agreed.

'Go on then,' said Billy.

'Go on what?' I said.

'Have a go.'

'No,' I said, 'I don't think so.'

'Go on,' repeated Billy. 'Be good for your article, wouldn't it?'

'I should really be getting back to the feast.'

'Only take a minute now,' said Billy, and thrust the knife into my hand. 'Quick, now. The lads need a dozen per platter.'

The three shuckers paused in their work and stood watching me, oyster knives in hand. I had no choice.

I took an oyster from the basket, scrubbed it, took it firmly in my right hand and then attempted to dig into it with the oyster knife in my left.

'Leftie, are you?' said the first man.

'Don't want any lefties round here,' said the second.

'Be careful!' said the third. 'Injury to one is an injury to all!'

I had a few more tentative digs. It was more difficult than it looked. I nearly stabbed my palm in the process several times.

'Careful!' said the first man.

'Careful!' said the second.

'Careful!' said the third.

'Would he be better holding it on the table?' said Billy.

'He would,' said the first man.

'He might,' said the second.

'He could,' said the third.

So I held the oyster tight to the table while I used the knife to slide between the upper and lower shells, eventually managing to crack it open, severing the muscle, the oyster, and indeed my hand in the process. The end result was not a pretty sight.

'Not bad,' said the first man.

'For a first attempt,' said the second.

'Bloody mess,' said the third.

'Only a nick,' said Billy, examining my hand. 'Here, come and rinse it under the tap.'

Alas, it was more than a nick.

'That might need dressing,' said Billy. 'I'll go and fetch the first-aid kit.'

While Billy went for the first-aid kit I sat and watched and bled as the oyster shuckers returned to their task and waiters and waitresses arrived with empty platters, and then left again with full ones. The feast was in full swing. When Billy eventually returned he quickly dressed my hand with a bandage and took a platter himself.

'Come on,' he said. 'I'll show you back up.'

On the way up to the Moot Hall – up worn stone stairs – Billy told me all about his life and times.

'I'm an honest hard-working man,' he insisted. I didn't think for a moment he wasn't. On the contrary. As well as working in the evenings as a waiter at various functions in the Town Hall he also worked for a local jeweller's, Hopwood, Son & Payne, '47 High Street. Watch and Clock Makers, Goldsmiths, Silversmiths, Jewellers, Opticians, Souvenirs & Pawnbrokers,' explained Billy. He was at pains to point out that he wasn't just a shop boy. He was a bona fide watch and clock repairer – 'Bona fide self-taught,' as he put it – and was the shop's roving repair man, heading out around the highways and byways of Essex on his Triumph, collecting, delivering and occasionally even fixing watches and clocks as he went. *And* he'd just picked up a new job as a rider on Sunday nights on the Wall of Death at Southend's Kursaal amusement park.

'You're a very busy man,' I said.

'I like to keep myself busy,' he replied. 'It's not good to have time on your hands, is it?'

'That's good coming from a watch and clock repairer,' I said.

Billy laughed. I liked him. He had a genuine

sweet nature about him; keen to help and eager to please.

As we made our way up the final few steps towards the Moot Hall we were greeted by a scene of chaos. Guests were rushing from the Oyster Feast, waiters and waitresses standing staring in amazement.

'What's happened?' Billy asked one of the waiters. 'What's the problem?'

'It's the mayor,' the waiter said.

'Mr Marden?'

'Is he all right?'

'Not really,' said the waiter. 'He's dead!'

CHAPTER 10

THE OYSTER'S LONELY
SUBTERRAQUEOUS SIGH

C onfusion reigned. Making my way down the steps towards the entrance of the Town Hall, I caught up with Miriam and Morley. 'It's ghastly!' said Miriam. It most certainly was.

We were beset by the sight and sound and smell of what Morley would normally have called 'the inevitable consequences of excessive indulgence'. (The inevitable consequences of my own excessive indulgence being something that he was often known to comment upon.) On this occasion, however, he had diagnosed the problem as something entirely other than it appeared.

'Crowd hysteria,' he announced, vigorously twitching his moustache. 'Or, rather, *mania*, hysteria deriving from the Greek *husteria*, of course, meaning – Miriam?'

'Womb, Father,' said Miriam, with some distaste.

'Precisely. Thank you. And since we have both men and women here *mania* seems more appropriate, does it not? Mania deriving from – Sefton?'

'The Latin?'

'Of course. Meaning?'

'Madness?'

'Yes. Insanity, frenzy. Crowd hysteria: crowd *mania*. Nothing more, nothing less. Not uncommon, but terribly dangerous. One person goes, and then the next, and then the next, and so on and so forth and before you know it – boom.'

'Boom?' I said.

'Yes, boom – you've got an epidemic on your hands. Or a riot. Revolution. Disaster. Whatever. Did you ever meet Charles Fort, Sefton?'

I had never met Charles Fort. Indeed I had no idea who Charles Fort was or under what circumstances I might possibly have met him. (The number of Charleses and Charlies that Morley at one time or another asked me if I knew and that I had certainly never met probably ran into the many hundreds, including Mr Chaplin, Mr Lindbergh, Mr Laughton, Mr Atlas, Mr Ives and Charles I of Austria. The mysterious Charles Fort was therefore just one among many.)

'Lived in London for a while,' continued Morley. 'Remarkable fellow. Excellent sense of humour. Collected curious phenomena. Very interested in crowd hysteria. All to do with thresholds of belief, Sefton. Once you get one person to believe something – voom!'

'Voom?'

'Voom, yes. It's an ignition point, d'you see?'

'I see,' I said, which I didn't. What I could actually see were men and women in evening dress variously tottering, staggering, fainting and indeed,

93

alas, violently throwing up in the street. If this was merely the power of suggestion then it was a pretty powerful suggestion. The poor, wretched vomiting souls were being kindly tended to by the Town Hall beadles, police officers, soldiers and by the Dagenham Girl Pipers, resplendent in their tartan. Shadowed by the stately Town Hall it was like a scene from the last days of the Roman Empire, shot on location on Flodden Field. 'What on earth happened?' I asked.

'Voom!' exclaimed Morley. 'Voom!'

'The mayor excused himself from the feast,' said Miriam, rather more helpfully, lighting a cigarette and busily wafting the smoke around, in an attempt to dispel the miasma. 'He left the Hall, and then the next thing we knew people were saying that he'd died and that the oysters had killed him and then—'

'Crowd hysteria took effect,' said Morley. 'As I say, voom!'

'Voom, or boom?' I asked.

'Voom and then boom, Sefton! Ignition point, explosion. As you can see.'

'I see,' I said.

'"O oysters come and walk with us, the Walrus did beseech,"' said Morley, with some logic that was apparent only to him. 'Miriam?'

'Lewis Carroll, Father.'

'Correct!' said Morley.

'What's happened to your hand?' asked Miriam.

'Not been fighting again, I hope,' said Morley. 'I have warned you, Sefton.'

'No,' I said, 'I just caught it on something.' I didn't mention that the something was the wrong end of an oyster knife.

'I don't know what all the fuss is about. I feel absolutely fine,' announced a rather elegant, bold-featured woman who emerged through the crowd to stand beside us. She looked vaguely familiar, but I couldn't quite place her. She looked like she might be a friend of Miriam's – perhaps a few years older. Immaculately dressed, made-up, hair elaborately waved, etcetera. Handsome, bordering on the beautiful. One of Miriam's London set? 'And you two look fine.'

'Of course,' said Morley. 'There's absolutely nothing wrong with the oysters.'

'Then how did the mayor die?'

'I have no idea,' said Morley, 'but I know for sure it wasn't the oysters.'

'But how do you know, Father?' asked Miriam.

'Last major outbreak of poisoning from oysters at a banquet like this was back in 1902, I think I'm right in saying, when the Dean of Westminster – Winchester? – one of them – and a number of others got sick from a batch of contaminated oysters.'

'Were they all right?' asked Miriam. 'Did they recover?'

'Oh no,' said Morley. 'They all died.'

'Father!'

'But all Essex oysters have been specially purified ever since. I'm surprised everybody doesn't know.'

'Of course they don't know, Father.'

'Well, they should. Because it means there's absolutely no chance of the mayor having being poisoned by oysters. No chance whatsoever. None.'

At which precise moment a distinctly pea-greenish-looking middle-aged male dignitary in full evening dress not a few feet away from us spectacularly vomited into the gutter, with the most extraordinary spongy croaking sound, like a giant frog having carefully ransacked the entire contents of its stomach and laid it all out for public examination. The malignant smells were beginning rather to take hold. The croaking sounds were growing all around us.

'Ah, yes,' said Morley. '"The oyster's lonely subterraqueous sigh." Miriam?'

'No idea, Father.'

'Byron, I think, *Don Juan*?'

'Oh, I love *Don Juan*. My dear, would you mind if I stole a cigarette?' asked the woman who had joined us, having produced a silver cigarette case from her handbag and found it empty.

'Of course,' said Miriam, delighted to find another dedicated female smoker. 'It is getting a bit . . . whiffy, isn't it?'

'It's just a shame, isn't it,' said Morley, utterly unperturbed by what was going on all around us, 'that it's not possible to install some kind of window into a man's stomach, to be able to study the movement of the gastric juices.'

'Father!' said Miriam. 'That's appalling.'

'Practical though,' said the woman, having lit her cigarette. 'Very practical, in fairness. It would be an excellent engineering solution to a human problem – if it were possible.'

'I have no doubt that one day it will be possible, my dear. Tiny cameras perhaps ingested or inserted, the equivalent of little windows into the human body?'

'Oh Father, really,' said Miriam.

'And I have no doubt that were we blessed with just such a window into the human stomach at this very moment it would prove conclusively that the oysters are perfectly good to eat,' said Morley. 'All this disorder' – he gestured around us, at the increasingly offensive scene, and then tapped his head with his forefinger – 'is not physical but mental. Honestly. Nothing that a good strong Mazawattee and a ginger snap wouldn't cure. Mental. Mental. Entirely – *entirely* – mental.'

'Yes,' I agreed. *Entirely* entirely mental.

'You two are not feeling any ill effects at all, are you?'

'No,' agreed Miriam and the woman, rather too swiftly, methought.

'There we are then. Sefton? What about you?'

I was in fact beginning to feel more than a little off-colour, though I hadn't actually eaten any oysters. In Spain there were often occasions in camp when the combined stench of one's fellow volunteers, corned beef stew, sour milk and Spanish cigarettes was capable of turning one's stomach

97

– plus the ever present stench of fear, of course. And death. That sweet, seamy, bloody smell.

'I'm absolutely fine,' I said.

'There we are. Proof positive,' said Morley, slapping me heartily on the back – which very nearly made me throw up. 'Disdain not the succulent bivalve. We used to feed you oysters when you were young, Miriam. Do you remember? All mushed up. Excellent baby food. Should be marketed as such. "Oysters for Infants, Adults and the Valetudinary. Oysters for All!" You know Henry VIII liked to start a meal with three or four hundred?'

'That's disgusting!' said Miriam.

'Symbolic foodstuff, you see,' continued Morley, 'the oyster. Consumption of large numbers signifying power. And traditionally associated with sex and death, as you know. I think I'm right in saying that at one time the oyster cellars of New York were to be identified by their glowing red lights . . .'

'As in . . .?' asked the woman.

'Precisely,' said Morley. 'I believe that in the old days one might go to an oyster bar to enjoy not only the taste of a juicy bivalve but also the pleasant company of women – in private booths provided specially for the purpose. Roistering and oystering.'

'How appalling,' said Miriam.

'I don't know,' said the other woman. 'I suppose it served a practical purpose. Two birds with one stone, as it were.'

'Exactly. Law of similarity, you see,' continued Morley. 'Ginseng, rhinoceros horn: they all resemble the human genitalia in one way or another, do they not?'

'Father!' said Miriam. 'Do spare us your ramblings, please. We are in polite company.'

'Oh, don't be concerned on my account,' said the woman. 'I've heard it all before. That's why it's assumed that those who consume oysters possess enhanced sexual powers, is it, Mr Morley? The resemblance?'

'Precisely!' said Morley.

'Oysters?' said Miriam, who could at times be as shockingly prudish as she could be shockingly shocking. 'Human genitalia? If not for the company's sake, Father, do please exert *some* self-control! Things are bad enough as they are, without you free-associating on the theme of human genitalia.'

'Free-associate on, Mr Morley,' said the woman. 'Don't mind me. I rather admire a man with a vivid imagination.'

'I'm sorry, I don't think we've met,' I said, holding out my hand to this remarkable woman who clearly seemed more than able to appreciate and understand Morley's – shall we say idiosyncratic? – conversational manner. He had a terrible propensity to pelt people with facts and ideas and associations. Most people – rightly – tended to duck. This delightfully unflappable woman seemed more than prepared to fling ideas right back at him.

'Oh, how silly of me!' said Morley. 'I forgot. Stephen Sefton, my assistant, this is—'

But at that moment a hush fell upon the crowd – and even upon Morley – as four ambulance men brought the body of Arthur Marden on a long white stretcher from the Town Hall. He had been stripped of his heavy regalia and his hands had been folded on his chest like some dead Plantagenet on his tomb. There were gasps of horror from the crowd. A Dagenham Girl Piper had the good sense to step forward and drape a tartan cape over him. Some people began loudly sobbing.

'Oh, how morbid,' said Miriam disapprovingly. 'You'd think they'd save it for the cemetery.' Like her father, Miriam sometimes rather lacked normal human sympathy and emotions. 'Life's not made of barley sugar, you know,' she often liked to remark – when in fact her own life was of course made almost entirely of barley sugar.

Morley at least had the restraint and good manners to allow the stretcher to pass before continuing with his introductions.

'Yes, Sefton, sorry, as I was saying, this is Amy Johnson, the aviatrix.'

'It's an honour to meet you,' I said, as the doors slammed on the ambulance and poor Arthur Marden was driven away.

Amy Johnson! Amy Johnson was at that time perhaps one of the most famous women in the world, the Bette Davis of the skies. Like everyone else, I was more than familiar with

Miss Johnson's empire-wide flying exploits and her many crashes and near-misses – in her personal as well as her professional life. Her many adventures, and the many ups and downs of her often tempestuous relationship with Jim Mollison, the equally famous aviator, meant that she was rarely out of the newspaper headlines. Amy Johnson was a bona fide celebrity. How on earth could I not have recognised Amy Johnson? I can only explain that she was far more glamorous in real life than she appeared in photographs; I'd only ever seen her in flying gear and goggles, climbing in and out of aeroplanes. She was dressed that evening in a gown that may well have been a Schiaparelli for all I knew; it was certainly, according to Miriam, 'scrummy'. She was also – of course – entirely goggle-free.

'It's a pleasure to meet you,' said Amy Johnson, whose manners were as impeccable as her flying was daring.

'I thought they were rather good, the oysters, actually,' said Morley.

'Rather like licking the bottom of a boat though, don't you think, swallowing an oyster?' said Miriam.

'I was thinking something else entirely,' said Amy Johnson, grinding out her cigarette beneath her heel.

'Have you all just met this evening?' I asked Amy Johnson.

'That's right. I've been reading Mr Morley's

work for years, of course, but we've never met. Although it turns out that the same man taught us to fly, funnily enough.'

'Yes. A Captain Matthews,' said Morley. 'Taught us both. Highly recommended.'

'You can fly?' I asked Morley, astounded.

'Naturally, Sefton. In years to come I believe flying will be as natural a daily activity as riding a bicycle or driving a car. An entirely safe and reasonable means of transport. There'll be aerodromes everywhere. Entire communities will be built around them. Homes will be provided with hangars and . . .'

Another man a few feet away succumbed to the effects of crowd hysteria, causing even Morley – thank goodness – to pause in his aeronautical reflections. (For those wishing to enjoy his reflections at greater length I would point them towards the little-known articles he wrote for *Aero Digest* magazine during the 1930s under the unfortunate pseudonym Ayre O'Naut. Morley's many and various pseudonymous works include his humorous – or at least purportedly humorous – pieces for *Punch*, as R.I.B. Tickler, and the health and fitness articles he wrote for *Physical Fitness* magazine as Mr Mussel. His use of false names and pseudonyms was partly an attempt on his part to avoid the Jack of all Trades label that was often – fairly or unfairly – applied to him and his work, partly to allow him to publish multiple articles in the same issue of a magazine, and partly simply to allow him to indulge in his simple love of word-play: see his long-running and often pun-packed 'Notes of an English Gardener', for example, as Mr Greengrass in *Nature* magazine, and his perfectly serious and unintentionally hilarious advice column as the rather astringent Mr Pickle in the *Daily Express*.)

'Positively Boschean, isn't it?' Morley remarked, at this latest addition to what was now no longer a trickle but a veritable tide of human ooze and effluvia.

'Mmm,' agreed Miriam. 'More Pieter Bruegel the Elder, wouldn't you say, Sefton?'

I grunted. 'But you don't even drive, Mr Morley,' I said.

'That's only because I'm too busy to do so,' said Morley. 'Driving for me alas is a necessity—'

'Which I take care of, Father, on your behalf, like so much else,' said Miriam.

'Thank you, my dear, you do, yes, indeed,' agreed Morley jovially. 'Flying on the other hand remains a pleasant leisure activity. An indulgence.'

'Isn't it just,' said Amy Johnson. 'You know the only time I really feel free is when I'm up in the air.'

'Did you fly in today, Miss Johnson?' asked Morley. 'I forgot to ask.'

'Yes, as it happens, into Stapleford Tawney. Booked out again first thing in the morning.'

'Essex has an aerodrome?' I said. I had not entirely caught up with the aeroplane age.

'It has several, actually,' said Amy Johnson.

'Oh, do keep up, Sefton,' said Miriam. 'This is 1937, man! It's not the 1920s!'

The fetid stench and the pathetic sight of men and women staggering around in confusion and despair was now such that whenever and wherever it had occurred it would have been difficult to concentrate on the conversation. I didn't care whether or not the chaos was the result of crowd hysteria, bad oysters, and how much or how little it resembled the work of painters I'd only half heard of. I'd had enough.

'Do you know, I might excuse myself actually,' I said.

'Are you OK, Sefton?' asked Miriam, managing a disapproving eyebrow-raise. 'Not feeling funny at all?'

'No.'

'Not even just a little bit?'

'No.'

'A teensy-weensy bit queasy? Just a little bit queer? In need of the smelling salts?'

'I'm absolutely fine, thank you.' I was in fact on the very point of heaving – as I'm sure Miriam herself must have been, though she'd never have admitted it. 'I might just go for a little stroll.'

'We'll see you back at our lodgings then, shall we?' said Morley, whose physical constitution was as strong as the proverbial ox's and whose mental make-up was entirely impervious to even the most noxious powers of suggestion.

'Yes,' I readily agreed. 'Where are we staying?'

'Just there,' said Morley, pointing to a hotel a few yards away from the Town Hall. 'The George.'

'Very convenient,' I said.

'Yes. Dates from the fifteenth century, I believe,' said Morley. 'Old coaching inn. One can just imagine the merchants of old travelling down from Yarmouth and Harwich, can't one, on their way to London, stopping off to rest and refresh themselves there. A slice of bloody rare roast beef and a tankard of foaming ale, eh?'

'Yes, Mr Morley,' I said, just.

'Or perhaps half a dozen oysters and couple of gins?'

'I'm going to take a little rest myself,' said Miriam.

'Very well, my dears,' said Morley.

'Goodbye, Miss Johnson,' I said, striding quickly away.

CHAPTER 11

THE AVIATRIX

I very happily wandered the ordinary streets of Colchester for half an hour or more – High Street and Crouch Street and Head Street, with their tobacconists and outfitters, and hardware shops, the confectioners and bakeries – slowly quelling any desire to vomit. Then, as is often the case in such circumstances, the tide of nausea having ebbed, I found myself feeling ravenously hungry. I'd not eaten since breakfast with Miriam back in Soho, which might as well have been a week ago, and so was delighted when I came across a brightly lit pie shop, McCluskeys, with a charming hand-painted sign depicting a shiny, steaming pie in a pie dish. (I should admit that McCluskeys was in fact to all intents and purposes just an ordinary house in an ordinary terraced street, with the kitchen and front room converted to commercial use – no Manze's, but highly recommended nonetheless.) There was a queue of people outside with their pie basins and mugs for gravy and the promise of all sorts of pies – without oysters – within. So I joined the queue. The talk in the queue was of course of the events at the Oyster

Feast, and of the death of the mayor, who was, I learned, 'a lovely fellow', 'far too young' and who most certainly 'didn't deserve the indignity of it'.

I'd only been waiting and eavesdropping on this fascinating back-street gossip a few moments when I noticed out of the corner of my eye a woman approaching. It was dark but there was something about her, something in the way she moved, something different. She had a bearing that was not a back-streets sort of bearing. And then I realised.

'Miss Johnson?' I said, as she approached. The aviatrix.

'Ah, Morley's assistant. I'm terribly sorry, I've forgotten your name. I met so many people this evening.'

'Sefton,' I said. 'Stephen Sefton.'

'Sefton, yes, that's right.'

'You've changed?' I said, rather redundantly, since she obviously had.

'Yes. I couldn't put up with that evening garb the whole time. I'm much more comfortable in this.' This was a fine fitted misty-blue woollen suit with a long skirt that vaguely resembled one of her flying outfits – and indeed she had a white silk scarf knotted cravat-style at her throat, as though she were about to mount a plane and roar off to Africa at any moment. Miriam would perhaps have described the outfit as practical and stylish, though she would of course have disdained the practical. 'Mr Morley went on with his daughter. I just thought I'd take a stroll. Off again early tomorrow.'

'Well, I'm just queuing for a pie here, Miss Johnson, if you'd like to join me?' Which is one of those sentences that one never expects oneself to say and which indeed one is utterly surprised to find sayable even at the point of its saying. Amy Johnson's reply was equally surprising.

'Do you know, Stephen Sefton, that is the most welcome invitation I've received in a very long time.'

Which is how I ended up spending one of the most peculiar nights of my life, after what had already been one of the most peculiar days of my life, sharing a meat and vegetable pie with two mugs of tea with one of the most famous women in the world in Colchester's back streets, discussing the meaning of life, flying, romance and the distant prospects of war. It was one of those intimate, unexpected evenings that one occasionally enjoys with total strangers, when one recognises in the other some deep quality or great fascination that goes unnoticed by those we know and love. The sort of evening that is often aided by alcohol, and which can often lead to complications.

'Are you heading back to the hotel?' asked Amy Johnson, after we left McCluskeys.

'I'll maybe call in to a public house on the way,' I said.

'Then I might join you, if I may?' asked Miss Johnson. And join me she most certainly did. In the Abbey Arms on St John's Green. And in the Live and Let Live. The Shoulder of Mutton.

The Goat and Boot Inn. The Duke of Connaught, the Flying Fox, the Royal Standard, the Wig and Fidget. Some of the pubs alas refused to serve women in the public bars and some were without saloons, but in others we found seats and drank quietly, deep in conversation, until we were interrupted and moved on. Miss Johnson was recognised by men and women everywhere – that double-take I'd noticed occasionally with Morley, but multiplied many times and which preceded the inevitable request for autographs. If I learned anything from my years with Morley, and as I was reminded most forcibly that evening with Miss Johnson, it is to permit the famous their privacy. They have so little they have to protect it with their lives.

'Can I ask you, Stephen, have you read my husband's book?' Miss Johnson asked me, once we were several pubs in; it may have been the Rose and Crown. Or the King's Head.

'Whose book?'

'Jim Mollison. My husband. *Playboy of the Air*.'

'I can't say I have, miss, no.'

'I'm so glad.' She had produced her silver cigarette case and was gently tapping it on its side upon the table as she spoke. 'Most of it's entirely untrue, of course.'

'I see.'

'It's amazing that you can live with someone for so long and yet apparently never know them at all, isn't it?'

'Yes,' I agreed.

'I wonder if perhaps the fault was mine.'

'There's always fault on either side in these circumstances,' I said, not wishing either to upset or offend her.

'Yes,' she said, ceasing in her tapping of the cigarette case. 'But you see we women have to spend so much time putting ourselves over and winning men over, that sometimes we lose sight of who we really are. The carapace becomes us. We lose our inner selves.' She took a rather mournful sip of her glass of gin. 'Women are like oysters really, Stephen.' She placed a hand on mine.

'Are they?'

'The harder the skin, the outer casing, the softer the heart. It takes something to prise you open, and then . . . You find you're simply consumed. Just like that.' She clicked her fingers and took up her cigarette case again.

'I'm not sure I quite follow, Miss Johnson.'

'No, of course, you wouldn't understand. I shouldn't be talking to you like this.'

'No, no, it's fine,' I said, laying my hand gently on her arm. 'Sometimes it's easier to—'

'You should ask Morley's daughter all about it; she'll know what I mean.'

'Miriam?'

'Pretty girl,' said Amy Johnson. 'Very pretty girl. When are the two of you getting married?'

'We're not getting married,' I said.

'Really? Oh. I assumed. Her engagement ring.'

'Miriam is always getting engaged to someone.'

'I see. So the two of you are not . . .'

'No, no,' I said. 'For better or for worse, I am entirely single, Miss Johnson.'

She looked at me rather curiously at that point, I thought, with some kind of realisation. And then she started talking about some of the flights she was planning – big plans.

'One must seize every opportunity that life presents one with,' she said.

'I couldn't agree more,' I said.

'When it comes to flying, I mean.'

I couldn't work out whether we were talking increasingly at cross-purposes or entirely along the same lines.

I went to get us another drink, for clarification.

The barman asked me if I'd heard the news.

'What news?' I asked, taking the opportunity to light a cigarette. 'About the Oyster Feast? Yes.'

'Len Starling.'

'I don't know Mr Starling, I'm afraid. I'm not from round here.'

'The Town Sergeant.'

'Ah,' I said. The Town Sergeant was the busybody fellow in the Moot Hall who had presented the mayor with his oysters. The man in the white tie and white gloves and the blue coat with brass buttons. The White Rabbit.

'Yes, what about him?'

'They've taken him in for questioning, apparently.'

'Oh dear.'

'On suspicion of poisoning the mayor at the feast.'

'Goodness me.'

'I'm not surprised,' said the barman, setting our drinks on the bar. 'Everyone knows about Len.'

'Knows what?'

'Nod's as good as a wink to a blind man,' said the barman, nodding over towards where I'd been sitting with Amy Johnson, meaning either something to do with Len Starling, or Miss Johnson, I wasn't entirely sure – though when I turned to take our drinks back to the table, I understood.

Amy Johnson had gone.

CHAPTER 12

BLUEBEARD'S CASTLE

She had left her rather handsome cigarette case. I pocketed it, finished both our drinks and returned to the hotel, where I then proceeded to drink French brandy by myself in the bar until late, in the full expectation of catching Amy Johnson and presenting her cigarette case to her on her return. I was sure we had more to talk about. When she hadn't returned by one o'clock I retired to my room.

I woke the next morning feeling about as rough as if I'd eaten a dozen bad oysters washed down with a gallon of Tizer, my sleep having been upset by dreams of a woman riding the wings of a biplane while I was the pilot and she was standing out on the wing and then suddenly she leapt off, and went sailing down towards the earth and there was absolutely nothing I could do to save her.

After washing and dressing I went straight down to reception and asked if I could leave the cigarette case for Miss Johnson. But Miss Johnson had apparently checked out early that morning. And the hotel was not in a position to provide me with a forwarding address. Which meant that I was in possession of Miss Johnson's handsome silver cigarette case until the next time we met. I examined the case: sterling silver, exquisitely and intricately engraved in an Art Deco style with what I assumed was Miss Johnson's very own Gypsy Moth aeroplane. I guessed that it was probably worth at least—

But I immediately put the thought from my mind. Under no circumstances would I even consider selling Amy Johnson's cigarette case in order to pay off my debts to Delaney. That would be utterly monstrous.

However, nonetheless, and coincidentally, Hopwood, Son & Payne, 'Watch and Clock Makers, Goldsmiths, Silversmiths, Jewellers, Opticians, Souvenirs & Pawnbrokers', at 47 High Street, Colchester, is just a few steps from the George Hotel. I had noticed it the night before. Since I was passing – and I was passing – and it was open I thought I might just make an enquiry.

Hopwood's – in case you don't know it – is a curious establishment, part high-class jeweller's and part emporium of tat. The shop's window display seemed to have been designed as a miniature Oyster Feast-themed stage set, with red curtains as the backcloth and various shelves, brackets, pads, stands, boxes, platforms and indeed Plexiglass hands reaching up and out and across a pale blue sea of fabric resembling a turbulent ocean, arrayed with sprays of rings, brooches, vanity cases, watch straps, spoons, tankards, baby rattles and teething rings, in an arrangement that suggested not so much the promise of luxury as the possibility of beachcombing for the flotsam and jetsam thrown up by a fancy goods shipwreck. At the centre of this tidal wrack, beneath a sign hanging from delicate silver chains announcing 'GENUINE PEARLS FROM GENUINE PERSIAN OYSTERS', was a large crude ceramic oyster shell displaying a shiny pus-yellow oyster at least half an inch in diameter and which looked suspiciously as though it needed lancing. The whole scene had the curious but no doubt intended effect of arousing in the passer-by the strong desire to explore what on earth was on offer inside the shop. If this was the flotsam and jetsam what cargo from distant Ophir – as Morley might put it – awaited inside?

Opening the door activated a loud tinkling chime and as I stepped across the threshold my entrance was mirrored by a sober-suited middle-aged man stepping through a curtain at the back of the shop. He wished me a cheery good morning, I wished him a cheery good morning in return: it was almost as if I had entered a stage set through the window display and was simultaneously viewing myself entering a stage set through the window display. This sense of strange symmetry and illusion was further emphasised by the illuminated and mirrored window recesses on either side of the shop, which displayed jewellery of all kinds and all kinds of everything – trophies, lighters, clocks, cutlery,

charm bracelets and a wide assortment of orna-
ments – in an endless mirrored distance. Instead
of the usual display cabinets there was a series of
small glass-topped display tables set out as if in a
restaurant, ready for intimate conversations *à deux*.
I made my way towards the back of the shop,
moving between tables of trinkets and snuff boxes,
past the earrings and the chokers and the jewellery
boxes, to the ring tables with their diamonds and
emeralds, every item with a tiny tag attached,
marked not with a price but with some cryptic
stock figure, presumably so that if you were interested in an item you had to ask the price – and
so the selling could begin.

(Morley writes about the complex psychological
mechanics involved in retailing in his popular
How to Run a . . . series of books – *How to Run
a Sweet Shop, How to Run a Fruit and Vegetable
Shop, How to Run a Surgical Supplies Shop*, etcetera
etcetera – a series that claims to reveal 'the secrets
of the successful retail experience from the perspec-
tive of both the shopkeeper and the customer'.
The advice in the *How to Run a . . .* books, as in
all his books, combines the utterly unobjectionable
and common-sensical with the completely unexpected and bizarre. 'You hook your customer,' he
writes, for example, in *How to Run a Fishing Tackle
Shop*, 'as Isaak Walton hooked his worm, *as though
you loved him.*' 'The good salesperson is possessed
of a dual personality,' he suggests in *How to Run
a Drapery Shop*. 'You should be yourself and yet

– simultaneously – your customer.' And 'The basis of all transactions,' he writes in *How to Run a Household Hardware Shop*, 'is the exchange of knowledge. You must be generous. It will often be the case that you must give away entirely for free much of what you know about screws and nuts and washers and hinges before it is possible to sell even a single screw or a nut, a washer or a hinge. In retailing, you must trust that the universe will provide.' Morley was often ahead of his time and occasionally beyond comprehension.)

But perhaps the most unusual and impressive thing about the unusual and impressive retail experience that was Hopwood, Son & Payne was a big illuminated clock face on the back wall of the shop that had no hands and a sign above it reading 'A Gift From Hopwood, Son & Payne' and a sign below it reading 'Timeless'. Like a low-hanging moon the illuminated clock bathed the entire shop and all its contents in an atmosphere of glittering sadness, like an Ali Baba's cave in Bluebeard's Castle. I was aimlessly admiring a bracelet with a jewelled clasp and strung with half a dozen rows of pearls beneath the light of this strange moon when the sober-suited shop assistant – Hopwood? Son? Payne? – came sidling up to me. He looked deathly pale in the shop's strange light and reflected in its many mirrors appeared almost like a ghost of himself. He spoke with that sinister, low, calm confiding voice beloved of ministers and salesmen.

'Ah, yes. A good choice, sir, if I may say so. A very good choice. Sir knows his jewellery, I take it?'

I most certainly did not know my jewellery.

'In the style of René Boivin,' he said.

'Rather beyond my price range, I fear.'

'You'd be surprised, sir. I could check for you if you'd like? It's for your wife? An anniversary present perhaps? Sir is looking to buy something special for a . . . special lady?'

'Sir is not looking to buy anything at all, I'm afraid,' I said.

'Oh,' he said, doing his best to hide his obvious disappointment. 'Then how can I help you?'

'I was looking for a valuation.'

'I see. For insurance purposes, might I ask?'

'No, no.'

'Security for a loan for sir? Or probate perhaps?'

'No.'

'For sale?'

'Well, perhaps for eventual sale,' I agreed reluctantly. I was rather regretting my decision to cross the threshold. What had seemed like a good idea I now realised was a terrible act of betrayal that would weigh heavily and for ever on my conscience. Then again, a debt of a hundred pounds to the likes of Delaney perhaps weighs even more heavily.

'These are not new goods, I take it?'

'No.'

'And they have been in the family for some time, or they're a recent acquisition?'

'It's a . . . recent acquisition.'

'Very good, sir. Very good. And you have the piece with you?'

'Yes, I do.'

'Could I see it, perhaps?' He held out his hands, as if in prayer or supplication.

I produced the silver cigarette case from my pocket.

'Might I?' said the shop assistant, extending his hands; and I gave him Amy Johnson's case, which was not mine to give.

'Mmm,' said the man. 'Interesting. Mmm. Very interesting.' He held it up close to his pale face for examination and ever so slightly licked his lips, I noted, with an intense curiosity that suggested that he was tempted to swallow the cigarette case whole and ingest it. He had a long poky nose and his hair was grey and receding at the temples. I almost snatched the thing back from him – I suddenly found him revolting. I resisted the temptation. 'I might need to call upon our silver expert, if I may, sir?'

'Of course,' I said.

He disappeared then behind the curtain beneath the moon clock face and within moments another man appeared. It was none other than Billy 'Bouncing' Ball, my friend from the Oyster Feast. He was holding the cigarette case carefully between his two index fingers, as though literally measuring its worth. He was in characteristic good humour and as before had not a hair out of place. A leather apron hung around his waist and a jeweller's spectacle loupe perched on his forehead gave him the appearance of a Dr Frankenstein mid-experiment.

'Stephen Sefton?' he said. 'Well well! Good of you to pop in! If I'd known you were coming I'd have baked a cake! Recovered from last night? You weren't taken ill, I take it?'

'No. Thank goodness. And you?'

'Between you, me and the gatepost, Mr Sefton' – he glanced around, in case there was a gatepost there to overhear – 'I wouldn't touch an oyster if you paid me! Though I'll happily serve them to others!'

'Terrible business with the mayor,' I said.

'Yes,' agreed Billy cheerfully. 'Absolutely. Anyway, this! This, Mr Sefton, is quite something you have here.'

'So you're a silver expert as well?'

'I dabble, I suppose you would say, Mr Sefton. I dabble. More of a humble lapidarist. Keeps me occupied.'

'You are a man of many talents, Billy Ball.'

'I do my best. Needs must and what have you. Now, tell me, is this yours, this little beauty?'

'No, it belongs to a friend of mine, actually,' I said. 'I just wanted to get a valuation on her behalf.'

'Oh. I see.' His face fell. 'Well, I'm afraid we're not able to offer valuations, Mr Sefton, without proof of ownership.'

'Really?'

'Yes. Mr Hopwood's very strict on that. Very

strict indeed. It's to prevent the shop being used for the purposes of – well, you understand.'

'Of handling stolen goods?' I asked.

'Yes, exactly. Not that I'm suggesting for a moment that you'd be trying to pass off stolen goods, Mr Sefton!' He laughed.

'No, of course not.' I attempted to laugh even louder.

'It's just, you can never be too careful these days, can you?'

'No, no.'

'Mr Hopwood's had problems in the past, that's all. East End villains and all sorts coming up here and trying to fence their ill-gotten gains, that sort of thing.'

'Of course. Yes. Terrible. Well, I'll return it to my friend and see what she wants to do with it.'

'That's probably best, Mr Sefton. Or, as I say, proof of ownership, that'd be fine.'

He carefully handed the cigarette case back to me, and I equally carefully tucked it into my jacket pocket. It felt hot and dirty – damaged, dangerous goods.

'Well, sorry we couldn't be of more help there,' said Billy.

'Not to worry,' I said.

'Are you staying for long in Colchester?'

'No,' I said. 'We have a pretty hectic schedule.'

'For this book of yours?'

'That's right. I think we'll be heading off today.'

'Well, it was very nice to meet you,' said Billy,

offering his hand – which I was of course unable to shake, due to the state of my own bandaged hand.

'Forgot about that!' he said, nodding at the bandage. 'How's it feel?'

'Fine,' I said. 'Thanks to you. Thank you again.'

'Not at all. Until we meet again!'

'Indeed.' That seemed unlikely. I had no intention of ever again serving oysters, or indeed of attempting to sell Amy Johnson's cigarette case.

CHAPTER 13

A KIND OF KNOCKING

Leaving Hopwood's, disheartened but with my integrity more or less intact, I made my way back to the hotel and was about to enter when Morley came purposefully striding outside, looking disturbingly trim and kempt, as always.

'Ah, Sefton! Excellent! Saw you through the window,' he said. 'We've set up HQ in the breakfast room.' He nodded inside and sure enough I saw his typewriter and reference books piled up, incongruous on a white linen tablecloth on a table set with tea and toast. I'm sure the hotel staff were delighted; wherever we went throughout the country, Morley always liked to establish a centre of operations where he could set up his beloved Hermes Featherweight and his vast stationery supplies depot and start banging out his articles, essays, columns and of course *The County Guides*. Basically he ran a low-cost, high-profit portable writing factory, with Miriam and me the only full-time operatives, with hotel staff and resources deployed as necessary. During my years with Morley I very often felt like Charlie

Chaplin in *Modern Times*, screwing endless nuts on an assembly line.

'We were wondering where you'd got to. Out for your morning constitutional? A matutinal stroll? Everything all right? You look rather as if you'd lost a shilling and found a farthing.'

Not quite. I'd found an expensive cigarette case but was still painfully short of a hundred pounds.

'Yes,' I said. What else could one say?

'You missed some excellent porridge.' Morley rated hotels and guesthouses almost exclusively on the quality of their tea and porridge. I remember once he returned from staying at the Hôtel de Crillon in Paris for some ceremony or other and all he could say afterwards was, 'Terrible tea and porridge.' There were guesthouses in the west of Ireland that he rated more highly. 'Well, what do you make of Colchester, then? Take any photographs?'

I didn't actually have the Leica with me. I was supposed to carry a camera and notebook at all times, to collect material for *The County Guides*, but half the time I forgot and the rest of the time I couldn't be bothered.

'No,' I said. 'I thought I'd get some photographs later. It's a bit quiet at the moment.'

'Quiet?' said Morley. He looked perplexed. 'As in somnolent?'

'I suppose, yes.'

'Colchester, Sefton?' He threw out his arms, gesturing towards the busy sunlit morning High Street. 'Somnolent, Colchester? The capital of

124

Roman Britain? The town that gave birth to Helena, the mother of Constantine, and possibly to Constantine himself? The oldest town in Britain? Our greatest garrison town? The town that in 1884 was the epicentre of Britain's most destructive earthquake? The town that indeed just last night witnessed perhaps the greatest outbreak of crowd hysteria since the dancing plague of the sixteenth century? And which saw its own mayor struck down before the assembled guests at a grand civic occasion? Somnolent, Sefton? I do sometimes wonder, sir, if you are sleepwalking through this life.'

I sometimes wondered it myself – especially when Morley went off on one of his jags. I could have done with a little something to make my sleepwalk all the sweeter, frankly, but it was too early in the day to start drinking. The only thing to do in the circumstances was to try to steer Morley elsewhere.

'You heard about Len Starling?' I asked.

'The Town Sergeant?' said Morley. 'Yes. Arrested. Nothing in it, Sefton. He'll be released by this afternoon, mark my words.'

'Do you think?'

'Absolutely certain. Lot of nonsense. Poor Marden died, goodness knows why, but of natural causes I have no doubt. And not poisoned oysters, for sure. Not that it stops people jumping to all sorts of ludicrous conclusions. Do you know, one of the women serving breakfast claimed that the

Oyster Feast was the target of the communists, for goodness sake, trying to kill off the great and the good! Total stuff and nonsense, the whole thing. I'm going to write an article today about crowd hysteria. Interesting case study. If only Mr Fort were here to view it for himself. But. All a distraction from the book, Sefton. We *must* focus on the book.'

He took me by the elbow, in his usual irresistible fashion, as though leading a horse to water, or a lamb to the slaughter.

'Now, Miriam has arranged for us to visit the Colchester Oyster Fishery, I believe. Few miles away, West Mersea. But she's just mentioned that there was some problem with the car yesterday, is that right?' He nodded again towards the hotel breakfast room, where I spotted Miriam busy looking languid over coffee – at which she was most definitely succeeding. 'I'm rather concerned, Sefton, to be frank. You didn't mention it before.'

Miriam winked at me through the window.

'Didn't mention what, sorry, Mr Morley?'

'The Lagonda, man! The problem with the Lagonda? You didn't see fit to mention it?'

'No, well, with everything that's happened.'

'No excuse, Sefton! A workman always looks after his tools, first and foremost. Doesn't matter what chaos may surround us. What do we do in a storm? What do we do in a crisis? Blame others, or take responsibility ourselves? Without the Lagonda, where would we be?'

126

'In Norfolk, Mr Morley?'

'Very funny, Sefton. I take it that's supposed to be a joke?' Morley could never quite tell. 'You know we rely on that car. *The County Guides* rely on that car. Our whole project. A modern Domesday Book doesn't write itself, you know.'

'No.'

'We can hardly cycle the length and breadth of the country, can we?'

'No, Mr Morley.'

'Unless we could find a bicycle that could fold and we could take it with us on trains and on buses . . . Hmm. Something worth thinking about, eh?'

'Yes, Mr Morley.' A folding bicycle? He often had these lunatic ideas. It was always best to ignore them.

'So what's wrong with her?' he said.

Miriam was now making faces at me through the window. It was rather distracting.

'Who?'

'The car, man! What was wrong with the car? Poor fuel consumption?'

'I'm not sure about the fuel consumption.'

'Losing power?'

'It may have been losing power, yes . . .'

'Is that it?'

'Well, yes. Although it was also making a rather funny sound.'

'Funny? Funny in what way, Sefton?'

'Just . . . funny.'

'Oh come on, Sefton. Describe, please. Knocking? Clunking? Clicking?'

'Erm . . .'

'Clanging? Rumbling? Roaring? What?'

'I'd describe it as . . . more of a knocking, Mr Morley.'

'Knocking, eh? Loud knocking? Quiet knocking? A rat-a-tat-tat? Or a tum-ti-ti-tum? Pounding? The sound of an actual door knocker knocking? A knocker-upper knocking? A—'

'A kind of metallic knocking, I'd say, Mr Morley. The sort of knocking you'd hear in a car.'

'Hmm. Doesn't sound good, Sefton, does it? Not good at all.'

'That's what I thought.'

'Where is it then?'

'The knocking sound?' I said.

'The car, man! The car.'

'We had to park a way away.'

'Come on then, chop chop, let's tend to the poor beast.'

We found the Lagonda parked where Miriam and I had left it the night before. I was always half-expecting the car to be stolen – it wasn't exactly an unnoticeable sort of a vehicle. (Indeed, on one very memorable occasion it was stolen, but that's another story.) On that fine Essex morning it was, thank goodness, quite simply there, in all its glory.

'The old white charger,' said Morley. 'Keys?'

The car had been fitted with a special key ignition

128

at Morley's request: in many ways he had the mind of a thief, and could always foresee opportunities for crimes and misdemeanours; the Lagonda was clearly an invitation to sin.

'I don't have the keys, I'm afraid, Mr Morley. I think Miriam has them.'

'Ah, well, fortunately I think I have a spare set.' He dug into the many pockets of his tweeds; he had his tailors, Davies & Co. – 'Oldest on the Row, and still the best,' according to Morley – make extra pockets everywhere in his suits, so that they became his home from home, equipped with every household item bar the kitchen sink. In fact, one wouldn't have been surprised if one of the pockets did indeed contain the kitchen sink, or at least a small folding version, of the kind that one used to find in the cabins of continental sleeper trains. Sure enough, in a key pocket there was an extra set of keys for the Lagonda – and the house, St George's, and all the rooms in the house, and its various outbuildings, and his other cars. If he'd produced a starting handle from his pockets I wouldn't have been shocked. 'Start her up, then.' He tossed the keys to me and then hoisted up the bonnet and started fiddling around inside.

The car was certainly making a very unhappy sound, and the longer Morley fiddled in there the unhappier it became. After a few minutes he slammed down the bonnet.

'That'll do, Sefton.'

I turned off the engine.

'Well?' I said.

'Did you say she started playing up in Ongar?'

'I think so, yes.'

'Something wrong with the place?'

'Not as far as I recall, Mr Morley, no, it seemed perfectly—'

'Dirty sort of place?'

'Dirty?'

'Lot of grit or anything lying around? Mud?'

'No, I don't think so, although there was a big delivery of sand and gravel while we were down in Becontree, and the car was sort of dusted with—'

'Dusted? What do you mean dusted?'

'Well, sort of dusted—'

'With sand and gravel? Good grief, man! Great Jerusalem save us! Why didn't you say so before? Sand and gravel, for goodness sake! Sand'll destroy an engine as quick and as sure as the Royal Navy setting its sights on Zanzibar, Sefton! Have you no idea whatsoever about the workings of the internal combustion engine?'

I did not.

'I'm sorry, I didn't think, Mr Morley.'

'Clearly. Sometimes I do wonder, Sefton, if it's a good idea to leave you and Miriam unattended with the Lagonda.' Sometimes I wondered myself if it was a good idea for me and Miriam to be left unattended, with or without the Lagonda. 'She is not a toy,' he continued – meaning the Lagonda. 'She is a valued member of our team.' He did have a terrible tendency to anthropomorphise, metaphorise, exaggerate and otherwise make things up. 'We need to get the old girl to a garage quick and have her looked at. Didn't we pass a place up on the High Street, by the Town Hall?'

'I don't know, Mr Morley, did we?'

'What are our rules, Sefton!'

'No funking, no shirking, no shilly-shallying? Or no shirking, no shilly—'

'Not those rules!'

'Always look on the bright side of life?'

'Nor that!'

I tried '*Interdum vulgus rectum videt*', one of Morley's favourite Latin phrases.

'In plain English, man! Common sense and observation, Sefton! Are they not our bywords?'

We had so many bywords it was difficult to know which words were bywords and which were just by-the-way words.

'What was it called?' asked Morley, consulting his mental file-card index for recent additions under 'Mechanics, Essex, Signs, Observed'. 'Harold J. Willett?'

'I'm not sure, Mr Morley.'

'Well, fortunately I'm sure. Come on.'

CHAPTER 14

A MECHANICAL APHRODISIAC

His mental filing system was accurate, as always. It was indeed Harold J. Willett and it was indeed on the High Street near the Town Hall.

Willett's is a pretty impressive outfit, comprising a large car showroom, garages and workshops. We managed to get the car there in one piece and were attended to by Mr Willett himself – or at least by a Mr Willett. There may have been several; Willett's was not a one-man enterprise. It was a little empire.

'Now,' said Morley, after a long conversation with Mr Willett about carburettors and air filters, and having made complex arrangements for the car to be thoroughly examined and fixed. 'I wonder if it might be possible for us to borrow something from you, transportation-wise, while the Lagonda is repaired?'

'Of course we can do that. No problem at all,' said Mr Willett, who looked and dressed and spoke like all car salesmen, then, now and for ever: just a little too sleek, the tie just too thick, the suit too sharp and too shiny, the speech both too eager

132

and aggressive, and wheedling. 'If you follow me, I can show you—'

'In fact I did wonder . . .' Morley swivelled around on his heels and began to make his way in the opposite direction towards what was undoubtedly the finest car in the showroom – a big black and cream convertible over by the window. 'A car showroom is the museum of the future, don't you think?'

'Yes,' agreed Mr Willett. I suspect that he – like me – had no idea in what sense a car showroom might be the museum of the future, though we were doubtless about to find out.

'A site of display and investigation, Mr Willett. In years to come, the car will be understood to be the most important cultural artefact of our time, never mind the most important mechanical device in history – with the possible exception of the button, the clock and the printing press, of course.'

'I'm sure,' said Mr Willett, who was beginning to look rather bemused.

We were approaching the big car by the window.

'Do you know Marinetti at all, Mr Willett?'

Mr Willett admitted that he did not know any Marinettis, although he did know the Morettis, who ran an accident repair service in Chelmsford – lovely bunch of chaps.

'Odd fellow, met him in Rome,' continued Morley. 'Many years ago. Grotty little café. San Calisto? Hangout of writers and artists, you know the sort of thing. Claimed that a sports car was more beautiful than a Greek statue. Absolutely correct of course. I mean, don't we all want to caress the hot breasts of a speeding vehicle?'

'Erm . . .'

We had arrived beside the big car by the window. And Morley was beginning to stroke it.

'Not my words, I hasten to add!' he said. 'I'm quoting Marinetti, of course. Italian. And quite an oddbod to boot, as I say. But you can see what he's getting at, can't you?'

'Erm . . .'

'The sensuous surfaces of the thing.' Morley, standing now at the bonnet of the car, leaned forward and embraced it. He really was a great car man. 'Look at this! The sheer girth! A car, Mr Willett, a great car, is a kind of mechanical aphrodisiac, wouldn't you agree?'

'I couldn't really say, sir,' said Mr Willett, with admirable calm, given that like me he had doubtless never seen a man embrace a car before, nor for a moment considered that a car was a kind of mechanical aphrodisiac, or indeed a mechanical anything, except a car; and even if he had thought it he would have been unlikely to express it with quite Morley's uninhibited enthusiasm.

(For Morley's always enthusiastic writing about cars, of which there is alas rather a lot, like the great vehicular torrent itself, which has swept through our age, and which like Morley's work is quite exhilarating at best and quite deadly at worst, see his monthly column in *Motor* magazine, which ran from 1934 to 1939, and which was often reprinted in motoring magazines around the world, including *Motoring, Motor Car, Motor World* and indeed – as I know, having had to conduct the negotiations myself with the editor, by telephone, with the aid of a Brazilian Portuguese dictionary – *Automobilismo* in Brazil. In one particularly popular article, entitled 'Unholy Union' (June 1936) Morley claims that 'When driving, there is a connection between man and machine that goes beyond the merely physical and takes us into the realms of the metaphysical. In driving, there is a transference between man and machine, just as there is between man and horse, or man and bicycle. This act of exchange amounts to an act of love, a love between man and machine that is the spirit of our age.')

'Is it not a relationship of love, our relationship with the car?' continued Morley, who had by now straightened up and was pacing round the vehicle, surveying it with pleasure.

'I suppose it is, sir, yes. A relationship of – ahem – love. Yes.'

'Do you remember your first car, Mr Willett?'

'Of course.'

'What was she?'

'A Morris Minor, 1931.'

'Ah, yes. Fine car,' said Morley. 'Fine car. The hundred pound car.'

This reminded me of my outstanding debt of

one hundred pounds. Perhaps I should try to steal a Morris Minor. I smiled benignly.

'And then an Austin 7 Tourer,' said Mr Willett, becoming quite caught up in his automotive memories.

'Ah, yes, the Tourer, the Tourer. We have an Austin saloon at home. The old gin palace.'

'Super car,' said Mr Willett. 'Super super car.'

Listening to Morley and Mr Willett becoming slowly intoxicated with their car talk was like listening to anyone becoming slowly intoxicated with car talk, and indeed like Morley talking to anyone about anything: it became very tiresome very quickly.

'Couldn't agree more,' I said, with no idea what I was agreeing to or about, but simply trying to bring the conversation to a conclusion. 'Couldn't agree more.'

'Cadillac V16, if I'm not mistaken?' said Morley, returning to stroking the bonnet of the car.

'V12 actually, sir. Convertible sedan. Very few made.'

'She is certainly a fine-looking creature,' said Morley. And it was. Red leather interior. Twin side-mounted tyres. The car had a kind of swagger about it that was difficult to define. Similar to the Lagonda, but slightly more aggressive, with more . . .

'American muscle,' said Morley admiringly, putting his finger on it exactly. 'That's what she's got, isn't it, Mr Willett?'

'Yes,' agreed Mr Willett. 'Similar to the V16, but on a much sportier chassis, so—'

'She really shifts, I'll bet?'

'She certainly does.'

Morley patted the flanks of the car as though he were patting the flanks of a thoroughbred race-horse. He was in a kind of trance. I'd seen it before when he was inspecting vehicles of any kind: tractors, bicycles, gypsy wagons. He loved anything and everything to do with speed and travel; he was a regular Mr Toad. He had even planned at one point to release a '78 of traffic noise, a sound that he genuinely believed was 'soothing'.

'We'll take her!' said Morley.

'I'm afraid this car is not one of those we offer to customers for loan while their own vehicles are—'

'Not for loan?' said Morley. 'Not for loan? Oh dear. Oh dear oh dear. Oh dear oh dear oh dear.' This was perhaps Morley's strongest expression of disappointment: the once, twice, thrice repeated 'Oh dear'. 'Oh dear.' Plus another! Catastrophe! 'What do you think, Sefton?'

'It's a nice car,' I said, not quite sure what I should have said. I certainly shouldn't have said 'nice'. Morley had a thing about 'nice'. 'Nice', according to Morley, was not a nice word. Fortunately he didn't notice – he was transfixed. I clarified. 'It would certainly do, Mr Morley.'

'Do?' said Morley. 'Do? This is a work of art, Sefton.'

'Not an actual work of art, of course,' I said.

'What? This car? She most certainly is a work of art, Sefton, if we judge a work of art – as we should – as something that has been designed for aesthetic appeal as well as mere functional purpose.'

'I suppose so, Mr Morley,' I agreed.

'A car serves all the purposes of art in our modern age, Mr Willett, does she not? She excites us. She intrigues us. And a car like this is surely the perfect advertisement for the fine taste and forward thinking of an establishment such as Willett's? This is presumably why you have her here so prominently displayed? She puts you in the avant-garde, does she not, Mr Willett? At the very forefront of the Essex motor trade?'

'Well, I suppose—' Mr Willett began modestly.

'And yet . . . and yet . . . And yet . . . she is also perhaps a four-wheeled memento mori, is she not?' Morley's conversation often changed tack unexpectedly in just this way – I always half suspected it was a tactic, to discombobulate the listener. It almost always worked.

Mr Willett gave a polite cough and glanced at me with a nervous expression: clearly none of this was the usual sort of talk in the showroom. But Morley was off and away again and there was no stopping him.

'The speed of the car reminds us surely that there is only motion in this life, and that we are all bound for the same ultimate destination, gentlemen. Speed is of the essence! Though not if that old bore Hore-Belisha has his way.' I had heard Morley's anti-Hore-Belisha speech before. 'In the future there will be traffic-control robots everywhere, Mr Willett, will there not, if we're not careful?'

'Possibly, sir.' Mr Willett glanced at me again, with signs of panic in his eyes. It was always difficult to tell where Morley's conversation might go next.

'With those blasted amber globes on their ridiculous striped barber poles! What do you think, Mr Willett?' Poor Mr Willett no longer knew what to think. 'A disgrace, frankly!' said Morley. 'Mark my words, gentlemen, if Mr Hore-Belisha has his way we'll all be riding horses again. Do you ride, Mr Willett?'

'I can't say I do, sir, no.'

'Pity. You may need to learn. Did you know that during the entire Napoleonic Wars with France—'

But this, finally, was enough wild rambling for Mr Willett, who was clearly beginning to despair of ever being able to follow what Morley was going on about and who presumably had work to do.

'All right, you can take the Cadillac,' he said. 'Until we get the Lagonda looked at and ready for you. It'll be Monday at the earliest now.'

'Excellent!' said Morley, ceasing immediately in his mad automotive oration. 'Excellent!' He shook Mr Willett's hand and gave me, I thought, a quick look of triumph. There was always – sometimes – a method in his madness.

'We have wheels, Sefton!' he exulted, as we left the showroom in the Cadillac. 'And what wheels we have!'

CHAPTER 15

WHAT HAVE THE ROMANS EVER DONE FOR US?

Miriam, needless to say, loved the Cadillac and certainly seemed to agree with Morley that it was indeed a kind of mechanical aphrodisiac: she insisted on referring to it, alas, as her 'Yankee toy'. She spent an inordinate amount of time merrily and pointlessly revving the engine outside the George Hotel, in absolute ecstasy, causing quite a hulla-balloo: the roar she managed to coax from the thing was really quite extraordinary, like an animal in heat.

'She was just the same when she got her first pedal car,' said Morley, who was momentarily distracted with yet more articles to file – a piece on spade mills for some guild newsletter or other, and a short piece on Maimonides for the *Jewish Chronicle*, all of which he somehow managed to write, edit and dispatch in the time it took me to rustle up a flask of tea and some dry biscuits from the hotel kitchens – but eventually we set off shortly before lunch for the famous oyster beds on the Essex coast.

While Morley and I had spent the morning

sorting out the Lagonda and procuring the Cadillac, Miriam had been busy catching up on all the local news and gossip. This was her forte. She was capable of eliciting information – and, frankly, almost anything else – from anyone. Apparently there had been no other fatalities from the oysters at the Oyster Feast and those who had been admitted to hospital had been released.

'Crowd hysteria,' said Morley. 'As I said.'

'Yes,' agreed Miriam. 'It does seem that poor Mr Marden really was just terribly unlucky.'

'Heart attack?' said Morley. 'Possibly. Could have been anything.'

'One bad oyster, possibly?' said Miriam.

'Nonsense,' said Morley. 'One bad oyster, out of however many thousand being eaten at the feast, and poor Marden's on the receiving end? Statistically highly unlikely.'

'Well, whatever it was, it was jolly bad luck anyway,' said Miriam, as if Marden had just been dealt a bad hand in a game of whist.

'Indeed,' agreed Morley, though of course he did not believe in luck, good or bad, in cards or in anything else. (For full details of his ideas about luck see his much reprinted article 'Get Lucky', which first appeared in the *London Gazette* on 24 October 1931, and which has been variously plagiarised, summarised, rephrased, represented and otherwise regurgitated by many others and indeed by Morley himself ever since. In summary: according to Morley, good luck is a skill, and bad luck simply the product of poor choices and over-looked opportunities. In other words, tough luck. He always had a touch of the Samuel Smiles about him.) Fortunately he did not seem to be in the mood for a discussion about the meaning of the mayor's good or bad luck. The poor man was dead, after all, and that was that. And we had work to do. 'Come on!' he said, as we finally left Colchester. '*Essex* won't write itself, you know.'

As we left Colchester in the Cadillac I glanced up, half expecting to hear the overhead chugging of Amy Johnson in her Gypsy Moth, waving us goodbye. But there was nothing. She'd gone. I patted her silver cigarette case in my suit pocket.

At high noon the vast salt marshes and intertidal mudflats of the Essex coast have the most strange and spectral appearance – almost as if one were in a desert approaching an oasis. It is a landscape without figures which forever promises mystery, misery and – most likely – fog. Distant creeks coil around dozens of uninhabited low-lying islands covered with lilac sea lavender and both land and water seem never-ending. Morley of course was absolutely in his element, imagining the place as it might once have been, when England and France were joined by land and mammoths roamed the marshes. He insisted that I make notes on all sorts of passing items of interest: the occasional cabin and poor dwelling, the wildlife, rose hips, samphire, faint evidence of ancient settlements. Starlings. Swallows. The white corona of the sun, which looked vaguely dyed yellow, apparently, and which reminded him of the colour of one of his favourite canaries . . . The conversation was as strange and as spangly as ever, Morley merrily riffing, for example, on the theme of Roman Colchester.

'Do you know, for all their achievements, what we really have to thank the Romans for, Sefton?' he asked, as we sped along.

'Aqueducts?' said Miriam, who was not one to be bested, even on very general questions of general knowledge.

'No, no, no,' said Morley. 'Not aqueducts, Miriam, absolutely not. Common misapprehension. We have the Greeks and Assyrians to thank for the development of aqueducts, I think you'll find.'

'Sanitation?' I said.

'Ancient India!' said Morley. 'Plenty of it there, thank you very much. Highly sanitised race, the Indians. Years ahead. We have the Harappans to thank for the development of public health and sanitation, Sefton, not the Romans. Are you quite up to date on your ancient cultures and civilisations? Does a Cambridge education not equip a man with such knowledge?'

Apparently not. My grasp of ancient cultures and civilisations was clearly not what it might have been. The Harappans? Who on earth were the Harappans?

'The roads, Father?' said Miriam. 'Didn't the Romans give us roads?'

'Hmm, close, my dear, yes, close, roads. Straight strong stone roads certainly. But what about the ancient log roads of Europe, eh? And animal tracks and trails? I fancy the history of the road began long before the Romans, long long ago in Ancient Egypt. And India. And China of course.'

'Irrigation, then?' said Miriam, with some annoyance. 'Medicine? Education? Wine? Public order? All or any of the above?'

'Mesopotamia, China, China, China again, and – guess what? – China. Remarkable culture really, isn't it?' said Morley. 'I wonder if there might be a book in it, you know? *What the Chinese Did For Us?*'

'We have more than enough books on our hands at the moment, Father,' said Miriam. 'Don't forget there's that book of folktales you're supposed to be editing. And that history of tartan.' It was down to Miriam to manage Morley's massive output – a management task that was in itself far beyond most human capacities, never mind Morley's actual endless production of the stuff, which was unimaginable.

'Ah, yes, the tartan book; I wonder if I can get something in about the Dagenham Girl Pipers?' said Morley.

'I'm sure you can, Father. I'm sure you can. But we must focus first on the task in hand, mustn't we?'

'Of course, my dear. What were we talking about?'

'China?' I said. Miriam shot me a glance of disapproval.

'Yes! Yes,' said Morley, returning to his theme. 'We underestimate the Chinese at our peril, Sefton. In years to come, mark my words, China will once again be the world's greatest empire. The Soviet Union will seem quite puny in comparison. Never mind the Roman. So . . .' He looked up from his notebook for a moment. He was always making notes: writing, drawing, making calculations. There are indeed many many more notebooks than there are books – a treasure trove for future scholars. (And for future reference, as I've often had to plead: please do not write to me, write to the estate, c/o Morley's London agent.) 'Do you want me to tell you?'

'Tell us what, Father?' said Miriam.

'What was the most important thing that the Romans ever did for us?'

'Oh yes, do,' said Miriam. 'Because I think I can safely say that we're totally fed up with this game now, aren't we, Sefton?'

'Well . . .' I said, havering. I probably spent half of my working life with Morley totally fed up and the other half amazed. It was a reasonable percentage.

'You really want to know the most important thing that the Romans ever did for us?' said Morley.

'Yes!' said Miriam. 'Do get on with it, Father.'

'The most important thing that the Romans did

for us was . . .' Morley paused for effect. 'The cultivation of oysters in brackish pools near their centres of settlement, of course!'

'Oh,' said Miriam. 'How disappointing.'

We arrived eventually in West Mersea, which is a place that specialises in the cultivation of oysters in brackish pools, and which is indeed rather disappointing, the kind of place that it's hard to believe still exists in modern England. One doubts it could exist for much longer, if it still exists at all, that is. It had all the appearance of a remote fishing village in the Highlands of Scotland or in Nova Scotia. Beyond the few houses and the chapels, the church, there were dozens of rather decrepit buildings clustered down by the beach that at first appearance seemed to be made entirely of salvaged materials – weatherbeaten planks, rusted iron and so on – and which on closer inspection turned out actually to be made entirely of salvaged materials. The place had all the aspect of a coastal slum.

'Marvellous!' said Morley, as we clambered out of the Cadillac, having parked in a muddy patch of ground by the largest of the buildings. 'Look at this! Human ingenuity in the face of nature's onslaught!'

'Oh God,' said Miriam, pulling off her driving gloves and lighting a cigarette. 'Not what I expected at all. Absolutely dismal, isn't it?' It was always impossible to know exactly what Miriam expected, though she always expected better, and dressed accordingly. Today she had gone for a nautical look, a silk dress in blue and white with a high belted waist, capped sleeves and bow collar, accessorised – as she liked to say – with a sailor's cap and white patent leather heels. Miriam and her outfit would probably have looked perfectly the part in a cool breeze on a yacht on a summer's day in the south of France. They were perhaps a little de trop in West Mersea in October.

'Cut on the bias,' she confided to me, when she caught me admiring her in the dress, though I had absolutely no idea what that meant. 'Rather flattering, isn't it?' I couldn't deny it.

Morley knelt down and took two handfuls of what appeared to be muddy gravel.

'As I thought!' he said, straightening up. 'Look at this, Sefton.'

I looked. 'Yes,' I said.

'Well?' he said.

'Muddy gravel?'

'Crushed and ground oyster shells!' he exclaimed. 'Marvellous! Used to be used as aggregate, of course, by the Romans. Very useful building material. Only trouble is, the buildings made from it tend to collapse.' He allowed the oyster shell gravel to run through his fingers. 'Anyway, lead on, Miriam!'

'Lead on, Macduff!' I said, in an attempt to ingratiate myself with the pair of them, with a little Shakespearean allusion of my own.

'It's "Lay on, Macduff,"' said Miriam.

'Spoken by Macbeth,' said Morley.

'"And damn'd be him that first cries, 'Hold, enough!'"' added Miriam. 'Meaning, roughly, let's fight to the death, before of course Macduff kills Macbeth in combat. Entirely appropriate?'

'Good try, though,' said Morley. 'Keep at it, Sefton. You'll get there.'

I was getting nowhere.

CHAPTER 16

FLITRATION & PURTEFICATION

Miriam had arranged for us to meet with an oysterman in West Mersea, a man named Vince, Vincent Ramsey, who had agreed to take us out on his oyster boat, and Vince it was who came lumbering towards us now out of the largest of the buildings, which was by far the most impressive and also almost entirely intact. I noted the sign above the corrugated double doors: COLNE OYSTER FISHERY FILTRATION & PURIFICATION. Except someone had done their best to change the spelling of FILTRATION to FLIRTATION, rubbing out the 'I' and inserting another artfully elsewhere. Or unartfully, rather: the word in fact spelt FLITRATION. PURIFICATION had been almost changed to PUTREFACTION: PURTEFICATION. Essex wit or Essex spelling? I couldn't tell which was which.

Vince – with his thick white beard and funereal gaze, his old pearl-buttoned waistcoat and flared, patched sailor's trousers – appeared to be auditioning for the role of a wise and ancient old seadog, a role for which it turned out he was ideally suited. He was a descendant, apparently, of an ancient Essex oyster dredging family and a Freeman of the River Colne, one of the four hundred dredgermen of the Colne Fishery Company who have the right to fish for oysters in and around West Mersea. He imparted this information to Morley in wise and ancient old seadog fashion through his vast salt-speckled seafaring beard while I took a few photographs of the fishing huts and Miriam did her best to pretend that she was in St Tropez.

'You've come as a jolly jack tar then?' said Vince to Miriam.

'One does one's best, Mr Ramsey,' said Miriam, with a sour pout. 'It's very kind of you to host us. I'm sure the trip will be invaluable for the book.'

'I'm sure,' said Vince. 'You mentioned money?'

'Yes, of course,' said Miriam, smiling thinly and producing from her handbag a brown envelope that presumably contained crisp unmarked notes. It is true that *The County Guides* was built largely upon the good-natured generosity of the English people but it also required the steady and continual greasing of palms. Vince took the envelope in silence, counted the money, nodded, and without a word turned to lead us down to his boat, moored off West Mersea's wobbly jetty. I wondered how much Miriam had handed over. Five? Ten? Twenty pounds? Morley rarely handled cash and seemed oblivious to the back-handers and bribes that made the books possible. Like all good men, like fools and the virtuous, he was incorruptible, though surrounded by corruption.

'I was just saying to my young companions here this morning, the English oyster at its best is absolutely unbeatable, isn't it, Mr Ramsey?'

'Mmm,' said Vince.

'I had the American oyster once, in New York. Grand Central Station. Have you ever been, Mr Ramsey?'

'No,' said Vince seadoggedly.

Morley spoke often of his travels, it seemed to me, not so much to boast or intimidate but simply because he couldn't imagine people who didn't live the kind of life he lived. His sympathies were broad, but his understanding strictly limited: for all his socialist convictions he was really an intellectual aristocrat, entirely removed from the dull everyday lives of the English working classes. It seemed pretty clear to me that Vince had probably never ventured much further than Colchester, and that even then that might prove something of a culture shock. Morley carried on, of course, regarding Vince in every way as his intellectual and social equal, regaling the poor man with his autodidactic oyster-lore.

'*Crassostrea gigas*. Creamier, milder sort of flavour than the English oyster. Not at all unpleasant. Merely bland. Also had a carpetbagger steak in New Orleans. Have you ever tried one?'

Again, Vince answered no.

'Well, can't recommend it. Like eating a soft

152

pillow made of meat and brine. What is it Pliny says?'

'Yes, we know, Mr Morley,' I said, in the hope that this might put paid to another rather one-sided conversation.

'*Nec potest videri satis dictum esse de his, cum palmas mensaurum divitum altribuantur illis.* Something like that?'

'Very probably.'

'And Juvenal, of course. *Circaeis nata forent, an Lucrinum ad saxum, Rhutupinove edita fundo Ostrea, callebat prime deprendere morsu.*'

'In English, Father, if you wouldn't mind,' said Miriam. 'I'm sure Mr Ramsey here would appreciate a translation.'

'Something about oysters, wasn't it?' said Vince.

'It was indeed, Mr Ramsey!' said Morley. 'It was indeed.'

'We have the Latin here too you know,' said Vince.

'Oh,' said Miriam, who like me had perhaps been rather quick to jump to conclusions about Vince. Perhaps he was a brilliant Latin scholar.

'Excellent!' cried Morley, who was always thrilled to meet a fellow autodidact. 'You know Latin, Mr Ramsey?'

'I don't know Latin actually, sir, no. But I know oysters,' said Vince, his beard billowing in the breeze.

'Take a note, Sefton!' cried Morley. 'A wonderful phrase, Mr Ramsey, if I may say so. "I don't know

Latin, but I know oysters!" I hope you don't mind if we borrow it for our book?'

'What's this book of yours again?' asked Vince.

We had by now reached his boat, which resembled a barge, wide across the middle and steered from a small cabin up front, and which was called the *Eileen* – 'After my dear mother,' explained Vince – though Morley of course insisted on calling it the *Syracusia*.

'Our book, Mr Ramsey,' said Morley, as we all clambered aboard the *Eileen*, 'is to be a portrait of Essex.'

'Warts and all?' asked Vince.

'I see no warts, Mr Ramsey,' said Morley, with his typical – and at times rather paper-thin – insouciance.

'You're maybe not looking hard enough then, are you?' said Vince, who started up the motor on the boat, and suddenly we were away. Essex receded.

Morley stood in the cabin with Vince. I took photographs at the stern, and Miriam fell into conversation with the only crew member to join us on the trip, a man introduced to us, improbably, as Mr Storey, who like Mr Ramsey seemed to have stepped onto the boat fresh from the set of a seafaring saga at Pinewood Studios. This was the age, of course, when men still resembled their work, and Mr Storey was the very model of a modern fisherman: unshaven, broad-shouldered, thick forearms bearing tattoos, cigarette stub

154

behind the ear, and with a cable-knit sweater that might actually have been knit from cables.

'Chilly out here, isn't it?' said Miriam, her outfit offering little protection against the cool offshore winds of the Essex marshes.

'Aye,' said Mr Storey, who was clearly apprenticing in Vince's salty seadog style of speech. 'Colder the better. Colder it gets, the sweeter the oyster. Increases the flavour, doesn't it? We like it cold. Last thing an oysterman wants is a mild autumn and winter.'

'Well, I can clearly cross "oysterman" off my list of possible career choices then,' said Miriam.

Mr Storey – rather to my dismay, but to Miriam's obvious pleasure – then removed his cable-knit jumper and draped it over Miriam's shoulders, exposing rather a lot of brightly tattooed torso under his vest.

Once we had journeyed far enough out into the breezy shallow bay beyond West Mersea, Vince cut the engine, dropped anchor, and explained to us the process by which oysters might be caught. There was a lot of talk about nets and winches and tines and such like but rather than actually laying the nets, which really would have been tiresome and taken far too long, Vince demonstrated the principle of the thing using a long iron rake to bring up a small haul of what looked mostly like mud and debris. This sopping mess he deposited onto the wide wooden table at the centre of the boat, where Mr Storey quickly picked an oyster shell from in among the jumble. Vince then cracked it open in an instant with what looked like a sharpened penny, making my own attempts with an oyster knife at the Oyster Feast seem even more utterly cack-handed.

He offered the oyster to Morley who took it and began to raise it to his lips – until Vince roared, 'No!' and knocked it from his hand. 'Ye shall not!' said Vince.

'No, no, no,' said Mr Storey, who was shaking his head and wagging a finger. 'Oh no, no, no, no.'

'All oysters have to go through the process back in the sheds,' explained Vince.

'The process?' asked Morley.

'Filtration and purification.'

'Filtration?' said Miriam. 'Sorry, I thought you said something else.'

'Ah!' said Morley, striking his forehead with the palm of his hand. 'Of course. I forgot. Flitration and purtefication!' Clearly I hadn't been the only one to notice the strange West Mersea orthography. 'Perhaps we might take a look, once we're back on land?'

'I suppose,' said Vince.

'You don't know what might happen, sir,' said Mr Storey, taking Morley's oyster and tossing it overboard, 'if you eat an unprocessed oyster. Anything might happen. You might end up like Arthur Marden.'

'Dead, you mean?' said Miriam.

'Take no notice of him,' said Vince. 'Even with

an unprocessed oyster the worst you'd get is an upset, just.'

'Exactly,' said Morley. 'That's what I've been saying.'

'Best to be careful though,' said Vince. 'I've been eating unprocessed oysters for years and they've never done me a drop of harm. But I'm an oysterman. I'd advise—'

'Never to put anything in your mouth if you don't know where it's been?' said Miriam. She was always at the ready with a chorus-girl remark.

'Something like that,' said Vince.

'Ah yes, the paradoxes of the oyster,' said Morley, oblivious as always to innuendo. I could tell that this little episode was slowly gathering itself into meaning in his mind. 'Take a note, Sefton.' I fumbled for the notebook in my jacket pocket. 'It dies to give us life, though threatening us with death. Was it Dumas who remarked that there is something so threateningly strange about the oyster that the only way to deal with them properly is to eat them?'

'No idea,' said Vince. 'That enough for your book though?'

'Oh yes,' said Morley. 'Certainly. Thank you, Mr Ramsey. Most instructive.'

'Right. We'll head for the layings and that's your lot.'

I hadn't even got my pencil out. Memory is a wonderful thing.

★   ★   ★

157

There's really not much to say about oyster layings; they're basically ugly little swimming-bath-sized pits dug into the mudflats, where the youngest oysters get deposited to fatten until they reach standard size. Morley of course found them fascinating.

'How does one measure the standard size?' he asked.

'Traditionally it's set by the mayor's silver oyster,' explained Vince. 'We bring him out before the feast and he measures one; if it's the right size, then the season's open.'

'The silver oyster?' asked Morley.

'Some ceremonial thing,' said Vince. 'He wears it round his neck.'

'Oh yes, I think I recall it. Like a chain of office?'

'Or an oyster necklace?' said Miriam. 'I rather liked the look of it.'

'Terrible business with the mayor though, wasn't it?' said Morley.

'I'm sure,' said Vince.

'It must have caused a great deal of distress locally.'

'Not really,' said Vince.

'No?'

I rather thought that Vince weighed his words here more carefully than usual – or even more carefully than usual. 'Never had a lot of time for Arthur Marden myself.'

'Why ever not?' asked Morley.

Again a pause from Vince. 'He was from Kent originally, wasn't he?' he said.

'Does that matter?' asked Morley.

'I don't like men from Kent,' said Vince.

'Men from Kent? What on earth's wrong with men from Kent?'

'They tried to invade us, didn't they?'

'The Kentish?' said Morley.

'That's right,' said Vince. 'I would have thought you'd have known, with all your interest in books.'

'They tried to invade you?'

'As I say. One hundred fishing smacks came up to the oyster beds near Leigh-on-Sea. They made off with over a thousand bushels of oysters.'

'That's terrible,' said Morley. 'And when was this? I'm surprised we heard nothing about it in the papers.'

'In 1724,' said Vince, and we set off back to the shore, tour concluded.

In our absence the Cadillac had drawn quite a crowd, half a dozen men, all of them dressed like Mr Storey, weather-beaten, tattooed, tightly belted and poorly clothed – fishermen in other words – and one of them I thought rather familiar. I fancied he was the man who offered to fight me outside the Town Hall the previous night. It was difficult to tell in broad daylight.

'Go on, get out of it,' Vince told them, as we trudged back up to the car.

'It's all right, Mr Ramsey. They're just curious about the car,' said Morley. 'Perfectly under-standable. They're—'

'They're a bunch of troublemakers is what they are,' said Vince.

'Go on, you heard him!' said Mr Storey, gesturing in no uncertain terms for the men to leave. 'Go on, Joe, you don't want any trouble now.'

Joe Cowley, that was it.

'Joe Cowley, of the Cowley Brothers?' I asked, as the men slowly turned their backs to us and wandered off, muttering among themselves.

'That's right,' said Mr Storey. 'Do you know them?'

'Not exactly,' I said.

'Who are they?' asked Miriam. 'Friends of yours, Sefton? They do seem a little . . . unwelcoming, if you don't mind my saying so.'

'They're independents,' explained Vince.

'Independent whats?' asked Morley.

'Independent bastards. Excuse me, miss,' said Mr Storey.

'Oystermen,' said Vince.

He explained that as well as the dredgermen like him who were part of the Colne Oyster Fishery there were other private cultivators and adventurers all along the Essex coast who liked to try their hand at raising oysters in the creeks.

'Ah, I see,' said Morley. 'Like small businessmen, attempting to fulfil their dreams, eh? Smallholders of the Essex waters? Prospectors for oysters, as the men of the Yukon were once prospectors for gold?'

'I don't know about that, mister, but I'll tell you what I do know: they're troublemakers. Sooner they're all wiped out the better.'

'Wiped out?' said Morley. 'That's a bit strong, if I may say so, Mr Ramsey, isn't it? A bit extreme?'

Vince expressed his feelings about how much he cared about Morley's opinion of his being extreme or not by hawking up an oyster-size spit ball and expectorating in the Cowley Brothers' general direction. 'Council are dredging the Colne anyway, which'll put paid to their layings. Bloody parasites.'

The Cowley Brothers and their friends jeered back, in language highly unsuitable, I have to say, in the presence of a lady; and I have heard – and have indeed myself used – much unsuitable language in the presence of ladies.

'I think you'd best be on your way, Mr Morley,' said Vince. 'We wouldn't want you involved in any trouble.'

And we most certainly would have been on our way, had it not been for the fact that at that moment a police car arrived and two policemen got out. As so often, there was no need for us to go looking for trouble: trouble had come to find us.

CHAPTER 17

AN AVERAGE ESSEX AFFRAY

'Gentlemen,' said a giant of a man in uniform, carefully squeezing out of the police car. He was what one might call an old-fashioned-sized policeman. Morley was one of those who had campaigned for the abolition of the minimum height requirement for the police, believing that it excluded the very type of men who should have been recruited, from all backgrounds and classes. (See his article, 'Police or Militia?' in the *Daily Herald*, 23 March 1937.) Nonetheless, even he was clearly impressed by the appearance of this behemoth in blue, who was possessed of the chiselled, sharp-jawed features of a matinee idol: he was Boris Karloff, played by John Barrymore. Miriam I thought I heard simper. In his uniform, and with his commanding height and presence, the policeman was in every regard the opposite of the grimy little fishermen gathered around us. His companion, however, was of rather more normal size and alarmingly fresh-faced, almost childlike in appearance: indeed he looked not so much like a policeman as like someone done up in a police uniform, as if the big man

162

were taking his son on a work outing. Together they looked like a music hall comedy duo.

'Mr Adkins,' said Vince, in unfriendly greeting.

'Vince,' said the giant policeman.

'Lost your way? Looking for a police box? There's none round here!' called out one of the men with the Cowley Brothers. 'Get back to Colchester where you belong!'

'Somebody call the police? Or the local circus?' called another man, to much merriment – referring, I presume, to the mismatched height and appearance of the two policemen.

The big policeman – Mr Adkins – ignored the men. He seemed rather more interested in us.

'Who are this lot?' he asked, not politely, I have to say, nodding towards us.

'This bloke here's a writer,' said Vince, 'and these are his . . . what do you call 'em?'

'Assistants,' I said, whatdoyoucallem not being a term I cared to answer to, though during my time with Morley I was often called much worse.

'Swanton Morley,' said Morley, going to shake the constable's hand. 'At your service.' The policeman showed a flash of recognition: Morley often excited a second glance among the aspiring lower and middle classes, his books being a mainstay among those who wished to pull themselves up by their bootstraps; and the average English bobby, I always found, was surprisingly aspirant and forever up-and-coming, the very epitome of ambition. In all my years with Morley I think I

163

met more ambitious self-educated policemen than I met intelligent KCs, upstanding Masters of City Companies, or insightful Viennese-style professors: the whole country was rife with bright young thrusting bobbies. But few of them possessed PC Adkins's sheer physical presence. 'My my,' said Morley, drawing back, hand duly shaken. 'That's a handspan and a half you have there, sir! A hand that shook the hand that shook the hand that shook the hand of Sullivan!'

'Sidney's the current British Police light heavyweight champion, actually,' said Vince. 'Isn't that right, Sidney?'

'Currently, yes,' confirmed the big-fisted policeman, as though conscious that the title might any moment be snatched away.

'Aha!' said Morley. 'Of course!'

'Look, Vince,' said the mighty Adkins. 'I won't beat around the bush.' You certainly wouldn't have wanted him to beat around the bush: the bush wouldn't have stood a chance. He produced a crumpled piece of paper from his jacket pocket. 'I'm afraid we've notice here from the council that the fishery's to be shut.'

'What?' said Vince. 'The fishery? What's wrong with the fishery?'

'With immediate effect,' said PC Adkins, holding up the notice.

'What's going on?' said Vince, taking only a cursory glance at the piece of paper. 'Is this some sort of joke?'

It was not some sort of joke. Adkins explained exactly what was going on.

'You'll be aware of the death of Arthur Marden?'

'Of course. And what's it got to do with us?' asked Vince.

'Further to police investigations it seems that there's the possibility the death may have been caused by the consumption of unpurified oysters.'

'Rubbish!' said Vince.

'Yes. I doubt that very much, Officer,' said Morley. 'The last major outbreak of poisoning from oysters was back in 1902, I do think I'm right in saying, when the Dean of Westminster – Winchester? – Westminster? – and a number of others got sick from a batch of contaminated Brightlingsea oysters at a feast not unlike—'

PC Adkins held up his not inconsiderable hand, which even Morley was obliged to obey.

'Thank you. We have information that the oysters for the Oyster Feast were supplied by the Colne Oyster Fishery, is that correct?'

'Of course they were supplied by the Colne Oyster Fishery,' said Vince. 'You know that. We always supply them.'

'Which is why the fishery's to be shut down with immediate effect, Vince. You understand.'

'Everything we produce here goes through the purifying plant.'

'Well, maybe something slipped through?' said PC Adkins's small and hitherto silent companion.

During the course of this exchange the Cowley

Brothers and their friends had sidled up close and were now standing alongside us.

'Problem then, Vince?' asked Joe Cowley. 'Caught out, eh? What you been up to? You been a naughty boy?'

'Hold on,' said Vince. 'Where's this stuff about unpurified oysters come from? Who gave you the information? Who was it? Was it Len Starling, or was it them?'

'I'm afraid I'm not at liberty to say, Vince,' explained PC Adkins. 'At this point all you're required to do is simply shut the plant.'

'Are you trying to stitch us up?' Vince demanded of the Cowleys and the other independent oystermen. The Cowleys and their cronies shrugged their shoulders and huddled close together.

'All we need you to do at the moment is shut the plant,' repeated PC Adkins.

'I'm not shutting the fishery,' said Vince. 'It's our livelihood.'

'Now you know how it feels!' shouted one of the independent oystermen.

'Yeah,' came the chorus of agreement.

'You—' began Vince.

PC Adkins held him back with a commanding arm. '*You* are going to close the fishery,' he told Vince. 'And *you*' – he pointed towards the Cowleys – 'are going to mind your own business. Go on, get away.'

'I said I'm not closing the fishery,' said Vince.

'In which case we'll have to do it for you, won't

we?' said PC Adkins. He nodded towards his featherweight companion, and the two of them began walking towards the purification building.

'You're not going anywhere near it!' said Vince, blocking PC Adkins's way.

Unfortunately, the underlying threat of violence that seemed to me to have been hovering ever since we'd arrived in Essex now fully erupted. The Cowleys pulled Vince back from holding back PC Adkins, PC Adkins pushed back against the Cowleys, and then Mr Storey weighed in, and then Vince, and the Cowleys' cronies, and before you knew it there was a full-scale brawl taking place before us.

I quickly ushered Miriam and Morley inside the Cadillac, locked them in, and offered what assistance I could to the Essex constabulary, though my bandaged hand prevented me from doing much apart from prising men apart. Order was quickly restored, I'm delighted to say, though I wouldn't have wanted to be on the receiving end of a blow from PC Adkins's truncheon. The fishery was closed. The crowd was dispersed. It was an average Essex affray.

We drove back to Colchester in uncharacteristic silence. Miriam dealt with matters in her usual fashion: toss of the head, leather gauntlets on, a quick reapplication of lipstick and the foot firmly on the accelerator, but Morley seemed rather shaken up. He abhorred violence of course but he also seemed to be occupied with something. He was sketching and writing in one of his fiddly German pocket notebooks. As we approached the outskirts of Colchester he slapped the notebook shut.

'Everything all right, Mr Morley?' I asked.

'Not really, Sefton, no.'

'Oh dear.'

'There's a problem here.'

'Problem?'

You never quite knew what kind of problem Morley might mean when he mentioned a 'problem': it could be a crossword puzzle sort of a problem, a conundrum, an intellectual sort of a problem requiring an ingenious solution; or it could be a practical problem, relating perhaps to the day-to-day running of his affairs, or the affairs of others, in which he often liked to interfere, and which required fixing; or it could indeed be a moral and spiritual problem affecting the whole of mankind, which might require his moral insight and guidance. This problem turned out to be all three sorts of problem in one.

'You know, man is so often his own worst enemy, Sefton.'

'Indeed, Mr Morley,' I said.

'We bring misfortune upon ourselves.'

'Yes. That's true.'

'I'm beginning to think there's more to the death of Arthur Marden than meets the eye.'

'Oh,' I said.

'Well, of course there is, Father!' said Miriam, banging the steering wheel. 'I've been saying that all along!'

'Yes. Which means it may be time for us to investigate further.'

'Oh no!' said Miriam, immediately slamming on the brakes. The Cadillac came to a screeching halt – excellent brakes, unfaultable – and all three of us were nearly thrown through the windscreen. Fortunately there were no cars behind us or Willett's would have had their Cadillac most comprehensively crunched. 'Oh no. No no no. *Non*-QED,' said Miriam. '*Non sequitur*, Father. Not. Happening.' The car had now come to a complete halt in the middle of the road.

'What on earth are you doing, Miriam?' asked Morley.

'I'll tell you what I am *not* doing, Father. I am not staying in bloody Essex a day longer.'

'What? Why?'

'Why?' said Miriam. 'Because we have a book to write.'

'Of course. We always have a book to write.'

'*And* we're falling behind again.'

'When you get to my age, my dear,' said Morley, 'you will come to realise there's nothing *but* falling behind, and so fall behind we inevitably must, until we can fall behind no longer. And if there's a mystery to solve I'm afraid we have no choice but to fall behind.'

'Oh no, but we do,' said Miriam. 'That's the

point. Just because there's a mystery to be solved it doesn't mean *we* have to solve it, Father. The police have clearly got everything in hand.'

'And *there*'s the problem I was talking about, Sefton.'

'Where?' I said.

'What?' said Miriam.

'I'm afraid the police are barking up the wrong tree,' said Morley.

'No,' said Miriam. 'Not again.'

'Oh yes,' said Morley. 'Again.' He had that familiar twinkle in his moustache. 'Barking up the wrong tree entirely.'

CHAPTER 18

A FEW DISCREET ENQUIRIES

Driving into Colchester, Morley explained to us the various trees that he thought *were* worth barking up, and which the police had somehow unaccountably neglected to bark up themselves: utterly convinced that Marden could not possibly have died of bad oysters, he was adamant that if the poor chap didn't die of natural causes the only possible explanation was foul play. He was beginning to suspect police involvement. He was beginning to suspect council involvement. He was beginning to suspect – well, it would almost be easier to say who he was not beginning to suspect of being involved.

Miriam, quite rightly, was having none of it.

'Non-sense, Father. Non-sense! This is like your Jack the Ripper thing all over again.' (Some years previously Morley had spent considerable time and money investigating the possibility that the Ripper murders were a Masonic conspiracy involving the police, Parliament, the judiciary and the royal family, a perennially popular theory so utterly appealing in fact to certain parts of the press – and indeed among Morley's many readers

– that its only possible disadvantage was its being entirely false.)

Miriam suggested – insisted, indeed, and doubly- and triply-insisted – that rather than a county-wide conspiracy it seemed much more likely that Vince Ramsey had perhaps allowed some unfiltered oysters to slip through to the feast, thus inadvertently causing the death of Arthur Marden. I agreed, and pointed out that this obvious answer was certainly to be preferred to all other more complex explanations – or, in Miriam's words, 'Occam's razor, Father! Occam's bloody razor!' Having experienced the frenzy of the kitchens during the feast at first hand, I explained that it was more than possible that Vince might have sought to supplement his oyster supply with whatever he could get hold of, filtered or unfiltered, or indeed that the Cowleys might have sought to undermine the Oyster Fishery's reputation by slipping in some of their own. Joe Cowley, I reminded Morley, was serving on the night of the feast – which was where I'd first met him.

But Morley merely scoffed at our suggestions. Vince Ramsey, he believed, was above suspicion, since he had everything to lose and absolutely nothing to gain by supplying unfiltered oysters to the feast. And even if the Cowleys had slipped in a few bad oysters of their own, they were guilty of mischief rather than murder: a bad oyster was merely a bad oyster and neither a necessary or sufficient cause of death. A more likely explanation,

Morley suggested, was that Marden's oysters had been *deliberately* poisoned.

'Oh really, Father?' said Miriam. 'You think he was singled out and executed by poisoned oyster? Really?'

'And why not?'

'Because! This is not *Black Mask* magazine, Father, *this* is Colchester!'

'A man is much more likely to die from a poisoned oyster than from a bad oyster, surely, Miriam?'

'Oh yes, of course! Of course! In the same sense that a man is more likely to die from being shot by an assassin than being randomly shot by someone armed with a weapon – both possibilities being equally far-fetched and preposterous and not even worth thinking about! Logic, Father? Laws of average? Statistics? Proof? Have you entirely lost your mind? I mean really, who under any circumstances would want to kill the Mayor of Colchester?'

'Which is indeed the question, Miriam. Which is indeed the question! Well done.'

'Gggrrr,' said Miriam. It was a very bad sign when she growled.

When we arrived in Colchester proper, having reached stalemate, we found the streets once again to be in chaos.

'Ah! City of endless excavations,' pronounced Morley. 'Renowned for it. The English Valley of the Kings! Take a note, Sefton. Might be a nice detail for the book. The topography *underlying* the Essex landscape – the world beneath! Subterranean topography! The city as a kind of palimpsest: layer upon layer, trace upon trace, like a parchment that has been used and reused and which we must learn to interpret.'

'No, Father,' said Miriam. 'No. No. Sorry. Not having it.'

'Having what?' said Morley.

'Your whole city-as-palimpsest and sub-topography thing.' She spoke with a crisp, bone-dry calm, which was a sure sign of her having entirely lost her patience, and which was indeed far more threatening than her usual weapons of conversation, which included the crushing aside, the dismissal with contempt, and the flick and slash of sarcasm. 'First,' she pronounced slowly and carefully, 'Colchester is not a city. Clearly. And second, I think you'll find these are roadworks rather than archaeological excavations.' I always thought she'd have made a wonderful Myrna Loy.

There were indeed chalked and painted signs here and there which explained the digging going on all around us – and which was indeed, as Miriam suggested, for the purposes of gas main laying, sewage pipe repairs and electric cable laying, rather than as Morley seemed to think, for digging up Roman ruins. But Morley of course was capable of romanticising even the humble modern hole and so immediately rephrased his remark: the civic triumphs of modernity were no less subject to his approbation and enthusiasm than the imperial triumphs of the past.

'Well,' he said, without a moment's hesitation, 'in that case: Colchester! Town of the future! Take a note, Sefton. Ruins as the foundations of the future!'

We enquired about the roadworks from various workmen along the way, who were more than happy to lay down their picks and shovels to admire the Cadillac, and its driver, and to explain to us what they were up to – until they were forced back to work by their foremen, of course. From what we could gather from these snatched snippets of information, Colchester was going through one of those periods of painful and often pointless spasm that will be familiar to anyone who has ever lived in any English town before or after the war. It was being 'developed'.

Morley was in principle rather sceptical of 'development', just as he was in principle rather sceptical of 'progress' and 'modernisation', but in practice he was absolutely fascinated by all things new, from Becontree to the most up-to-date novelty and gadget, and in particular anything involving electrification – he had a Magnetophon, for example, imported from Germany, which took pride of place in the dining room back at St George's – and he now insisted on leaping out of the car at every opportunity to ask about the various electrical and plumbing works being undertaken by the working men of Colchester. As a consequence the journey took some time longer than the some time longer it was already going to take.

'If it's good enough for the Soviets it's good enough for us,' he announced to a set of bemused workmen who were trying to do something tricky with a ladder and a lamppost by the side of the road. He then proceeded to explain to them Lenin's vision of communism – 'Soviet power plus electrification' – which required the building of massive dams and hydroelectric plants across the whole of Russia and beyond. (For a more extensive summary of this impromptu roadside lecturette, see his essay, 'The Great Electrificator' in *Morley's Mighty Bear: A Children's History of Russia*, 1930.) In the time-honoured polite English tradition of dealing with madmen and eccentrics, the men listened, smiled, nodded and then completely ignored Morley and got on with their work, fitting whatever complicated new lamp it was that was required to develop Colchester. I hauled Morley back into the car, again. And again.

When we arrived at the George Hotel, there was a telegram waiting for Morley, from an old friend of his, living in Colchester, and inviting us to dinner that evening.

'Wonderful!' said Morley.

'No,' said Miriam, 'not wonderful,' and proceeded to announce that she had had quite enough of

Essex and of Essex people in general, and of Colchester and Colchester people in particular and that she was going to go and pack ready for our departure, which in her opinion could not be soon enough.

'Gentlemen, as far as I'm concerned you two can enjoy barking up as many trees and dining with as many of Father's old friends as you like. I, meanwhile, I am going to do the sensible thing and rest and relax here until it's time to leave. Let me know, Father, when you've solved the so-called "mystery" of the death of Arthur Marden and then perhaps we can be on our way?'

'Jolly good!' said Morley, as relentlessly positive as ever. 'Sounds like a plan!' He then briefed me on what the plan might actually be: to combine work on *The County Guides: Essex* with 'a few discreet enquiries'. (Among Morley's papers there is an unfinished manuscript entitled 'A Few Discreet Enquiries', which appears to be notes towards some kind of account of our various adventures in the English counties, his memoir of our time together. Like so many of his projects it was begun but never finished.)

'Do we really have time for discreet enquiries this afternoon, Mr Morley?' I asked as we left the hotel, armed with fresh notebooks and my camera. 'Might they not perhaps wait until tomorrow? Are there not some articles you need to begin or finish or . . . something? Do we really have enough time to—'

In reply, Morley shook both wrists at me, displaying his two watches – the luminous and the non-luminous.

'Never enough time, Sefton,' he said. 'Never enough time. Come on!'

The plan was to take a walking tour of the town, beginning with the Town Hall and taking in Jumbo, the water tower, and some of the old Roman ruins, but on our arrival at the Town Hall, just before five, we were immediately waylaid. To Morley's delight, and to my considerable consternation, we discovered that there was to be a meeting of the town council and all its committees – all sixteen of them, according to the meeting agenda, including the Watch Committee, the Finance Committee, the Housing Committee, the Highways Committee, the Town Development Committee, the Members' Allowances Committee, and committees on committees on committees. The public were more than welcome to attend, though I could think of no good reason why they would want to. With the sleek and well-nourished councillors arriving to go about their relentless council business, and despite my protestations, Morley insisted that we too should attend, in the hope that this might be a good place to start with our discreet enquiries and also in the process that we could witness and write about – in his words – 'the magnificent and majestic workings of English local democracy, renowned throughout the world from the time of Gladstone'. As it turned out, the meeting was neither majestic nor magnificent. What Gladstone might have made of it I can only imagine.

Despite being continually shushed by other members of the public in the public gallery, and by the journalists who were taking notes, and indeed by the councillors themselves, Morley did his best to brief me on the complex procedures and pageantry of what I was witnessing, explaining the role of the Clerk to the Council, the councillors, the aldermen, the Lord Lieutenant and the High Sheriff. 'Sort of a minor mayor, Sefton, the High Sheriff, minus the fancy trimmings. The traditional role is to attend executions, I believe, and to hob-nob with grandees.' This last comment earned him a hard stare from the oafish-looking High Sheriff and a reprimand from the extremely unhappy Clerk to the Council.

The first matter on the agenda was of course the death of the mayor and the announcement of procedures for the appointment of his successor. Morley's sotto voce comments on this subject – 'Ah, yes, the glamour of the English mayoralty, the lustre never dims, Sefton! Usually attracts entirely the wrong sort, of course' – drew many disapproving glances from every corner of the room and I feared we were on the verge of being ejected from the chamber before the meeting proper had even begun, had it not been for the fact that someone else was ejected before us.

The councillors were busy taking turns to stand and solemnly express their sympathies and condolences. 'This'll take a while,' said Morley – and it did.

After a quarter of an hour or more of condolences the man sitting next to me leaned across and nodded towards the next councillor preparing himself to stand and speak. 'You and your friend'll enjoy this!' he whispered to me. I very much doubted it.

'Councillor Basil Dunbar,' announced the Clerk to the Council, with barely concealed contempt, and Councillor Dunbar raised himself stiffly from his seat.

'Independent by name and independent by nature,' whispered the man sitting next to me, presumably meaning Mr Dunbar, who indeed proved to be extremely independent by nature.

Mr Dunbar, we learned later, was universally referred to as the 'anti-council councillor', though it might be more accurate to describe him as the anti-everything councillor. Wearing an ill-fitting houndstooth jacket that was at least a size too large and a bright purple poorly knotted tie that matched his purple and poorly knotted features, he began with the necessary few words of condolence before launching into the most extraordinary denunciations and condemnations. He was warned several times by the Clerk to the Council to mind his language and to respect the chair, but he did neither and indeed continued making all sorts of wild accusations, his little fists balled in anger as he spoke. According to the man sitting next to me, who was a regular at the council meetings – 'Much better than what's on in the variety halls, and it's free' – hardly a meeting of Colchester's town council had gone by in living memory when Dunbar hadn't been led out, carried out, escorted out or ordered out of the chamber. On one or two occasions he had even tried to sue the council officers for wrongful ejection.

On this particular occasion Mr Dunbar took the opportunity to denounce both Arthur Marden personally and council policies generally. According to Dunbar, a handful of local worthies, including Marden, had been busy for years dividing up Colchester for their own advantage like a personal fiefdom, installing gas and electric cables that no one wanted and that no one would use. He also complained that the council plans to dredge the river would disproportionately affect the oyster layings of the West Mersea independent oystermen compared to the layings of the mighty Colne Fishery Company, who were in cahoots with the councillors. There was a lot of other stuff too, but the gist was in his conclusion: 'Colchester,' he pronounced, 'is a rotten borough run by rotten people.'

When the Clerk to the Council asked Mr Dunbar to withdraw his comments about the council in general and Arthur Marden in particular, Mr Dunbar refused.

'As you know, I am not saying anything now that I would not say and did not say to the mayor when he was alive,' he said. 'The man was a—'

181

But before he could carry on he was roughly seized by two of the Town Hall beadles and ejected from the council chamber.

'Told you,' said the man sitting next to me. 'Excellent entertainment, isn't it?'

'Yes,' I agreed. It was certainly something.

I turned to Morley.

'What do you think, Mr Morley? A couple of ha'pennies short of a shilling?'

'On the contrary, Sefton. On the contrary. I think we may have found the very person with whom to begin our discreet enquiries, have we not?'

CHAPTER 19

LOOSE SCREW

It was too late, however – and thank goodness – to proceed any further with our discreet enquiries that evening, since we were due to join Morley's old friend, Edward Mountjoy, for supper. This was both a relief and a chore; meeting Morley's old chums was one of the many dubious pleasures of my time working with him. Over the years we visited with, were visited by – and for my part was often absolutely bored stiff listening to – the great and the good of English society, and often of the Scots, the Welsh and the Irish also. Among the writers with whom we enjoyed sherry, seed cake, tea, coffee, bridge, brandy snaps and cigarettes, were John Galsworthy, Rebecca West, May Sinclair, Charles Scott Moncrieff, Somerset Maugham, Hugh Walpole, H.G. Wells, Compton Mackenzie, E.F. Benson, Rose Macaulay and Arnold Bennett. (And what was truly surprising was how closely these allegedly freethinking souls all seemed to conform quite happily and unselfconsciously to national stereotypes: the English were all terribly class-bound; the Irish predictably garrulous, and often drunk;

the Scots dour and massively argumentative; and the Welsh of course anti-everything but wonderful singers. Maybe it was just because they were writers.)

Among Morley's other friends and acquaintances were Winston Churchill, Anna Pavlova, Jacob Epstein, Mistinguett, the Barrymores and the Aga Khan. Mr Pablo Picasso, I can report, is a demon at croquet, and Jessie Matthews – whom Morley absolutely adored, and with whom he liked to duet on her theme song, 'Over My Shoulder' – was something of a handful. But by far the most numerous among Morley's many friends were the unsung and the unknown of Olde Englande: the country doctors and solicitors, the headmasters and headmistresses, the farmers and stout yeomen who then made up the bulk and the backbone of English society, a backbone, for better or worse, that has long since bent and doubled. Edward Mountjoy was just one such doughty English soul.

Mountjoy was one of Morley's old croquet partners; 'the best one-legged croquet player in the country', according to Morley, a title for which there were in fact a surprising number of contenders, apparently, many old soldiers having lost limbs in the war and taken up croquet as the next best thing to actual combat. Morley and Mountjoy had forged their friendship at a tournament in Bristol, so the story went, when Morley had come to Mountjoy's rescue when the poor fellow had lost an essential screw in his metal leg and Morley had provided both a spare and a spanner. Mountjoy's inevitable and unfortunate nickname for Morley was, therefore, I learned, the Indispensable Spanner: Morley in return referred to Mountjoy as Loose Screw Mountjoy. Loose Screw was also a ceremonial deputy lieutenant, whatever that was, and a retired officer in the Essex Regiment. When Mountjoy had discovered that we'd be spending the weekend in Colchester, *sans* Lagonda, he had immediately telegrammed Morley and invited us to visit. When Miriam had earlier declined the invitation to dine she had pointed out that she had spent quite enough time in the company of Loose Screw at croquet tournaments in her childhood, so it was Morley and I who were now sharing the old soldier's Saturday night scratch supper of cold poached fish and potatoes.

Mountjoy was a widower who lived with a number of other retired army officers in a large and pleasant house on a leafy avenue in Colchester. Large, pleasant and rather damp, it has to be said: there was a compensating fire set in the wood-panelled dining room of such intensity that I thought it might be enough to burn the whole place down. Damaged old soldiers – damaged old souls – feel the cold. I cooled off from the heat with several gins before dinner – Morley, of course, sticking to water – and was now enjoying the free-flowing wine that was being generously poured at the dinner table by the officers' well-practised housemaid, a woman of ruddy complexion, remarkable embonpoint and indeterminate age named Mrs Wildy.

'Sure we can't tempt you with a touch of the old plink-plonk?' Mountjoy asked Morley.

'No, thank you,' said Morley.

'Abstainer?' asked one of the other officers, named Goodbody, seated at my left, whose rosy cheeks and red nose suggested that he most certainly was not.

'I am,' said Morley.

'Ne' mind,' said Goodbody, gleefully spearing a potato with his one good arm. What had happened to his other arm I did not ask. 'Ne' mind.'

'Good man,' said another, Bolger, who wore a monocle on one eye and a black patch on the other and who insisted on smoking a pipe all through dinner, though he was continually wiping beads of perspiration from his brow. The room really was very warm.

'Good man,' we all agreed, raising our glasses in a toast.

'To the Indispensable Spanner!' proclaimed Mountjoy.

'The Indispensable Spanner!' came the chorus.

'Right parry,' said ruddy-faced Goodbody.

'Left parry,' said the Cyclops Bolger.

'Forward lunge!' declared them all, draining their glasses.

It was turning into a long evening. I busied myself gazing at the peculiar contents of the room's vast leaded-glass display cabinet: odd bits and pieces of porcelain, regimental photographs, a collection of gulls' eggs, piles of books by the likes of E. Phillips Oppenheim and William Le Queux, a few Loeb Classical editions, and some thing or other floating in a jar. I wondered what it might be – and what it might be worth. My debt to Delaney was once again playing on my mind.

'Labrador testicles,' said Goodbody, munching enthusiastically on a large soft-boiled potato. 'Harris. House dog. Greatly missed.'

During the course of the meal Morley had been offering the assembled company his various considered thoughts about Colchester, and they in turn had been offering their own. I had been instructed by Morley to take notes on this great meeting of minds, which I did, occasionally, on a napkin, my notebook once again having eluded my grasp. Colchester, all the retired soldiers seemed to agree, perhaps not surprisingly, was the perfect place for soldiers to retire, though they admitted the place did have its problems.

'The thing you have to realise about Colchester, Morley,' said Mountjoy, 'is that it's a town with a bishop but no cathedral.'

'Yes,' agreed Morley. 'Yes, I know.'

'But in fact the very opposite is the case, if you catch my drift?'

Morley may have caught Mountjoy's drift, but I was struggling. The gin was taking effect.

'The opposite of a bishop with no cathedral is a . . . cathedral with no bishop?' I said.

'Exactly. No one's in charge is the problem. Hence the reputation for . . . what might one call it? The atmosphere of—'

'Lawlessness?' I said, thinking back to Joe Cowley threatening me outside the Town Hall, the scuffle down at the oyster plant in West Mersea, and the ever looming threat of violence and disorder.

'No, no, lawlessness isn't right, I don't think. I don't think we're lawless, are we, gentlemen?'

The officers chuckled in a good-natured fashion, though I have to say that all of them looked as though they might become utterly lawless without a moment's hesitation.

'No, no, not lawless at all,' said Mountjoy. 'On the contrary. It's a very lawful sort of a town. The problem is the lack of leadership. A strong leader is what's required.'

'Hear, hear,' agreed all the officers.

'Bring back Wellington!' said one of them, whose name was either Gerald Edwards or Edward Gerald – my napkin notes are rather jumbled.

'John Wayne,' said Bolger.

'John Wayne!' said Goodbody, and then more quietly, 'He loves John Wayne.'

'Churchill'll do,' said Gerald Edwards, or Edward Gerald. 'Churchill'll do.' Churchill'll do what he did not make clear. (Do far too much, according to Morley, who was a friend but not a fan: he thought Churchill had made an utter fool of himself over the abdication and over India.)

'I think what you have to understand,' said

another, a genial, plump fellow who'd introduced himself only as Charlie, who sported a beret on his rosy round bald head, who made little baby pig-grunts as he ate, and who had the terrible habit of breaking wind fore and aft quite unexpectedly without apology during the course of conversation, 'is that we're – [parp] – basically a garrison town with no one to fight.'

'Which is a good thing, surely?' said Morley.

'Of course,' said Charlie. 'Absolutely. Except that it means that things can sometimes get, what is it they say now – [parp] – bottled up?' No chance of anything of his being bottled up.

'Exactly,' said Mountjoy. 'And then before you know it they're at boiling point, and . . . Well. Men will be men, won't they, eh?'

There then followed a discussion of examples of men being men which was not for the faint-hearted – soldier talk, which took me back to Spain – and I think I can safely say that both Morley and I were relieved when the conversation turned to the death of Arthur Marden.

'Have you seen the paper?' asked Mountjoy.

'*The Times*?' said Morley.

'*Colchester Gazette*,' said Mountjoy.

'Journal of record,' said Charlie.

'Unfortunately not,' said Morley. 'No, I haven't seen it.'

'The chap Starling's been released.'

'There were murmurations around the table at this news.

189

'But some other chaps have been arrested – supplying bad oysters, apparently. Colne Oyster Fishery men?'

'Absolute nonsense,' said Morley. 'The whole thing. They'll be released tomorrow. I ate those oysters myself, there was absolutely nothing wrong with them.'

'I thought a lot of people got sick at the feast?'

'Mass hysteria, gentlemen,' said Morley. 'Nothing more, nothing less.'

'Ah,' said Mountjoy. 'Yes. Seen it in war.'

'Mass hysteria?' said Morley.

'Killing frenzy,' said Mountjoy. 'Very similar. Dangerous. Blood on your hands is one thing. Blood welling in your boots is quite another.'

'And you know there are rumours that Marden's daughter has left the town?' added Charlie.

'Really?' said Mountjoy.

'Yes. Mrs Wildy was saying. Isn't that right, Mrs Wildy?'

'She's perfectly entitled to leave the town, is she not?' asked Morley.

'Have we got a copy of the paper?' Mountjoy asked Mrs Wildy, who was once more doing the rounds with the wine.

'It's through in the drawing room,' she said. 'I'll just go and fetch it for you, shall I, sir?'

'Please, Mrs Wildy.'

I squinted at the large tapestry hanging over the credenza at the end of the room. It depicted some Roman ruins, set in an unlikely undulating wooded landscape, surrounded by a border of leaves and flowers. Exceedingly ugly, but excellent condition, well preserved, fine stitching.

'After Aubusson,' said Goodbody.

'Worth a bit?' I said.

'No idea,' he said.

'Hundreds?'

'No idea.'

'One hundred?'

'Possibly.'

Mrs Wildy returned with the *Colchester Gazette*. 'Here we are.'

Mountjoy read the front page. The newspaper reported that Len Starling had indeed been released by the police after questioning.

'Why on earth did they take him in for questioning in the first place, I wonder?' said Charlie.

'I assume because he was the person who served the oysters to the mayor shortly before he died,' said Morley.

'Yes. Though we all know that the Town Sergeant and the mayor had had their "differences", shall we say,' said Mountjoy.

'Differences?' said Morley. 'Starling and Marden? What sort of differences?'

'I'd rather not say,' said Mountjoy.

'But between friends?' said Morley.

'I'd really rather not say,' repeated Mountjoy.

'Come come,' said Morley. 'I'm only wondering because—'

'Do you know Starling?' I quietly asked Goodbody.

'Not really,' he said. 'I believe he's a cottager.'

'A whattager?'

'A cottager. You know, lives out in a cottage, on the edge of town. And Marden was a staunch Methodist, so I think maybe—'

'Change of subject,' said Mountjoy.

'But—' began Morley.

'I said change of subject,' repeated Mountjoy, fixing everyone at the table with an expression of piercing force.

The room went silent. The cordial atmosphere was suddenly gone: all you could hear was the ticking clock, the heavy laying down of silver cutlery, and the rushing of the fire. Even Morley could tell that this was not an avenue of conversation that was going to be worth pursuing.

'And what about Marden's daughter?' he asked Mrs Wildy, wisely changing the subject. 'She's gone away, you say?'

'Florence? That's what I heard, sir, yes.'

'Grief-stricken,' said Charlie. 'No doubt. To lose one's father, in such appalling public circumstances.'

'Or,' said Morley.

'Or what?'

'Or perhaps she is in some way implicated in the death of her father and so she's fled?' The room fell silent once again. Having retreated down one path it seemed that Morley had unwittingly blundered down another equally dangerous avenue.

'Don't be so ridiculous, Morley!' said Mountjoy,

with a tone as sharp and fixed as a bayonet. 'I know you've started getting involved in these sorts of things recently – I read about that business in Devon—'

'Yes, pretty rum stuff, wasn't it?' said Charlie. 'And Norfolk! That was rather grisly also.'

'But I hardly think it's on to start throwing around accusations about the mayor's daughter.'

'Absolutely not,' everyone agreed, in unison.

'I'm not throwing around accusations, my dear Mountjoy,' said Morley. 'I'm merely asking. Do you know her, Marden's daughter?'

'Florence?' said Mountjoy, his face flushed. 'Well, we've met of course, but I couldn't say I know her. I think all of us here have met her at some time. It's a small town, Morley.'

'I've met her a few times,' said Charlie. 'Perfectly pleasant young lady. Nothing at all to suggest that she'd be involved in the death of her father.'

'Anyway, I thought it was a bad oyster that carried him off?' said my ruddy-faced companion.

'I rather doubt that,' said Morley.

'What other possible explanation is there?'

'There are always other possible explanations,' said Morley. 'I'm sure the autopsy will give us some clues.'

'I'm sure it will. So we should probably wait and see then, shouldn't we?' said Mountjoy. 'Black is black and white is white. And anything else is speculation.'

'Speaking of speculation,' said Morley, rather

recklessly, it seemed to me. 'There was a meeting at the Town Hall today, and a chap named Dunbar made all sorts of accusations.'

'Old Miseryguts?' said Charlie.

'Don't take any notice of Dunbar,' said Mountjoy. 'The man's a bloody spoon – pardon my French, Mrs Wildy. Sworn enemy of all that's good in this town. He'd say anything to traduce Marden's memory.'

We agreed to disagree about what had led to the death of Arthur Marden and the plight of Marden's daughter, and retired back to the drawing room. Charlie sat at the out-of-tune piano and parped and jangled his way through a couple of Noël Cowards, a few regimental songs, something from *Ruddigore* and a memorable rendition of 'Up Girls and At 'Em', Goodbody sat smoothing a walking stick with some sandpaper, and Bolger read *The Times*, with a magnifying glass. Morley and I eventually made our excuses around 11 p.m. and left. Mountjoy drew me aside as we were leaving.

'Does he ever talk about . . . you know?' he asked.

'I'm afraid I don't know,' I said.

'His son?' asked Mountjoy.

'His son?' I said.

'You do know he had a son?'

'I . . .' I had heard mention of a son, but it was one of those few subjects – his dead wife was another – that Morley was not willing to discuss.

'Hmm,' said Mountjoy, patting me on the back. 'Probably best.'

Morley was keen to discuss the evening as we walked back to the George Hotel but I had no interest in spending any more of my evening in discussion with Morley about the evening, which would only make what was already a long evening all the longer. I reminded him that he doubtless had articles to write – which he did, obviously, something on autumn foliage for *Country Life* and something else on the relationship between modern literature and the art of the crossword puzzle for *Time and Tide,* and also his usual book-of-the-day to read before sleep, something called *The Road to Oxiana,* which he was greatly looking forward to, apparently – and I suggested he went on ahead and got started while I enjoyed an evening stroll to contemplate the eternal verities before bed.

Of course at that time I was incapable of contemplating any sort of verities except through the bottom of a glass and had no more intention of taking an evening stroll than I had of taking responsibility for myself and for my actions. The pub, whatever it was called, was filled with rowdy soldiers and thick with smoke. It stank of alcohol and sweat. There was no Amy Johnson to talk to. But there was the promise of entertainment: just as I arrived and ordered a drink, in the corner of the bar, set apart with a few chairs and a couple of standard lamps, a woman in a black evening gown in rather full-blown make-up with a huge feather boa began slowly removing first the boa, and then her gloves, and her gown, until I realised too late, to my surprise, that she was a he. I'd seen quite enough of that sort of thing in Soho over the years. I drank up quickly and left.

By chance, as I arrived back at the hotel, Miriam was also arriving back.

'Enjoy your night in?' I asked.

'Yes, thank you, Sefton.'

'Just popped out for a breath of fresh air?'

'That's correct. You too?'

She took one of my cigarettes, which I had not offered.

'How are the discreet enquiries going then?' she asked.

'Your father's still convinced that Marden's death was foul play.'

'I blame the influence of bad novels and films,' said Miriam.

'And where did you go tonight?' I asked, lighting her cigarette and my own.

'Am I my brother's keeper?' she said. 'The Regal, since you ask.'

'Cinema?'

'Of course the cinema, Sefton. The Regal? What else would it be?'

'By yourself?'

'Not that it's any of your business.'

'What did you see?'

'*Mountain Justice.*'

'Never heard of it. Any good?'

'Usual sort of thing. Tyrannical father, daughter

attempts to break free, ends up murdering him, Gothic depiction of a remote and backward community, contrasted with the fabulous glamour of the city. Sound familiar?'

'Sounds terribly formulaic. I'm not sure I'll be rushing to see it.'

'Josephine Hutchinson has excellent eyebrows.'

'Glad to hear it.'

'But she's no Bette Davis.'

'Well, who is?'

'And George Brent's no Bogart.'

Miriam gazed out dreamily at the silent street before us. She was half lit by one of Colchester's new electric street lights. 'Who would you have play you in a film of your life, Sefton?'

'I'm not sure,' I said.

'Sheila Terry might be good – for me, I mean. Or Dorothy Lamour? Don't you think?'

'Maybe.'

'Maybe?' She struck what I took to be a Dorothy Lamour pose.

'Definitely.'

'And you could be Claude Rains.'

'I'm not sure that's a compliment.'

'Or Peter Lorre?'

'Thank you.'

'I might write about it in my column. My imagined life on stage and screen. I imagine a lot of women share such fantasies.'

'I'm sure they do,' I said. 'And how is the column?'

'It's coming along.' She finished her cigarette, ground it out, and looked at me. I'd seen the look before. It meant 'Don't ask me any more questions.' I ignored it.

'Can I ask, do you ever feel like an oyster, Miriam?' I said, recalling my evening of discussing the Meaning of Life, Death and Love with Amy Johnson.

'I beg your pardon?'

'It's just something that Amy said.'

'Amy?'

'Miss Johnson, the aviatrix. She said that women were like oysters and that sometimes it took something to prise them open, and then—'

'Do you know, Sefton, I have never heard anything quite so revolting and preposterous in my life,' said Miriam. 'I'm surprised a woman like Miss Johnson was interested in sharing such . . . insights with you. Goodnight.' And she swished before me into the hotel, head held high.

CHAPTER 20

THE 'COTTAGING' EXISTENCE

'A fine Sunday morning!' said Morley. 'Cerulean skies. Bright sunshine. Essex at its finest, eh?'

'It is damp and it's autumn—'

'Nonetheless.'

'And it's Essex, Father.'

'Nonetheless, nonetheless.'

'*And* it's Sunday,' added Miriam, for good measure.

'Sleep well, Sefton?'

'I can't say I did, Mr Morley, no.'

'Hmm. Oh dear. Troubled conscience?'

'I don't know,' I said. I didn't know because my conscience was almost always troubled.

'The role of insomnia in human life and in human history: rather interesting, isn't it?'

'No, Father,' said Miriam truthfully, loudly buttering some toast. 'It is not.'

'The cause or the consequence of cruelty, do you think, Sefton? I'm never sure.'

'Erm.' It usually took several cups of coffee and cigarettes to bring me up to Morley speed in the morning and I was only one cup of coffee in.

'Tyrants always lie awake, do they not? But saints also. Most works of man – for good and ill – are the product of disturbance and discomfort.'

Miriam crunched her way through her toast.

'Lack of sleep: too much energy, or too little conscience?' continued Morley. 'What do you think, Sefton?' Breakfast with Morley was like sitting an Oxbridge entrance exam, every day, before 9 a.m. 'Too much energy, too little conscience?'

'One of the two, I'm sure, Mr Morley,' I said.

(For Morley's definitive statement on the matter of sleep and sleeplessness see *Morley Goes to Bed: On the History of Sleep and Insomnia, with Recommendations for Natural Sleep Remedies* (1930), in which he rails against pharmaceutical sleep aids – 'the chemical cosh' – and recommends instead various old-fashioned techniques such as warm milk and lukewarm baths, and a very precise sleeping posture, involving lying on a hard mattress on the right side of the body, stretched out with the arms relaxed, palms cupped, head only slightly raised and with the face 'not clogging the pillow', which leads to wrinkling, apparently; plus of course the adoption of what he always liked to call 'a healthy philosophy of life'. He cautions also against the consumption of alcohol, the use of tobacco, snuff, tea, coffee, sugar and all other treats or stimulants at any time of the day but in the evenings in particular. It was, in other words, not a regimen that anyone but Morley would have been able to follow.)

Over breakfast Morley restated his firm opinion that Marden had almost certainly been deliberately poisoned, treating us to his latest theories about who the murderer or murderers might be. Miriam did her best to drown out the sound of these half-formed hypotheses with the scraping of toast, continual interruptions and requests to the waiting staff for different types of Tiptree jam. ('So, logically, the murderer must be—', 'Do you have the Tiptree Greengage Conserve, by any chance?' 'The Mulberry?' 'The Blackcurrant?' 'The Quince?') Since we were due to collect the Lagonda the following morning and this would in all likelihood be our last day in Colchester, Morley thought it might make 'a pleasant diversion' – in his words – to try to wrap up the mystery for the Essex police before we left.

'Oh, I'm sure they'd be absolutely delighted, Father, for you to stick your nose in where it's not wanted – absolutely delighted! Don't you think, Sefton?'

'Delighted,' I agreed.

'Though can I say again – just to be clear – that this is an undertaking in which I will play no part whatsoever.'

'But we need you, Miriam!' said Morley.

'Do you though, Father? Or are you simply intent on pursuing your own little investigation, whoever or whomsoever might be prepared to assist you? As usual.'

'Oh no, no,' said Morley, suggesting – rather

cannily, I thought – that as well as wrapping up the small matter of the mystery of the death of Arthur Marden that we should also simultaneously be spending the day gathering more material for the book on Essex, in order to ensure our hasty departure on the morrow. 'Surely an entirely sensible and legitimate use of our time, Miriam? And many hands make light etcetera, eh?'

Eventually – after much father–daughter back and forth, and three rounds of toast and half a dozen pots of marmalade and jam later – Miriam kindly agreed to join us. By ten o'clock we were back on the road in the Cadillac. And I had a headache.

Our first stop was to be Len Starling's cottage, Morley to try to find out what exactly it was about his relationship with Arthur Marden that Mountjoy and his friends had suggested was 'difficult', Miriam and me to gather notes and photographs on Starling's reputed 'cottaging' lifestyle. As usual, Miriam was driving, I was taking notes, and Morley was talking, talking, talking and talking, delivering himself on this occasion of a rather long short history of the English cottage, its construction, its symbolic meaning, its recent evolution and – well, I'll abbreviate.

'The true ornament of the English countryside,' he enthused, as we negotiated the little lanes and avenues around Colchester, avoiding the interminable roadworks wherever we could, 'the English country cottage! The cottage life! The cottage style! The dream of every Englishman!'

I remember there was a moment during this discourse at which I glanced across at Morley in his foursquare tweeds, as he gesticulated his way through some fascinating point about the relationship between English Romanticism and the cult of the cottage, and it occurred to me that *he* was in fact the dream of every Englishman, *Morley* the English country cottage: low-born, high-minded, entirely natural and yet cultured, appropriate for all sites and circumstances, from the retreat in the grounds of a stately home to a labourer's humble dwelling, the very image of Olde Englande, embodied in one man.

'The dream of every English*man* perhaps: but *not* every English*woman*,' said Miriam, who of course represented everything that was not English country cottage style. Hers was rather what one might call contemporary metropolitan international style: tailored, structured, extravagant, *sparkling*.

'The cottage homes of England! / By thousands on her plains,/ They are smiling o'er the silvery brooks,/ And round the hamlet fanes,' said Morley, foursquarely.

'The cottage homes of England/ Alas, how strong they smell!/ There's fever in the cesspool,/ And sewage in the well,' replied Miriam, sparkling.

I was never quite sure if they'd rehearsed these sorts of routines – they were so practised and so strange. But it was just what they did. They had a wide repertoire of light verse that they used to entertain each other. At least it wasn't nonsense verse – it was really very very tiresome when they recited nonsense verse.

Thus, in summary, our abbreviated journey.

Len Starling's cottage was indeed one of those cottages that Englishmen – and whatever Miriam said, doubtless some Englishwomen – dream of, a thatched and weatherboarded place of the kind that we had seen dotted here and there throughout our travels in north Essex, an echt English cottage, no larger than the size of half a tennis court, and utterly perfect of its kind: the weatherboard freshly painted white and the thatch as crisp as if it had only just been cut and trimmed by an ancient whiskery thatcher with his bill hook and his knife.

If the cottage was symbolic and idyllic then the garden was – well, the garden really was something else. *What* it was, I wasn't sure. The front of the cottage was separated from the road by a white wooden fence which was planted in behind with a bulging herbaceous border. Morley was quite envious. 'Lovely big border,' he remarked, as we climbed out of the Cadillac. 'Isn't it, Sefton? Absolutely gorgeous. A classic English border.' (Morley suffered terribly from border-envy. He tended his own borders back at St George's – or at least supervised the tending of his own borders – with relentless care, in an attempt to create an impression of naturalness that was in fact anything but. 'Gardening is a cultural rather than a natural pursuit and phenomenon,' he writes in *Morley's*

Lovers of the Green Way: Biographies of Great Gardeners and Their Gardens (1929), 'and gardeners work like artists by tricks, devices, cunning and with sleight of hand.') It was what was hidden directly behind this lovely big English border that was truly strange and surprising. Behind the border was an area that was the very opposite of gorgeous, the counterpoint to the border planting: it was a kind of blank space of shingle, which had been piled in mazy circles here and there, which looked to me just like so many messy scribbles in the sand. There were also half a dozen small rocks standing up like mini-dolmen, and a few grassy-looking plants.

'My goodness,' said Morley, as we strode up the winding stone path through this strange landscape towards the cottage. 'What do you think, Sefton?'

I thought it looked rather like the grim landscape at West Mersea.

'If I'm not mistaken I think what we have here is a Japanese garden, is it not – in Essex! Do you remember visiting the Ryoanji temple garden in Japan, Miriam?'

'I can't say I do, Father, no.'

'You were very young.' Morley had stopped to gaze at the strange scene before us. 'The dry land-scape gardens of Japan! Might be worth a book, eh?' (And eventually, inevitably of course it was: see *Morley's Great Gardens of the World: A Guide and Gazetteer*, 1939.)

'Come on, Father,' said Miriam, pushing Morley

along towards the cottage and indicating that I should do likewise.

'Incredible culture of gardening in Japan. Serene planting, rocks used to symbolise landscape features, gravel intended to represent the sea, careful pruning: the entire effect meant to create a calm, relaxing, comforting atmosphere around the *ryokan* or the *tera*, if I remember correctly. Which is exactly what we have here, I believe. In miniature. In Essex!'

'Yes, you said, Father,' said Miriam. 'Very good.'

I had to admit, I rather liked it. It was rather different, and rather soothing: you somehow felt as though you were arriving somewhere else, in a different world, with different rules, a place slightly at a tangent.

Miriam, entirely practical, knocked loudly on the door of the cottage.

'I mean, as much as anything it's all just rather witty, isn't it?' continued Morley, staring back at the garden. 'The whole thing. The surprise of it, sort of tucked behind the border. You'd never know, would you? The opposite of the English country garden, behind what one supposes is an English country garden! Restricted palette, careful arrangement. A Japanese garden, in Essex!' He really did like it. 'I think Mr Starling must be rather a remarkable man? Don't you think, Sefton?'

I had no idea. But I could say this of him: he was certainly light on his feet.

No sooner had the echo of Miriam's knocking

died away than the top half of the cottage's front door swung open, as if on a cuckoo clock or in a stable, and there appeared Mr Starling – or least the top half of Mr Starling, as though he had been divided in two. He was in his shirtsleeves and waistcoat, with no tie, and wearing a brown house apron, upon which he was busily wiping his hands.

'Yes?'

'Mr Starling?'

'And you are?' He did not seem in welcoming mood. I remembered his sad and courageous face from the Oyster Feast. If anything he now seemed even sadder and braver. 'What are you? Are you all journalists?'

'No,' said Morley hesitantly. This was, I suppose, strictly true: Morley was of course a journalist by profession and by instinct, Miriam had her new press card from *Woman*, but I was most certainly not a journalist, so strictly speaking, we weren't *all* journalists. Morley clarified. 'No, we're not all journalists. And those of us who are journalists aren't *exactly* journalists. *Nulla dies sine linea*, certainly, but I would describe us more as . . . *littérateurs*.'

'No thank you,' said Mr Starling, who was about to shut the top half of his door.

'My name is Swanton Morley.'

'Swanton Morley?' said Mr Starling, hesitating. 'The People's Professor? You were at the Oyster Feast?'

'That's correct, sir.'

'Well.' Mr Starling adopted a rather more welcoming tone: Morley could sometimes have that effect on people. (I should say, he could also have the opposite effect.) 'Well. What can I do for you, Mr Morley?'

'I wondered . . .' Morley sometimes found it difficult to lie. Fortunately it was not a difficulty that either Miriam or I ever really struggled with.

'We're writing a book about Essex,' said Miriam. 'As part of a series, *The County Guides*. You may have heard of them?'

'I can't say I have, miss, no.'

'Well, you shall, sir,' said Morley. 'You shall.'

'And so we were wondering if you might be able to . . .' Miriam began, but clearly amid all her toast-scraping she hadn't been listening very closely at breakfast and seemed to have forgotten the purpose of our visit.

'We're interested in cottaging,' I said. 'For the purposes of the book.'

'Ah,' said Mr Starling. 'Well, I can't claim to be an expert, but I certainly do like to dabble. Please, come in.'

And he opened the lower half of the door and we entered his cottage home. During all my years with Morley I never ceased to be amazed at how easy it was to gain access to people's houses. It was just lucky none of us were thieves or ne'er-do-wells.

Mr Starling's stable door led directly into the front room of the cottage, which was furnished simply with a deal table, four chairs, an old leather chaise longue, a set of cupboards, and some faded watercolours hanging on the wall, depicting what I assumed were Japanese landscape scenes. There were simple flat-wick burner lamps and a couple of candles in holders on the mantelpiece above the fire.

'I was just admiring your Japanese garden,' said Morley.

'Well, inspired by Japan, but also by the salt marshes of Essex, actually,' said Mr Starling.

'Ah!' said Morley.

'But that's what I said—' I began.

'Yes, an interesting comparison and combination – which wouldn't have occurred to me before, I have to say, Mr Starling. Quite delightful and very observant of you. Have you ever been to Japan?'

'I have, actually,' said Mr Starling. 'I was at one time a personal assistant to a gentleman who worked with the Sumitomo Group.'

'Aha!' said Morley, giving a little bow. *'Hajimemashite.'*

A conversation then followed in Japanese, in which Miriam and I were of course unable to participate. The conversation went on. And on: Japanese appears to be a language with an awful lot of words. (In the introduction to *Morley's Le Mot Juste* (1927), his popular guide to language learning, there is a table indicating the number of essential and functional words required to communicate in different languages and Japanese indeed scores rather highly, just below Chinese and

Korean, languages in which Morley could also boast at least some functional level of fluency.) Miriam examined her fingernails. I began quietly whistling a tune and eventually gave a loud cough, just to remind Morley that we were here for purposes other than for him to practise his Japanese. He took no notice, of course, but fortunately Mr Starling did.

'Mr Morley?' he said. 'I think your friend here wants to ask you something.'

'Yes, Sefton?' said Morley.

I looked at my watch, which was always a sure way to get Morley moving.

'Ah, yes. Of course. Excuse us. It's very rare that one gets the opportunity to practise one's Japanese. I was asking Mr Starling about my essay, Miriam, do you remember, the one based on *The Tale of Genji*?'

'I can't say I do, Father, no.'

'To do with the Japanese concept of *mono no aware* – difficult to translate.'

'The pathos of things,' said Mr Starling.

'Exactly!' said Morley. 'That's right! The pathos of things. And Mr Starling was just explaining about his life here and in Japan: he makes his own beer and wine, you know – he's almost entirely self-sufficient.'

'How marvellous,' said Miriam, gazing round at the rather spartan surroundings. 'One can clearly achieve quite a . . . remarkable state of . . . cosiness by the efforts of one's own hand.'

'Well, we do our best,' said Mr Starling.

'*Mono no aware* indeed,' said Miriam.

Morley then began asking Mr Starling – in English, thank goodness – about William Cobbett, and about *Cottage Economy*, and about nutting and blackberrying, but neither Miriam nor I could bear the prospect of any more cottaging talk, in whatever language.

'I wonder if we might see the rest of your garden, Mr Starling?' suggested Miriam.

'Oh yes, of course,' said Mr Starling. 'Do come through.'

Miriam turned and gave me a triumphant wink.

The front room led into the kitchen, which had the usual big black range, an old sink propped up on bricks, a tiny table, two chairs, and a ham wrapped in muslin hanging by the back door. There was a washboard in a bucket in the sink, thick with fresh white suds.

'Oh, I do hope we're not disturbing you,' said Morley.

'Not at all,' said Mr Starling. 'Sunday's our wash day.' There were dark uniforms and white shirts hung over by the window.

'If your garden here is as spectacular as the garden at the front,' said Morley, 'I really do think you have created something quite unique.'

'Well, thank you. I don't know if we can live up to that billing!' said Mr Starling. 'But let me show you.' And he opened the door to the rear of the cottage.

'Well, well, well,' said Morley.

The garden at the back of the cottage was quite unlike the garden at the front. It looked at first to be more like a traditional cottage garden: there were flowerbeds and vegetable beds, a hen house, a little rough hut that looked to contain some geese, but then one noticed something rather strange. It took a few moments to work out what it was but once it was obvious it was really very obvious: the garden appeared to have no boundaries whatsoever; there seemed to be no fences nor hedges nor walls separating the cottage garden from the vast Essex landscape beyond. This gave the garden the impression of limitless expanse, as if it were a part of the landscape rather than separate from it, the cultivated plants merging with the natural fauna and flora, clumps of cultivated this clustering with wild circles and drifts of natural that. Again, Morley was terribly impressed.

'Well, well, well,' he repeated. 'Well, well, well. Quite extraordinary. An open garden? Just on a practical point: how do you deter the foxes and the vermin?'

'We're very vigilant,' said Mr Starling. 'We do have to be careful.'

'You'd have to be,' said Morley. 'Wide open to attack. This is the very opposite of what we might usually expect a garden to be, is it not?'

'I'd never really thought of it like that,' said Mr Starling.

'Yes,' said Morley, who had taken off along a

pathway through the grass, like a dog having picked up a scent, the three of us hurrying along behind him. 'I mean, the derivation of the English word "garden" is – I think I'm right in saying, aren't I, Sefton? – closely associated with notions of a boundary, is it not? From the Old English *geard*, meaning "fence", the Vulgar Latin *gardinum*, meaning "enclosure" and of course the Hebrew origin of the word "garden", which is . . . Miriam?' He clicked his fingers, as if summoning a waiter, or a thought. Morley occasionally had these little lapses, when he required a helping hand. 'The original Hebrew?'

'I'm afraid I don't recall the original Hebrew, Father.' Miriam was not always able or willing to provide a helping hand and alas my Hebrew was not all it could be.

'Ah, well. Anyway. You have quite revolutionised my idea of the garden, Mr Starling! You have turned it upside down and inside out, as it were.'

'That's terribly kind of you, Mr Morley. I really don't know what to say. All we're trying to do here is to create our own little piece of heaven.'

It looked as though someone in the near distance was burning leaves; you could only just see them through the thick grey smog. I realised now that Morley was striding on towards them, his curiosity disguising his curiosity.

'Well, you have quite succeeded, sir. Paradise haunts your garden.'

'Thank you, Mr Morley,' said Mr Starling.

'That's very kind. But there's really no need to go any further now.' I thought a note of panic had perhaps crept into his voice. 'We should really stop here.'

'Oh no, let's go on!' said Morley. 'There's more to explore, isn't there?'

Starling hadn't moved. Morley was surging on. He called back.

'Is this your co-creator perhaps, up ahead?' said Morley, as he approached the figure in the smog. 'The Eve to your Adam?'

As we grew closer the figure stepped out of the fog towards us. It was PC Adkins.

None of us said anything for a moment. Miriam gave me a look, which I did not return. And then Mr Starling caught up with us and broke the silence.

'This is Sidney,' he said. 'He does a lot of the heavy work for me in the garden.'

'We met at West Mersea,' said PC Adkins, who was dressed in an old blue boiler suit, which, I have to say, rather gave him the appearance of a criminal.

'Yes, yes. Indeed. That's right,' said Morley, without any hint of surprise or embarrassment. 'How lovely to see you again! How's the investigation going into the death of Arthur Marden? I hope you don't mind my asking?'

'Not at all, sir,' said Adkins. 'Very well, thank you, sir.'

'Good. Any leads at all?'

'We're following several lines of enquiry.'

'Nothing at all about a batch of bad oysters, I suppose?'

'Not as far as I'm aware,' said PC Adkins.

'I never expected there would be,' said Morley. 'Absolute nonsense.'

'Really?' said Mr Starling.

'Absolutely,' said Morley. 'Never believed it for a minute. Total fantasy. Boadicea died from eating poisonous leaves in Epping Forest, I think. But Marden died of some natural cause.'

'Yes. I'm sure you're right,' said Mr Starling. 'Natural cause.'

'Almost certainly,' said Morley. 'Either that . . . or he was murdered.'

'Murdered?' said PC Adkins. Did he exchange a glance with Starling? I can't recall exactly.

'Which is highly unlikely,' said Morley. 'As my daughter keeps telling me. Anyway,' he said, changing the subject. 'I was just saying to Mr Starling here that you have created something quite remarkable in these gardens, Constable. Quite unexpected and quite quite delightful.'

'Thank you, sir,' said PC Adkins.

'The notion of a garden with aesthetic as well as utilitarian features is one of many things we might learn from the East, don't you think, Mr Starling?'

'I do, Mr Morley, yes.'

'I think it's sometimes assumed that there is perhaps only one way of making a garden,' he said, 'but one realises by your fine example here that there are of course many possibilities and many paths, as it were, to pleasure. The gardens of the Persians, the Islamic garden – a rich variety of possibilities available to us all, if only we might imagine. To have created one remarkable garden would be something, Mr Starling, but to have made two!'

'I can't claim responsibility for them both, alas,' said Mr Starling. 'I'm responsible for the front and Sidney is responsible for the rear.'

'And what a rear, Constable!' said Morley, to Miriam's dismay. 'What a rear you have here!'

'You should have seen it in the height of the season, Mr Morley,' said PC Adkins. 'The green sea kale, the red poppies, yellow sedum. Lavender, santolina.'

'I'm sure it was magnificent,' enthused Morley. 'Congratulations.'

After some dreary discussion about the finer points of plantsmanship we eventually began walking back up to the house, Morley successfully having taken Mr Starling and PC Adkins entirely into his confidence. I could never quite distinguish Morley's tactics from his personality: the two were inextricably linked.

'Now, just going back to Arthur Marden for a moment,' he said, as we'd almost reached the cottage. Was this a ploy, or was it pure disinterested enquiry? 'I'd be intrigued to know what you two fellows made of him?'

216

'Made of him?' said Mr Starling.

'Yes. I just wondered if the poor chap had any, you know, any enemies at all?'

'Enemies?' said Mr Starling.

'People who might have been glad to see him go? Anyone who had – shall we say – "differences" with him?'

'Not as far as I'm aware,' said Mr Starling. PC Adkins remained silent. 'He was an upstanding upholder of the traditional values of Colchester and the council.'

'Very good,' said Morley. 'Man after my own heart.'

'Why do you ask?' said Starling.

'It's just we heard this chap Dunbar in the council chamber, didn't we, Sefton? Quite a performance he put up, making all sorts of accusations about Marden.'

'Oh well, I think it's common knowledge that Basil had a grudge against Marden,' said Mr Starling.

'And who is this Basil with a grudge?' said Miriam, who had remained unusually quiet during the course of our conversation. She seemed quite fascinated by PC Adkins.

'This Basil Withagrudge is Basil Dunbar, my dear, an independent councillor,' said Morley. 'Bit of a loose cannon, would that be a fair description, Mr Starling?'

'Yes, I think so.'

'He struck me as an angry man, I have to say,'

said Morley, 'but not as someone capable of murder.'

'I don't think there's any suggestion that Mr Dunbar was implicated in the death of Mr Marden,' said PC Adkins.

'No, no,' said Morley. 'I'm not suggesting he was. That would be quite preposterous. Doubtless you've looked into all of this anyway?'

'I'm afraid I'm not at liberty to say, Mr Morley.'

'No, no, quite understandable. I've said from the very beginning that there is no way that Marden died from eating a bad oyster. Utterly ridiculous. The poor fellow either died of natural causes – or, as I say, he was bumped off.'

'Bumped off?' said PC Adkins sceptically.

'Possibly by his daughter.'

'His daughter?'

'Florence?' said Starling. 'You think Florence killed her father?'

'She has disappeared, I believe. Nowhere to be found.'

'That hardly makes her a suspect,' said PC Adkins.

'Does it not?' said Morley. 'Well, if it doesn't I don't know what does.'

'Motive?' said PC Adkins. 'Opportunity?'

'Motive for a daughter to kill her father?' said Miriam. 'I can't think of any possible motive. Can you, Father?'

'I think in the end we'll find that Marden died of a bad oyster,' said PC Adkins reassuringly.

'That affected only him?' said Morley. 'In which case it was either jolly bad luck or it was carefully administered to him by someone?' He looked pointedly at Starling, who looked pointedly away.

'Do excuse my father, gentlemen. He reads a lot of crime novels from America,' said Miriam. 'He sometimes confuses fiction with reality. Come along now, Father.'

'It's been a pleasure,' said Mr Starling.

'Very nice to meet you again, PC Adkins,' said Morley.

'Likewise,' said Adkins.

We drove away from the cottage with Starling and Adkins standing together by their fine English border, waving us goodbye.

'Father!' said Miriam. 'What on earth do you think you're doing?'

'I'm trying to flush out the truth about the death of Arthur Marden.'

'By embarrassing and humiliating those two men?'

'Embarrassing and humiliating? Does it not strike you as strange that the man questioned by police about the death of Arthur Marden not twenty-four hours ago has a serving police officer involved in the investigation assisting him in his garden? One's suspicions are aroused, surely?'

'I don't think it's *those* suspicions it arouses, Father.'

'What? What do you mean?'

'Well, it's pretty obvious, isn't it?'

'What is?'

'The pair of them are living together, Father.'

'Living together?' said Morley.

'Yes, living together, Father.'

'I see.'

'Do you think it's possibly their living arrangements that Marden objected to?' I asked.

'Why on earth would anyone object to that?' asked Morley. 'Two men living together, pursuing their cottaging dream?'

'Oh, Father,' said Miriam.

'Like bachelor farmers?' continued Morley. 'Why would anyone possibly object to that?'

We drove on in silence for some time, Morley mulling over some notes in his notebook.

'I still have a rather queer feeling about the death of Arthur Marden,' said Morley.

'You're not the only one,' said Miriam.

'I wonder if we might just pop in and say hello to Mr Dunbar?'

CHAPTER 21

PROOF! PROOF!

Basil Dunbar lived in an old narrow house by the Balkerne Gate, which was once of course – I say of course, though admittedly I had never heard of it and had absolutely no idea – the Roman west entrance to Colchester. (For anyone as ignorant as I was, see Morley's extensive remarks about the Balkerne Gate in *The County Guides: Essex,* in which he compares the gate to various other surviving Roman gates in Europe and concludes, not surprisingly perhaps, that what is frankly a rather pathetic English ruin is in fact the finest in the world. If you were to believe Morley, the Balkerne Gate is basically the Roman Forum, the pyramids of Giza, the Acropolis, Ephesus and Petra, all combined – and in Essex.) Dunbar's was a home both mean and overstuffed, a sorry show-room of stop-gaps, imitations and it'll do: ancient linoleum and gas lights; a big fat ugly radiogram; an elaborate wooden mantel around a tiny fireplace; mirrors hung on chains like torture instruments; and two great grey bulbous armchairs; that eternal familiar sort of English home that always somehow speaks of absence, loss and some unidentifiable sadness.

After the episode at Len Starling's cottage, Miriam had decided that she had had enough of wild-goose chases for one day – and possibly for ever – and had determined to retire to the hotel until it was time for our departure.

'Good luck in your quest, Father,' she said, not without a hint of sarcasm.

'Thank you, my dear,' said Morley, oblivious to her tone.

'Let me know when your discreet enquiries are concluded and we can all move on.'

'Will do!' said Morley. 'Will do!'

Dunbar, I have to say, had greeted us very warmly – rapturously even – on our arrival.

'The People's Professor!' he declared, flinging open his front door, hurriedly swallowing something or other he'd been chewing. 'I'd heard that you were in town, Mr Morley, but I had not for a moment imagined that you might deign to visit us here, in my 'umble, 'umble—'

'Yes,' said Morley, interrupting Dunbar's Dickensian self-humbling, 'I heard you speak at the council meeting, Mr Dunbar, and I have to say I was rather intrigued.'

'Well, please, please, do come in! Come in! Come in! Come in!' He was almost panting with excitement. 'This is an honour, sir! An absolute honour! Mrs Dunbar! Mrs Dunbar! We have visitors!'

'Visitors?' called Mrs Dunbar, from the back room. 'Visitors, Mr Dunbar? Visitors?'

The Dunbars were not perhaps accustomed to entertaining on a Sunday. Or – by the look of it – on any other day.

Dunbar ushered us into the back room, where he and Mrs Dunbar had clearly been enjoying a Sunday lunch. An old newspaper covered their tiny dining table.

'My goodness,' said Mrs Dunbar, standing up and standing back, touching her hair, as though in shock. She wore a wrapover Sunday house dress that had perhaps seen the mangle and the hot iron on one or two occasions too many. Mr Dunbar wore a dull brown Sunday suit of similar vintage and wear. 'We weren't expecting visitors.'

'This is my glamorous assistant,' said Mr Dunbar. 'I'm only joking! This is my wife, Mrs Dunbar.' Mrs Dunbar gave us a weak smile.

'Hello,' said Morley, giving her a weak smile back.

'This, Flo, is Mr Swanton Morley,' said Mr Dunbar. 'The People's Professor? You've read him in the papers.'

'Of course,' said Mrs Dunbar, half curtseying. 'It's an honour to meet you, sir. Basil reads all your articles,' she said. 'He's a great fan. Aren't you, Basil?'

'I am, I am,' agreed Basil. 'A great fan.'

'Well, I am honoured,' said Morley, raising Mrs Dunbar from her half-curtseying position.

'And this, Flo, is . . .' began Dunbar, nodding towards me.

'My own glamorous assistant,' said Morley.

With four of us standing awkwardly in the room there wasn't much room to move.

'Well, can I fetch you both a slice of tongue?' asked Mrs Dunbar.

'That's very kind, Mrs Dunbar, but no thank you,' said Morley. I shook my head.

'A cup of tea, perhaps?'

'A cup of tea would be absolutely delightful,' said Morley. 'Thank you.'

'Basil?' She looked to Basil for permission to make tea.

'Yes,' said Mr Dunbar, 'tea is a good idea, Flo.'

'We've no cake,' said Mrs Dunbar. 'If I'd known you were coming I'd have . . . I could always . . .'

'Thank you, my dear,' said Basil. 'Tea will be sufficient. Mr Morley is famously frugal.'

Personally I'd have very much liked a slice of cake. We'd not eaten since breakfast and I was short on cigarettes.

Mrs Dunbar excused herself and squeezed out to go and prepare tea in the back kitchen.

Dunbar seated Morley and me at the table. I had the view of the yard: blank brick walls and nothing else, not a plant or a weed, nothing, nothing at all but a blank wall.

'Well, Mr Morley.' Dunbar was clearly absolutely chuffed: he puffed out his cheeks with pleasure, 'puffling', as Morley might have it. ('PUFFLE (verb): to puff with pleasure or surprise.' For other examples of Morley's nonce words and neologisms see his pamphlet, 'Words – And How to Invent Them', 1930. Morley always rather fancied himself as Shakespeare, though he was closer to Edward Lear.) 'I have to say I am uncharacteristically lost for words.' Dunbar snorted slightly at his own little joke. 'But I'll be honest, I have no idea why you're here!'

'As I say, Mr Dunbar, I was very impressed by your . . . performance in the council chamber. My colleague and I here . . .' Morley looked in my direction for support. He was having one of his George Washington moments. He needed a surrogate liar.

'. . . are writing a book about Essex,' I said, 'and are interested in providing some sketches and portraits of regional and local politics and the . . . characters involved.'

'Well,' said Mr Dunbar, sitting up rather straighter in his seat. 'I don't know about being a character, but it is certainly a subject on which I have strong opinions.'

'Quite,' said Morley. 'Quite quite plain from your speech in the council chamber.'

'I see it as my job to make this council account-able,' said Dunbar. 'To the people of Colchester.'

'And you clearly feel you have an uphill struggle on your hands, by the sound of it?' said Morley.

'I'm afraid so,' said Mr Dunbar. 'As far as I can

see, the council is run for the benefit of its councillors and not for the benefit of the town.'

''Twas ever thus, Mr Dunbar,' said Morley. ''Twas ever thus. *Sic semper tyrannus*. And what about Arthur Marden?'

'Marden?'

'The mayor?'

'Ex-mayor,' said Dunbar. 'You know he's dead?'

'Yes,' said Morley.

'Do you need to take notes?' asked Dunbar.

'Notes?' asked Morley.

'About what I say.'

'Oh no. No, no, no,' said Morley.

'Are you sure?' said Mr Dunbar. 'I wouldn't want to be misquoted or misunderstood.'

'No, no need,' said Morley. 'It's all up here.' He tapped his head. 'And my assistant here takes notes for me. Don't you, Sefton?'

I reached into my pocket for my notebook, which I knew wasn't there, and which Morley doubtless knew wasn't there; fortunately the mere act of looking for it seemed to have satisfied Mr Dunbar of our bona fides.

'Arthur Marden?' Morley prompted.

'Marden?' Dunbar gave a sharp dismissive laugh. 'Marden was harmless. Marden was only ever a pawn in the game,' said Dunbar. 'He wasn't a big player.'

'So who are the big players?'

'In Colchester?' said Mr Dunbar.

'Indeed, in Colchester,' said Morley.

'Milk and sugar?' asked Mrs Dunbar, nervously popping her head round the door.

'Neither for me, thank you,' said Morley.

'Milk and three sugars if you have it, Mrs Dunbar, thank you,' I said, as she disappeared again.

'Who are the big players in Colchester?' asked Morley.

'The big players in Colchester? The big players in Colchester are the same as they are everywhere, Mr Morley.'

'I'm sure they are. Just remind me, though? For our readers, who may not be as familiar as you are with Essex council politics.'

'It has nothing to do with being familiar with Essex council politics,' said Basil. His brow furrowed. 'This is *Realpolitik*, Mr Morley. This is the politics of the boardroom. The politics of government. The deals and the arrangements behind the scenes.'

'Ah. I see. The politics of the hidden hand? The Machiavellian workings of town hall politics?'

'Yes. Correct. And as always and everywhere, the big players in the game are the landlords and the landowners. The people with inherited wealth, the upper classes and the arriviste businessmen. The paymasters.'

'Ah. I see, Mr Dunbar. Are you by any chance a communist?' Morley could often be rather to the point. 'I hope you don't mind my asking?'

'I certainly do not mind,' said Dunbar. 'And I

227

most certainly am not. I am an independent, Mr Morley. I pride myself on my independence.'

'Excellent,' said Morley. 'I am of a similar mind myself.'

'Independent of Mind and Independent of Spirit,' pronounced Dunbar. It was the slogan of Morley's ill-fated British Liberal Independent People's Party (founded 1931, foundered 1935). Morley preferred not to talk about the BLIPP. Suffice it to say he was not a natural political leader – he found the views of many of his supporters unsavoury and uncongenial. And it probably didn't help that the party was called the BLIPP. 'The BLIPP?' said Dunbar, smiling with pleasure at the memory of it.

'Indeed,' said Morley. 'Gone but not forgotten. So are you suggesting Marden was taking money from people, in order to influence council policy?'

'That's exactly what I'm suggesting,' said Dunbar.

'That's quite an accusation.'

'Well, it's quite a scandal,' said Dunbar. 'It deserves telling. It deserves telling to the widest audience possible. It deserves the kind of audience you command, Mr Morley.'

'Do you have proof?' asked Morley.

'Proof? Proof? I have been gathering proof my whole life, Mr Morley!' said Dunbar. 'This is our chance to expose them, sir. Together we could work on a campaign to expose and root out the canker at the heart of local government in this country!'

'Well, we'll see, shall we, Mr Dunbar?'

Morley was often pestered by cranks and crackpots who sought to enlist him in some campaign or cause. There was the Society for the Prevention of Smoking Among Girls, for example, a cause that Morley believed in but for which he felt Miriam had prevented him from expressing his public support. There was the Campaign for Peace Through Silence, another cause that in principle he supported but for which he felt his loud vocal support was perhaps inappropriate, given the nature of the campaign. Plus all sorts of personal crusades by men and women bearing grievances and grudges who saw Morley as a potential high-profile supporter and ally. I spent much of my time at St George's and on the road replying to the endless petitions and importunities of England's great disgruntled: I have never seen the contents of an MP's postbag but I think I probably have a pretty good idea of what they have to put up with.

'And what about Marden's daughter?' asked Morley.

'His daughter?'

'Florence? Did you ever come across her?'

'No. Can't say I did. Why? Do you think she might be involved in the conspiracy as well?'

'We'll just have to think about that.'

'You never know,' said Mr Dunbar. 'You never know.'

We briefly exchanged polite conversation with Mrs Dunbar when she returned with our tea and then Dunbar took us upstairs to what he called his 'office', which was the tiny front bedroom of the house, crammed from floor to ceiling with shelves and papers. Actually, 'crammed' is wrong; 'crammed' implies that the room was merely full, that what was there was perhaps merely a throng of paperwork, a busy little gathering of material. It was not a throng. It was not a gathering. It was an explosion. It was chaos. There seemed to be no order to the room at all: papers had been piled, bundled and stacked to form a rockfall of paper, an avalanche of evidence. It was a place, in its way, as ruined as the Balkerne Gate next door. Dunbar stood at the doorway, staring ahead, eyes swivelling frantically from left to right and back again, as if searching for something. Morley and I stood shoulder to shoulder on the landing.

'Now,' said Dunbar, rubbing his head like Aladdin rubbing his lamp, wishing for wishes, seeking guidance. 'I know it's here somewhere.'

'What *exactly* is it you're looking for, Mr Dunbar?' asked Morley.

'Proof!' said Dunbar.

'And what kind of proof exactly?'

'Proof, Mr Morley, that will reveal what's behind all this. The full extent of the conspiracy. The paperwork.'

'You certainly have quite a lot of paperwork,' I said.

'Of course,' said Dunbar. 'I have to. I have council minutes and agendas going back thirty years. And look, if you' – he had started burrowing into his hoard – 'if you carefully cross-reference them with the newspapers and company reports and . . . all sorts of other sources, you're able to read between the lines and begin to see what's actually happening here.' He held two pieces of paper triumphantly in his hand. 'See! Proof!' He grabbed some more. 'Proof!' And then more. 'Proof!'

'I see.' Morley looked at me despairingly. 'That sort of proof.' And then, mumblingly, '*Argumentum non probatur*, Sefton.'

Mr Dunbar began gathering armfuls of paper but Morley put out a kind and restraining arm: if there was one thing he understood it was obsession.

'Mr Dunbar?'

'Yes?' said Dunbar, continuing to ferret away at the papers.

'Mr Dunbar.' Dunbar ceased. Morley chose his words carefully. 'This material is so interesting and so significant that I think it's probably going to take all of us some time to work through the implications of what you're saying.'

'Oh yes, oh yes,' said Mr Dunbar. 'The implications are huge.'

'Massive,' agreed Morley.

'Yes.'

'And you're really going to have to quarry your way in to dig up all your evidence.'

'Yes, quarry in,' said Mr Dunbar.

231

'Quite an excavation.'

'Indeed.'

'So I think perhaps today is not the time to begin.'

'No?' said Mr Dunbar.

'Perhaps we could return another time to help you dig through the material more thoroughly?'

'Yes, that would be excellent, Mr Morley. That would be excellent! Thank you!'

Morley thus skilfully extricated us from what might have been a rather long afternoon's paperchase.

'Good God,' I said, as we got back into the Cadillac. 'Mad.'

'Now, now, let's not dismiss him out of hand, Sefton.'

'He was a raving lunatic.'

'Hardly. Perfectly harmless and rather charming, I thought.'

'But all that paperwork? It was absolute chaos.'

'Nothing wrong with chaotic paperwork, Sefton. You should remember, young man, that Britain and indeed the entire British Empire has triumphed in large part precisely because of our chaotic paperwork!'

'I don't think so, Mr Morley,' I said, lighting a cigarette and starting up the engine.

'Oh yes, absolutely. Mark my words,' said Morley. 'As administrators we English have always been rather indifferent – which is of course the art of

232

true mastery. And what does indifference rely upon for its smooth and proper functioning?'

'I don't know, Mr Morley.'

'Chaotic paperwork, Sefton! If no one quite knows what's going on then things just sort of – well, they go on. Look at the Spanish. And the Romans. And the Germans, I dare say. Terribly well organised, the lot of them – and their empires hence doomed to failure.' (This theme of the importance of messy versus tidy paperwork is one that Morley elaborated upon some years later in an article, 'Paper Work and Print Runs' in the *International Paper Manufacturer's Magazine*, August 1939. His own approach to paperwork was, I have to say, according to his own crude categories and typologies, rather more German than it was English. He was *fanatically* well organised.) 'Mr Dunbar with his paperwork seems to me in fact the archetypal Englishman, and a jolly good thing too.' If I had a penny for every time that Morley claimed during our time together that the average eccentric was the archetypal Englishman I would be a wealthy man.

We were about to drive away when Dunbar came rushing out of his house.

'I've found it!' he said, running up to the car. 'I've found it!'

Morley pulled down the window of the car.

'Mr Dunbar! Lovely to see you again. Found what exactly?'

'A crucial piece of evidence.'

'Really? Crucial in what regard?'

'It's Ken Cowley.'

'Ken Cowley?'

'Yes! The High Sheriff. You talking about excavating made me think.'

'Excavating?' said Morley. 'Really?'

'Yes. Cowley's been in a long-running dispute with the mayor over the electrification of the town.'

'I see.'

'All the roadworks.'

'All yes, we had noticed.'

'Cowley and his family run an oil company. They have everything to lose with the electrification of the town.'

'Mmm,' said Morley. 'Interesting.'

'And there's more! When you mentioned the quarrying I remembered that Marden had sold Cowley some land many years ago – a part of what used to be the site of one of his old quarries, for Cowley to use as a depot.'

'Right-o,' said Morley.

'Don't you see?' said Dunbar.

'I'm not sure I do, Mr Dunbar, no.'

'Cowley might have felt that Marden had swindled him on the deal, and so years later, and now with the electrification of the town taking place, he has been driven to take his revenge!'

'Yes, well, that's certainly one possibility, Mr Dunbar. Thank you for raising it.'

'Shall we go to the police?'

'Erm. I think we might perhaps conduct our own enquiries first.'

'I'll come with you!' said Mr Dunbar, ready to yank open the door of the Cadillac and jump right in.

'No, no. I'm afraid I – we . . .' Morley looked to me in panic to come up with a convincing lie.

'We have some meetings – important meetings – to attend to first, Mr Dunbar.'

'On a Sunday?'

'Yes, we're really working flat out at the moment, to try to get this next book completed.'

'Oh. OK. So what do we do now?'

'I'll tell you what, Mr Dunbar,' said Morley. 'Shall we sleep on this thing with – what's he called again?'

'Ken Cowley,' said Mr Dunbar. 'The High Sheriff.'

'Yes, with Mr Cowley. We'll sleep on it tonight and get to it first thing tomorrow. How about that?'

'Well, I suppose I could see if I could find some more proof tonight.'

'Yes. Good idea. Excellent. And we'll maybe pay a call on Mr Cowley tomorrow, just to get his side of the story.'

'Is that wise?' said Mr Dunbar. 'If we suspect him of murdering Marden?'

'Well, let's not jump to any conclusions. These matters require careful handling, Mr Dunbar.'

'Yes, of course. Right.'

'Where might we find Mr Cowley? Is he local?'

'He has a mill down by the Hythe.'

'And he's not related to the Cowley Brothers, by any chance?' I asked.

'The Cowley Brothers?' said Mr Dunbar.

'They're independent oystermen out at West Mersea,' I said.

'Probably,' said Mr Dunbar. 'There's a lot of Cowleys. Do you want me to come with you tomorrow?'

'Erm . . .' said Morley.

'We'll call for you, Mr Dunbar,' I said.

'Yes. That's it. We'll call for you. Thank you very much,' said Morley. 'You've been very helpful.'

As it turned out, Mr Dunbar had been very helpful, though not at all in the way he'd intended.

CHAPTER 22

KURSAAL

We retired to the hotel to join Miriam, exhausted from our dealings with the utterly wearisome Dunbar, who was, I realised, basically Morley without Morley's iron self-discipline, his good luck, his moustache and his charm. I met many such men during my years with Morley, men with great passions and enthusiasms who were – thankfully – too disorganised to cause anyone any harm. The dangerous ones were those with the energy *and* the organisation. As Morley might say, *Nisi Dei gratia, sim,* and *Hunc tu, Romane, caveto.*

While Morley set to work in the hotel dining room, racking his brains, making notes and diagrams, forging connections, trying to piece together what he regarded as all the various 'clues' about the death of Arthur Marden – 'When is a clue not a clue, Father?' asked Miriam. 'Answer: when it's a red herring!' – Miriam and I busied ourselves with a very thorough and very challenging and robust Essex afternoon tea: sandwiches thick with paste, and crusts, slabs of yellow-buttered fruit cake, scones and cups of scalding tea. No oysters. The food was soothing and delicious but – as seemed to be the Essex way – tempers soon became rather frayed. Perhaps it was something in the Essex air, something to do with Marconi perhaps down in Chelmsford, the peculiar atmospherics of Essex? (For Morley's theories about the effects of radio waves on the weather and on the human atmosphere generally, see 'On the Matter of Airwaves', an article in *Wireless World* in May 1920. 'The catwhisker,' he writes, 'may be introducing all sorts of interference into our lives which we are not yet able to comprehend.') Or maybe it was just Miriam, who brought with her wherever she went her own peculiar weather system.

The problem began when Morley suddenly announced, from deep behind a pile of papers, that Miriam and I were to be dispatched forthwith to Southend for the purposes of research for the book. Miriam, mid-way through a substantial scone, was not impressed; and when Miriam was not impressed, mid-scone or not, she was not one to keep her thoughts to herself. She did not believe in suffering in silence. (Morley, in an article 'Suffering and Silence', published in *Soul and Spirit* magazine, May 1927, and apparently inspired by the teachings of an unnamed holy man he had met on his travels in China, India and Tibet – but who I rather suspected, having seen Morley's methods up close, was in fact a composite figure, or amalgam, or indeed entirely a figment of his imagination – suggested a method for dealing with suffering which he called the Simmer. 'Put your troubles not to boil, but to simmer,' he writes. 'This simple act of reducing the heat beneath our worldly woes – the adoption of the method we might call the Simmer – would greatly reduce the sum of human suffering.') Suffice it to say that Miriam did not simmer and had little or no interest in reducing the sum of human misery.

'Think of it as a little holiday treat,' said Morley. 'An evening off.'

'A holiday treat?' said Miriam. 'An evening in Southend?'

'If it's good enough for the East End,' said Morley.

'Then by definition it is not good enough for me.'

'Miriam!' said Morley. 'That is hardly the spirit in which we're working, my dear.'

'The spirit in which we're working? Oh, do come on, Father,' said Miriam, 'and don't be so bloody self-righteous for once!'

'Self-righteous, Miriam? Me?'

Miriam snorted in response. It's true that Morley could sometimes be a little self-righteous.

'And I would thank you,' he continued, 'not to use bad language on a Sunday.'

'I'll use whatever language I like on whatever day I like,' said Miriam.

'Whichever,' corrected Morley. 'There being only a limited choice of days.'

'Whatever,' said Miriam.

'Ssshh,' I suggested, noting that a number of our fellow guests had paused in their afternoon tea tea-cup tinkling to listen in. It made no difference.

'Have you ever even been to Southend?' Miriam asked her father.

'No, but I hardly think that's the—'

'And am I right in saying that your favourite holiday destination is in fact Italy?'

'Yes, but—'

'Somewhere delightful like Alassio, for example?'

'That's true,' said Morley. 'But that's not to—'

'A grand resort for the grandees of Europe? Do you know the Grand Hotel?' asked Miriam, turning to me.

'I can't say I do, Miriam, no.'

'Absolutely marvellous. You really should go. Best martinis on the whole of the Italian Riviera.'

'I'll bear that in mind.'

'And the English Library,' added Morley. 'Just across the way. Wonderful. Testament to Anglo-Italian relations.'

'And there we are,' said Miriam, addressing me. 'Totally *unlike* Southend. Why on earth would anyone go to Southend when they could just as easily go to the Italian Riviera? Or the French, for that matter? The Negresco in Nice is simply divine.' She really meant it.

'Because, Miriam,' said Morley, with considerable restraint.

Miriam wriggled her nose: it was one of her

all-time and all-purpose favourite expressions, signalling just about anything from disgust to desire. This time it was a wriggle that clearly signalled dismissal.

'You really can't beat the English seaside resort,' continued Morley. 'A testament to the triumph of hope over experience.'

'The triumph of the utterly dull over the completely dreadful,' said Miriam.

'Give the place a chance,' said Morley. 'And anyway I'm concerned that we don't have enough material for the book. We've already lost a couple of days with the Lagonda being out of action, and what with the Oyster Feast fiasco we've fallen behind again.'

'We're always falling behind, Father,' said Miriam.

'Precisely,' said Morley. 'Which is why – as I always say – it's so important to try to keep up. *Tempus volat hora fugit.*'

'Whatever you say, Father,' said Miriam, finishing off her scone, and meaning of course that she didn't give a damn about whatever he said.

'What would you like us to cover in Southend, Mr Morley?' I asked, having myself finished a substantial plate of good paste sandwiches, and therefore feeling strong enough to attempt to calm the discussion.

'The Kursaal of course,' said Morley.

'The What-all?' said Miriam.

'The Kursaal,' repeated Morley. '"By the Dome It's Known!"'

'I'm sorry, Father, you've lost me.'

'The Kursaal. "By the Dome It's Known"? Because of its beautiful big dome. Considered a folly at the time, but now quite an attraction.'

'Nope, none the wiser,' said Miriam.

'Are the pair of you in any way in touch with what's actually happening in the real world?'

In all honesty, Miriam was never perhaps in touch with what was happening in the real world, and during those years I was doing my absolute level best – with every chemical assistance – to avoid it. I occasionally picked up *The Times* – Lindbergh in Munich, the Duke of Windsor in Berlin, killings, bombings, fascists – but soon managed to put it down again. It was all too much, everywhere, never mind keeping up with the latest in amusement park news from Essex. How Morley managed it I'll never know. (He sometimes boasted of reading every local newspaper in the country, every week, which was certainly possible: he had a crate of newspapers delivered to St George's every day, plus a sack of periodicals.)

Undeterred by our lack of interest and know-ledge, Morley briefed us on exactly what he was looking for: photographs of the grand entrance pavilion at this place called the Kursaal, which was not just an amusement park, apparently, but which also housed a circus, a zoo, a ballroom and goodness knows what else.

'The word Kursaal, as I'm sure you know, Sefton, is German, meaning, roughly—'

242

'A Cure Hall?' I ventured.

'Well, yes, strictly speaking. Very good.' He was always slightly disappointed when others knew something that he thought only he knew. Though he had the considerable advantage of knowing more about most things than most people. 'Though I think more colloquially we might refer to it as a spa.'

'A spa?' said Miriam. 'There's a wonderful spa in Rapallo. Minty Greene has been. She lost three pounds in three days. But she did have food poisoning.'

'Not that sort of spa, Miriam,' said Morley. 'It's a funfair and amusement park.'

'Oh dear,' said Miriam. 'Though I do rather like the funfair at the Porte d'Orléans.'

'Very similar,' said Morley. 'I thought we might do a chapter on the Kursaal in the book: the association of the funfair with the ancient fair and the market square, which is of course the centre of the *polis* and—'

'Oh, of course it is, of course,' said Miriam.

'Yet at the same time the funfair as the place where the world gets turned upside down, where one gets whizzed and whirled and de-centred, as it were, which is what makes it so remarkable and so potent a symbol of the modern age.'

'Is it, though?' said Miriam.

'A place where one is thrilled by machines,' continued Morley.

'Well, I do love to be thrilled by machines,' said Miriam.

'Who knows what we'll think of in the future, eh?' asked Morley, warming to his theme, and beginning to talk only to himself, as so often. 'Yet more speed, more intensity, more machine-made experiences. Where technology leads, so our pleasures and desires do surely follow. The Kursaal represents what the future might hold: a world of endless pleasure in which we are forever dodged, shaken up, twisted, helter-skeltered and generally made delirious. A world of perpetual self-indulgence.'

'Well, I don't know about you, Sefton, but you have certainly sold it to me, Father.'

'So that's decided then. We'll say a few photographs, some notes and we'll convene again in the morning and head off, shall we?'

'Very good, Mr Morley,' I agreed.

'Miriam?' said Morley.

'And you'll have solved your mystery by then?'

'Oh yes,' said Morley. 'Won't be long now.'

'As the monkey said when the train ran over its tail,' said Miriam.

'Exactly.'

'Oh, very well then, Father. Anything has to be better than sitting around in Colchester.'

And so Miriam and I left Morley to draw his improbable conclusions and we drove to Southend in the Cadillac, a journey lasting a good couple of hours but remarkable only for the fact that there was not a cross word between us the whole time: Miriam had apparently exhausted herself in argument with her father. Of course we discussed Morley's theories about the death of Arthur Marden and agreed that the most likely explanation was indeed the most likely explanation, that Marden had died from eating a bad oyster. It was, as it were, an open and shut case.

'I can smell it!' she suddenly exclaimed.

'Smell what?' I asked.

'The sea! And I can see it!'

'The sea?'

'Southend Pier!' she cried. 'Longest in the country, I believe.' She lit a cigarette. 'Certainly something to boast about, Sefton, isn't it?'

Southend's Kursaal is not difficult to find: basically, once in Essex, head for the coast, follow the traffic, and eventually you'll find it. You can't miss it: Southend is the Essex coastal destination and Southend is the Kursaal. (Clacton-on-Sea was at that time a distant second to Southend; too far from London for a day trip, before Butlin's transformed its fortunes.) Once parked we paid our money and passed through the turnstiles, joining the massed ranks of the East End and Essex – couples mostly, done up in their Sunday best, down for the weekend or out for the evening, promenading, enjoying themselves in that rather dutiful way in which the English excel. In the hallowed entrance hall – the dome – there were some depressing-looking children's rides, ridden by depressed-looking children, and a man in rather worn and ratty tails was plonking away on a grand piano.

'Debussy?' said Miriam.

It could have been Debussy, I suppose, but it was in fact a thick and soupy version of 'I Do Like to be Beside the Seaside'.

The whole place was rather like that: promising but misleading, disorientating, simultaneously grand and terribly shoddy, a kind of parody of luxury. Beyond the entrance hall you made your way down a passage, like a narrow street, an east coast English souk, thick with jostling crowds, lined with stalls on either side, a confectioner, a tobacconist, a darts stall, a fortune teller – to whom we gave an especially wide berth, after our recent experiences in Westmorland – and then you emerged outside into the sparkling lamplit wonders of the amusement park proper, the promised land. Kaleidoscopic colour. Hot fat and sugar. Sticky fingers. Shrieks of pleasure. Candyfloss. Kisses. All the fun of the fair.

The Kursaal has no doubt long since been exceeded by other amusement parks, but at the time – I think I'm right in saying – it was one of the few places in England, the Pleasure Beach at Blackpool and Dreamland in Margate being possibly the only others, where adults could go to feel like children and where children went to feel like adults; not everyone, after all, can make it to Soho. The Kursaal then was a place in and of itself, unique and vast – twenty acres or more – a pleasure dome, a small town within a town. After just a few minutes of wandering it was difficult to tell where you were, which was presumably the intention: you were trapped in a house of fun, a world of play.

Purely in the interests of research, Miriam and I visited various sideshows and amusements: the shooting gallery; the carousel; Ring the Bell; the Hall of Mirrors; the House of Horrors; the House of Destiny; the Odditorium; the Aboriginal Village, featuring 'real life Eskimos and Ashantis', who I rather fancied were from Southend and outlying areas; and a 3D Last Supper, with moving life-size models set to a musical background of Bach's Matthew Passion. Miriam's favourite exhibition was something called the Midget Mansion, a small house built to midget-size specifications, so you had to bend down to see in through the windows, where you could spy a family of very glum-looking midgets seated on midget-sized chairs drinking tea from midget-sized cups at a midget-sized table. It was not, I have to say, a very edifying spectacle, either for the spectators or, doubtless, for the midgets. I took some photographs – and was told that I was not allowed to take photographs. The Lady Lion Tamer, thank goodness, was on a tea break and something called A Grand Giggle was closed but we were able to attempt to Knock the Lady Out of Bed – a task in which I singularly failed but at which Miriam immediately succeeded, the buxom and scantily clad young woman falling at Miriam's first throw – and we also admired the antics in the Monkey Village.

It was, if nothing else, invigorating, not least because absolutely everywhere there were people, even on a Sunday night in early autumn, pushing past, jostling, shouldering their way through, flocking to the Palais de Danse (which boasted 'OFFICIALLY THE FINEST DANCE FLOOR IN ENGLAND') and to the Bumper Cars, to the Mont Blanc, the Caterpillar, the Jolly Tubes, the Ghost Train and the Petboats, and to all the various other events and competitions, including a play with 'A Star Cast of Wonder Children', apparently, and another promising simply 'Freaks'. 'Probably one and the same,' said Miriam, who had taken my hand and was busy leading us towards the busiest attraction of all, the Cyclone.

CHAPTER 23

UP AND DOWN AND ROUND
AND ROUND

Everyone now has of course experienced something like the Cyclone. Indeed in a sense – at least in a Morley sense – the Cyclone is now what we all experience, all the time. (In an article written in the dark days of 1940 but never published Morley, at his lowest ebb, described the twentieth century as 'a dream-land become a horror, a never-ending rollercoaster of spectacle and event'.) But to experience the Cyclone back then, back when you didn't know what to expect, when you didn't even really understand what it was, this thing, some thing you'd maybe read about that they had in Blackpool or in Coney Island, a *rollercoaster ride*: it was still something strange, something hard to under-stand. How you had to climb into those little carts, with all the other people climbing into their little carts, how you're all together but also somehow isolated and apart, and how you have to wait and wait and then finally how it starts moving and juddering forward and you realise it's too late, that it's begun and there's no going back. And the ground beneath you starts slowly inching away, the whole dense glow of the Kursaal opens up before you, and the town, and old England and the vast unarguable sea, and up and up until finally you come to a sudden stop, a pause, the peak of the rackety wooden hill and how everyone is silent – the sheer shock, the pleasure of it – and all you can hear is the sound of the gears grinding and the sounds below, but then an even greater silence descends.

And then it's that moment, the moment when you know something is about to happen, something unavoidable: the thing you know is always coming. *That* moment. And I remember Miriam turning and looking at me and her eyes were wide open and she was unsmiling and it felt as though I might almost look within her and see what she truly was inside: defiant, terrified, gleeful, expectant. And then – then it feels as if something has snapped, as if a cord has been cut, and you start falling. Down and down and descending down and it feels like you might crash through the whole machinery and go plunging into the earth itself. Miriam is screaming. Everyone is screaming. The speed is increasing by the second, the wind is pushing up against you, the bumps and shakes as the coaster twists and turns and you keep falling down to earth, nothing to stop you, and it feels as if something were moving through you – life itself passing through you. And then the sound of the grinding again as the whole thing begins to slow and suddenly it's over, the whole pointless dizzying experience, almost as quickly as it's begun.

We sat there for a moment, hands still gripping the metal bar in front of us.

'Shall we do it again?' said Miriam.

And so we did. And again. And again. A part of me wished we could ride the Cyclone for ever, Miriam beside me, that we would never be separated and never grow old and that nothing bad might ever happen except the sensation of the ride and the thrill of the moment. But eventually of course Miriam grew tired of the Cyclone and the Tannoy announced the last ride of the Wall of Death and so we joined the crowds heading for the last show of the night.

The Wall of Death sits like a big wooden barrel under its own spotlight, scratched and scarred, perhaps twenty feet tall and double that in diameter. It was overrun with people. We climbed up the wooden steps as others were making their way down, up to a parapet surrounding the top of the barrel, the whole structure shaking slightly as we did so.

'Do you think it's safe?' asked Miriam. 'I'm sure it's safe,' she reassured herself.

Dozens of people were standing two or three rows deep, staring over the edge down into the wooden drum below.

'He's just coming on,' said the man beside Miriam, and sure enough at that moment a big heavy door opened in the side of the Wall. Cries went up as the rider stepped through and banged the door shut behind him and acknowledged the crowd; he went over to his motorbike, and people were going wild. It was Billy Ball. Billy Ball of Hopwood, Son & Payne. I'd forgotten entirely that Billy was the stunt-rider.

The Wall of Death is like a one-man Cyclone, on the horizontal. After a few revs of the engine Billy started some slow counter-clockwise laps round the bottom of the Wall, leaning further and further over until suddenly, imperceptibly, he'd somehow gone from the vertical to the almost horizontal. It was incredible; Morley later explained the physics to me, which was something to do with friction and centrifugal force – or was it centripetal? Or both? Basically, whatever it was, it meant that instead of going crashing down on the bike Billy was able to come corkscrewing up to the very top of the wall at a terrifying speed, before slowly corkscrewing back down to the bottom again. And up and down, up and down, racing round, cutting the engine, dropping down, roaring up again, an entirely monotonous yet surprisingly satisfying spectacle. The whole place was shaking, the crowd cheering and shouting, the noise was incredible and the speed quite terrifying: it was as if the bike were heading directly for you. To my amazement the crowd at the front were reaching out to touch him, which would surely have knocked him off, and some lads were even throwing pennies, presumably with the intention of doing damage to the bike. The whole thing felt incredibly dangerous – not least because the structure was swaying slightly as the bike accelerated again and again, the front tyres flicking the safety wire that ran around the rim of the Wall. Yet for all its obvious dangers the performance was like a well-crafted story: there were peaks and troughs and surprises. First Billy rode with both hands. Then one hand. No hands. For the finale he even put on a blindfold – and for the encore to the finale he wore the blindfold and rode backwards!

Miriam was gripping my arm.

'Wow,' she said.

'Indeed,' I said. *Wow* was indeed the word.

'Wow, wow, wow,' she repeated.

'Yes.'

'Now *that's* what I call a show.'

'Yes,' I agreed again, 'he's very good.'

'And absolutely gorgeous,' she said – and I suppose he was. He was wearing a short dark military-style jacket with epaulettes, and jodhpurs, and a beret, and knee-length cavalry boots: he looked as though he'd just ridden across eternity to deliver good news. When he finally dismounted the bike and turned off the engine and waved up at everyone the whole crowd exploded with applause as if he were a conquering hero; people were stamping their feet and yelling and it felt like the whole platform might collapse. Quite a show.

'Come on,' she said, and we descended down to the bottom of the viewing area. 'Quick.'

'What?' I said.

'We *have* to meet him.'

I must admit I didn't share Miriam's sense of urgency – I'd met Billy, after all – but anyway I had little choice since the crowd was surging down the steps and on to other amusements.

We wandered round and then clambered between the wooden and steel supporting beams towards a wide wooden door set into the Wall.

'This must be the entrance,' said Miriam. She banged on the door.

'Hello?' she called. There was no answer. 'Hello?' she repeated.

'There's no point asking for your money back,' called a voice from behind the door.

Miriam looked at me, perplexed.

'I'm sorry Briton's not here, but every Sunday is Tornado's day off.'

'What's he talking about?' said Miriam to me.

'I have no idea,' I said.

'We're not here for our money back,' shouted Miriam through the door.

'It's me, Billy,' I shouted. 'Stephen Sefton, from Colchester.'

The door opened and there was Billy in all his Wall of Death glory – beret, boots and all.

'Billy,' I said.

'Mr Sefton, sir! If I didn't know better I'd say you were following me!'

'We're here writing our book.'

'Ah,' he said. He peeked his head around the door to see if anyone else was around. 'Sorry about that.'

'Sorry for what?' asked Miriam.

'You never know who's going to be here when you're finished,' he said.

'Fans?' said Miriam.

'Sometimes. But sometimes people get very annoyed,' he said.

'Why?'

'If they've come up from London.'

'I don't see why they should be annoyed,' said Miriam. 'You were fantastic!'

'But there's no Briton,' said Billy.

'Briton?' I said.

'The lion.'

'The lion?'

'Yes, Tornado and Marjorie ride the Wall with him. He used to fit on the bike but now he has his own sidecar.'

'Right,' I said.

'A lion in a sidecar!' said Miriam. 'How fabulous!'

'They groom him and clip his claws on a Sunday, see,' said Billy.

'Very good,' I said.

'So people are sometimes upset on a Sunday, when it's just me.'

'I see,' I said.

'Well, anyway, we didn't come to see the lion,'

said Miriam. 'We came to see *you*. And *you* were magnificent.' Miriam was like a skilled musician: she could make the word 'magnificent' last for a very long time and lend it all sorts of depth and colour.

Billy smiled, clearly delighted. 'Do you want to come in?'

'Do we?' said Miriam, meaning 'We most certainly do.'

'I should tell you, miss, you can't smoke in here,' said Billy.

'Of course,' said Miriam, stubbing out her cigarette.

He let us into the tiny amphitheatre that was the base of the Wall. I looked up. It gave you some idea of what it must have been like being a Christian thrown to the lions.

'Can I just say again, that was *absolutely amazing*,' said Miriam, standing very close to Billy and giving such massive emphasis to the words '*absolutely*' and '*amazing*' that they might as well have been banner-advertised on the back of a plane.

'Well thank you, miss, that's very kind of you.'

Miriam had already made her way over to the motorbike.

'Mmm,' she said, patting the seat on which Billy had only moments ago been so firmly perched.

'She is a beauty,' said Billy.

'Indeed she is,' agreed Miriam.

'She's an Indian Scout.'

'Really?'

'She has a 740 Flathead engine,' said Billy. 'Made by the Hendee Motorcycle Company of Springfield, Massachusetts.'

'Is that right?' Unfortunately Miriam was so good at feigning interest that it was sometimes difficult to tell when she was genuinely interested in something. On this occasion, however, she really was interested: she loved anything involving speed, danger and men in uniform.

But Billy rather misread her interest. He seemed to think she was interested only in the machine, when she was really interested in what the machine could do, and indeed what she could do with the machine.

'Lots of the parts are hand-made,' he said. 'The footboards, the fenders. A rider's only as good as his ride, miss.'

'Quite,' said Miriam, noticeably wriggling with pleasure. 'And she's so low!' She perched herself sideways on the seat of the bike.

'Low centre of gravity gives her more predictable handling on the horizontal, miss.'

'I see.'

'You have to keep your body in the centre of the bike.'

'Would you mind?' said Miriam, gracefully swinging a leg over and manoeuvring herself fully onto the bike.

'No, not at all,' said Billy.

As Miriam positioned herself into a low comfortable riding postition I was reminded for a horrible moment of Pasiphae, wife of King Minos and the contraption she'd had Daedalus construct so that she could consummate her passion for the bull. I managed to put the image quickly from my mind.

'You can use the footboards during the stunts, miss.' Billy unself-consciously assisted Miriam to position her high-heeled feet into the appropriate position.

'The saddle is so wide,' said Miriam.

'Again, for ease of handling. And if you look, all the controls are on the left-hand side here and within the handlebars, to keep them away from the rider's feet.'

'Yes,' agreed Miriam, rather breathily, I thought, firmly gripping the handlebars and rotating her wrists back and forth.

'That's because the bikes were originally developed for the Chicago police,' continued Billy, 'so they could keep their right hands free to shoot off their revolvers.'

'Shoot off their revolvers. Of course,' said Miriam, pretending to fire a gun. 'And hence your outfit, I presume?'

'I suppose,' said Billy. 'I've never really thought about it. It's Tornado's idea.'

'Mr Smith?'

'Yes.'

'Mr Morley did want a photograph of Mr Smith, for the book,' I said, vaguely recalling one of Morley's endless requests.

'I have signed photos if you want one,' said Billy.

'Thank you,' I said. 'That would—'

'And can I ask,' interrupted Miriam, 'what's it like, actually riding the bike?'

'Well, to be perfectly honest, miss, once you're up to speed it's just like riding on a very long very straight road.'

'Does it not give you a headache, going round and round like that?'

'No.'

'Not at all?'

'No. The faces of everyone sort of blur together, which can be a bit confusing at first, but as long as you concentrate on the tricks and the ride you're fine.'

'Yes, but what does it actually *feel* like?'

'What does it feel like?'

'Yes,' said Miriam, with a hint of a purr, I thought. And was she batting her eyelids?

'It feels pretty good,' said Billy. 'It sort of takes your mind off things.'

'Like meditation?'

'I don't know, miss. Takes a bit of getting used to anyway. Like anything. But it's worth it in the end.'

'Of course,' agreed Miriam.

'At first when you go round and round the blood sort of rushes to your hands and feet. But you soon adjust to it.'

'Quite,' said Miriam. 'And tell me, how on earth does one end up riding on the Wall of Death?'

'I only ride once a week, when Tornado Smith is off.'

'But how did you learn?'

'Well, I ride a motorbike anyway, so it only took about six weeks to learn to ride the Wall.'

'Just six weeks?'

'Or thereabouts. You start off just going round and round the bottom here until you can do it smoothly and then you put one wheel on the bottom of the ramp' – he stamped on the curved bottom of the Wall – 'and you keep doing that until you're confident. And then eventually you just have to take your courage in your hands, get her up to speed, look up and lean left and . . . well. You're away.'

'How exhilarating!' said Miriam.

'It is,' said Billy. 'That's just the word for it, miss: exhilarating.'

Miriam was by now settled very comfortably on the saddle and was leaning forward. 'I don't suppose?' she asked.

She was always keen to try new things. And she was never shy to ask if she wanted something.

'No, I don't think so, miss,' said Billy.

'Under no circumstances?'

'Absolutely not. It's against the rules, I'm afraid.'

'You don't strike me as someone who necessarily plays by the rules,' said Miriam.

'I'm sorry, miss.'

'I'm sure I can't be the first girl to ask? Please?' She reached out and touched Billy's arm, looking at him with a mixture of determination and pleading, her eyes wide.

Billy looked at me. I looked at him.

'Well, I suppose, if Mr Sefton is happy enough to let you.'

'Mr Sefton is not my keeper, I'll thank you for knowing,' said Miriam, stiffening slightly in the saddle.

'If you're sure?' said Billy.

'Do you know, Billy, I don't think I've ever been more sure of anything,' said Miriam.

And then this is what happened. It all happened very quickly. I wasn't able to prevent it – and it's possible I wouldn't have prevented it even if I could. Billy produced a length of rope from a box of tools, moved Miriam into position in front of him on the bike and asked me to help lash them tightly together. Which I did. There were things that had happened in Spain – and this was an uncomfortable reminder.

'You can't stay down here, Mr Sefton, I'm afraid,' said Billy. 'Just in case.'

'Just in case of what?' I asked. My mind had wandered.

'Nothing's going to happen, Sefton,' said Miriam.

'Are you sure about this, miss?' asked Billy again, once they were tightly bound.

'Let's do it,' said Miriam, her voice low.

I banged the wooden door behind me, looked back nervously, just once, and then ran up to the top of the viewing platform as Billy began revving

261

the engine. I wondered if Miriam had any idea how dangerous it was. By the time I reached the parapet they were slowly circling the bottom of the Wall – and then Billy accelerated and the two of them became a blur as they raced past, once, twice, three times. The sight had a strange effect on me that even now I find difficult to describe. Suffice it to say that I was both glad and disappointed when they finished.

By the time I'd got back down Billy had untied Miriam and the two of them were happily laughing and chatting.

'Utterly fearless, isn't she?' said Billy.

'Alas,' I said.

'Thank you, gentlemen,' said Miriam, giving a little bow.

'So are you heading back to Colchester?' I asked Billy.

'Yes. Up bright and early in the morning and back in the shop.'

'Where do you work?' asked Miriam.

'Hopwood, Son & Payne. It's a jeweller's on Main Street.'

'We're heading back that way ourselves. Perhaps we can offer you a lift?'

'No, thank you. I'm riding the bike.'

'Well, in that case perhaps you could offer me a lift?' said Miriam.

'I could, miss, I'm not sure.' Billy looked at me, seeking, I suppose, permission.

'It's me that's asking, not Sefton,' said Miriam.

'Yes, of course,' said Billy. 'It's not the Indian. It's just my Triumph.'

'I'd love to ride your Triumph,' said Miriam.

'If you're sure?'

'Quite sure.'

'It's quite a journey, riding pillion, miss.'

'Oh, I think I'll cope. Sefton's fine on his own, aren't you, Sefton? You don't need me to hold your hand, do you?'

I had no choice but to agree.

Billy locked up the door to the Wall of Death and we began walking through the now deserted Kursaal, the crowds already having departed. Suddenly there was the sound of a siren in the distance, and then all the lights went out.

'What on earth?' said Miriam.

'Power cut?' I said.

'Ah, no, I forgot,' said Billy. 'It's the blackout experiment.'

'The what?' said Miriam.

'The blackout experiment.'

'Never heard of it,' said Miriam.

'Have you not read about it, miss?'

'No.'

'They're trying these blackout experiments all over the country. Wartime conditions, they say. You get the siren and then the blackout – to give warning of the approach of enemy aircraft. We should get moving,' said Billy. 'Or we'll never get home.'

And so the three of us ran through the deserted

Kursaal, in the dark, to the sound of sirens, Miriam taking Billy's hand and me following on behind.

I drove back alone through Essex, thinking all the time about Billy riding with Miriam. The last thing I heard her say was, *'Non sto più nella pelle.'* She was, I think, referring to his Triumph.

CHAPTER 24

OIL AND DIRT

I t was our last morning in Colchester – a damp windy autumn morning that promised only wind and rain and yet more wind and rain. We couldn't leave soon enough.

Of all the counties we visited, Essex seemed to me one of the most strange and one of the most difficult, perhaps the most truly incomprehensible; indeed, it was 'trickier than Tibet', according to Morley, in *The County Guides*, and he should know. (See *Morley's Tibetan Tales*, 1930, a book more packed with escapade, and featuring more tricksters, more holy men, more princesses and charlatans than any of his other unbelievable tales of adventure.) *Essex* itself sold more copies than *Wiltshire* and *Hampshire* combined, more than *Leicestershire* and *Warwickshire*, but many fewer than the books on the Ridings, or even on Northumberland. Which counties sold, and why, remained a mystery to me, though Morley thought it had as much to do with the effects of folk memory as it did with the quality of the books themselves. People think they know Yorkshire, though they may never even have visited. They think they know Cornwall and Devon. These places have cultural resonances. They have mental associations. They have a certain *aura*. Len Hutton. The Brontës. Amy Johnson.

But Essex? Who could be said to know Essex? What did Essex represent? What was Essex all about? Many of the counties refused easy summary but Essex seemed to refuse us entirely, defying us as it seemed to defy itself, unable to decide whether it was a place of retreat or a site of attack, seaward-facing, London-looking, Janus-faced, unevenly split and equally uncomfortable in its bulging new towns, its dead and dying ancient villages and its scabby Victorian seaside resorts. In the great parade of the English counties, Essex wore the most ill-fitting suit: it was the odd one out, odder even than Bucks and Shrops and Rutland. It was not really a place at all, I thought, except a place of miscegenation, a dumping ground, a departure point, a place of no return.

I had woken – clearly – in a foul mood. I had barely slept, horribly conscious of being alone and tormented with a sense of both physical lack and terrible desire, a feeling worse even than the morning after some foolish one-night stand and that familiar feeling of being utterly spent and exhausted, yet without satisfaction and still yearning for something more and something better. My mouth tasted gamey and rotten, though I hadn't even been drinking; it was as if I were chewing through my self. My dreams featured Miriam and

Amy Johnson, and not in a good way. I could barely be bothered to shave and put on my suit and tie. I struggled even to get out of bed – yet I was also filled with the impulse to get up and leave and just walk until I could walk no further, until I dropped down, finished, to escape that feeling of entrapment and despair that had haunted me ever since I'd returned from Spain and that may in fact have been with me always, though I hadn't known it. Sometimes the feeling was overwhelming; sometimes I felt that I was just waiting for it finally to overcome me, and to take me down to where I belonged; it was almost as if I could see it, waiting for me, out of the corner of my eye.

It was the sight of Morley, oddly, in the hotel's breakfast room that kept me from going under entirely. The sight of him, bolt upright, tucked away in the corner, tapping away at his beloved Hermes Featherweight, his cup of strong black tea trembling beside him, as though registering the movement of his soul. It occurred to me, seeing him there, that he too was alone, that he too was waiting and was lost. Besides, I had nowhere to go without him.

After a perfunctory breakfast of black coffee and cigarettes for me and the usual bowl of steel-cut oatmeal and fresh-minted pronunciamentoes for Morley – reflections on the meaning of life and its relation to the meaning of architecture, on Mandeville's *Fable of the Bees*, and the trouble with Oscar Wilde, the future of the BBC – we went to Willett's garage to collect the Lagonda.

'I'm sure Miriam will be joining us later,' said Morley.

I wasn't so sure. I thought she was – actually, even now I don't like to think what it was I thought. To distract myself I asked Morley if he had managed to solve the puzzle of the death of Arthur Marden. I was surprised by his answer.

'We shall leave Essex defeated, I fear,' he said.

It was one of the only times during all my years with Morley that I heard him admit to the prospect of defeat. Essex, it seemed, had beaten us all.

Over the door of its workshop and garage Willett's advertised itself with a sign promising 'Prompt, Efficient and Economical Service that Always Leaves Our Customers Satisfied', a proud boast but one that might easily have been replaced with a more accurate sign promising, 'Pompous, Condescending and Supercilious Service that Always Leaves Our Customers Feeling Foolish', the true boast of all self-respecting car showrooms and repair workshops the length and breadth of England. We handed the keys to the Cadillac over to Mr Willett, who silently examined the vehicle for signs of damage, before handing us back the keys to the Lagonda. It was good to see the old girl: over the years the Lagonda, like the family dog or a stout pair of shoes, became a reliable friend. Without the Lagonda there would undoubtedly have been something missing in our lives; and as for me, the Lagonda was just about the closest thing I had to a trusty companion.

Mr Willett examined the summary of repairs provided to him by his mechanics, a summary consisting of several sheets of closely typed onionskin paper.

'So it was giving you a rough ride, is that right?'

'Yes,' I said, 'that's right.'

'Losing power?'

'Not noticeably,' I said – but that was because Miriam was driving the car far beyond its capacities.

'Poor fuel consumption?'

'Yes. We had to stop a couple of times.'

'Surges and stalls?'

'Yes.'

This interrogation went on for some time, until I decided I would answer no more.

'I think you have all the details, Mr Willett,' I said, rather impatiently. 'The only question is – is it fixed?'

'Oh yes,' said Mr Willett. 'It's fixed.'

'Good,' I said, and was ready to leave it at that.

'And what was the problem?' asked Morley.

'Dirt,' said Mr Willett.

'Dirt?'

'Yes. You see you get these tiny little specks of dirt that build up on your filter and prevent the flow of air into the carburettor, and they can disrupt the ratio of fuel to air – it's like the engine is choking on dirt.'

'Exactly as I suspected!' said Morley. 'Choking on dirt! Exactly.' He was absolutely thrilled. Even if he couldn't solve a problem Morley always liked to think that he knew how he would solve a problem, if only he knew how – and so he discussed the problem of dirt in engines and details of the repairs for what seemed like an eternity with Mr Willett, while I refamiliarised myself with the Lagonda. The walnut dash. The rear wing curves. The big chromium-plated exhaust pipes on the side. It was a beauty. I could understand the fascination. But for me the main thing was that they had fixed it: for Morley, the conversation about *how* they had fixed it was just as important, if not more so.

'Any time you're back in Colchester, be sure to visit us again,' said Mr Willett, once we had agreed to pay a king's ransom for the work and the hire of the Cadillac. Morley of course didn't care about the money. I cared a lot: the cost of the repairs alone would have made a significant dent in my debt to Delaney.

'So, Mr Morley,' I said, as we drove away from the workshop. 'That's us then? We can go?'

'Well, actually, there is just one more thing,' said Morley.

'One more thing what?'

'You remember Mr Dunbar yesterday mentioning something about the High Sheriff Ken Cowley having been at loggerheads with Marden about the electrification of the town?'

'Yes,' I said, very vaguely. 'Very vaguely.'

'Well, I've arranged for us to pay a visit to Mr Cowley, just in case.'

'Just in case?'

'Just in case there's something we've missed.'

'What about Miriam?' I asked.

'We can pick her up when we've finished, Sefton. She'll be fine, I'm sure. We must allow her to have her beauty sleep. She's clearly exhausted.'

Indeed.

Cowley's Mill is just outside Colchester, on the Hythe, on the River Colne. The mill itself is an industrial-agricultural style of building, of the kind that's now familiar throughout the country, but which back then was still rather unusual outside dock areas and factories; it was basically a big corrugated-iron hut, built around a steel frame, a building of no architectural merit whatsoever beyond its simple practical purpose. A boiler house and a water tower were bolted on the side and some small cranes stood looming out the back.

'Not so much dark Satanic mill,' said Morley, 'more corrugated Satanic shed, eh?'

There were a couple of very smart-looking vans lined up outside the mill, which proclaimed that Cowley's Mill provided 'Oil, Polish, Paraffin, Lamp Glasses, Lamps and Wicks for Business and Domestic Use'.

'Tidy little business,' said Morley. *'Lux mundi,* eh?'

Having announced ourselves to the site foreman we were shown into Ken Cowley's office, which sat above and within the big metal hut like a captain's cabin overlooking a ship: set up high on metal girders and accessed via a narrow metal staircase, with windows half tilted lengthways, it granted a perfect view of the dozen or so people toiling away in the building below. The place was freezing – cold, damp and humid all at once. On Cowley's desk sat piles of paper, which riffled slightly in the breeze from the mill and the river outside. When we entered, Cowley was speaking loudly on the telephone and vigorously smoking. He waved us in and indicated for us to sit down on two thin metal chairs in front of his desk. He was a man with an oversized belly and a too-loud voice who glistened rather under the office lights; indeed, he had all the appearance of having at some stage actually been dipped in oil. After he had finished his conversation he slammed the phone down and pointed to us.

'Tea?' he asked Morley.

'Tea?' he asked me, before Morley had replied.

'Three teas,' he told the foreman, who was hovering by the door, and who immediately departed.

'You can't get the staff, can you, eh?'

'Quite,' agreed Morley, who as far as I was aware had no staff problems at all: he had Miriam running his day-to-day affairs, me to assist, Mr Humphrey his occasional butler, Mrs Brittain his 'Maid of all Work', his cook Mrs Christie, gardener and estate manager Mr Henry, and plenty of people from the village for all other purposes in times of need. There was no staffing crisis back at St George's.

'Now, how can I help you gentlemen?' asked Ken Cowley, grinning widely and looking at us properly for the first time, at which his face instantly clouded and darkened and his grin vanished. 'Hold on, weren't you at the council meeting on Friday?'

'Were we?' said Morley, caught momentarily off-guard.

'Yes, you were. I remember the pair of you. You were causing all sorts of trouble.'

'Ah, yes,' said Morley. 'That *was* us, Mr Cowley. Yes, of course. We are . . .' He looked across to me to dig him out of yet another hole. I considered for a moment allowing us to be ejected from Cowley's Mill so that we could get out of Essex as quickly as possible. Then again, Morley was my employer, and I needed the work.

'We are writing a book about the magnificent and majestic workings of English local democracy,' I said, without conviction, 'renowned throughout the world from the time of Gladstone.'

'That's it!' said Morley. 'That's it.'

'And we're interested in speaking to those people who are involved in running the local council.'

'I see,' said Cowley, flattered, as everyone is always flattered, by the prospect of appearing in a book – until, that is, they actually appear in a book. (At any given time Morley was usually fighting at least one case of libel, defamation or

273

slander. Serious matters of course were left to his lawyers in London but Miriam and I often had to deal with the everyday disgruntled, irritated and annoyed. One man, a shopkeeper in Cumbria who shall remain nameless but whose premises Morley had described in print as 'rather grimy' – which they were – demanded a written apology, which Morley duly provided, along with the gift of a mop, a bucket and a stiff-bristled broom.)

We drank our tea – served, grudgingly, by the foreman – and Morley wasted some time asking Cowley pointless questions about the functioning of the council and the role of the High Sheriff, until eventually he brought matters round to the death of Arthur Marden.

'Very unfortunate,' said Mr Cowley. 'Great loss, great loss.'

'I understand that you and Mr Marden didn't always see eye to eye,' said Morley.

'I don't know who told you that,' said Cowley.

'Just council titter-tatter, I suppose,' said Morley.

'Well, local politics, Mr Morley. Can be a messy business.'

'And things were *messy* between you and Mr Marden?'

'I wouldn't say messy, no. We had our differences, certainly.'

'Differences?'

Cowley leaned back in his chair. He seemed to glisten ever more brightly under the lights. 'You're a businessman, Mr Morley, are you?'

'I am a writer and journalist, sir.'

'But you work for yourself or you work for someone else?'

'I work for myself, sir, and always have done.'

'So basically you manufacture and supply goods or services to others, yes?'

'That's one way of putting it, yes,' agreed Morley. 'If we understand words as goods or services.'

'So you'll understand me.'

'I always do my best, sir.'

'Well, the situation is this, Mr Morley: I'm running a business here and I want to protect my business, just the same as you want to protect your business, don't you?'

'I suppose I do, yes.'

'So if someone came to you, say, and they said – let's imagine – they were going to replace all the books and newspapers in the world with some other form of communication, I don't know what it would be . . .'

'Radio waves?' said Morley. 'Telephones? Electromechanical machines—'

'Whatever. You would try to protect your career as a writer of books, would you not?'

'I'm sure I would, yes. Or I might learn to adapt to the new—'

'Because if you don't protect your business, who is going to?' said Cowley.

'No one?'

'Correct, Mr Morley. No one.'

'So you felt that Marden presented a threat to your business interests?'

'I did, Mr Morley, I did, I'll be honest with you. But it wasn't just about the business; and to be clear, I had no argument with the mayor himself. I enjoyed good relations with him over the years. I simply felt that he was going too fast for the town. Pushing things forward that really require a lot more time and reflection.'

'You wanted to slow it up, the electrification?'

'Yes. I think that's what a town council is for, Mr Morley. It's to put the brakes on schemes that have maybe got out of control. To act as a fail-safe mechanism.'

'You are in fact describing the healthy functioning of democratic and accountable government, sir!'

'Exactly,' said Mr Cowley. 'Which is why I was always . . . agitating – behind the scenes, you understand – or encouraging, you might say, a more considered approach. There are very big issues at stake here, Mr Morley, not just in Colchester, but throughout the country, as I'm sure you're aware.'

'Just remind me of the big issues at stake?' I asked, having just about kept up with this fascinating conversation.

'What I mean is, gentlemen, we have gas lamps and oil lamps everywhere being converted to electricity but we still don't know if it's safe! Does that seem sensible to you?'

'Electricity?' asked Morley.

'Yes.'

'Not safe?' said Morley. 'I think you'll find—'

'I think you'll find, Mr Morley,' said Cowley, raising a hand, 'that nobody really knows if electricity is safe or not.'

'But—'

'But oil, on the other hand, has stood the test of time. The Romans used oil—'

'The Chinese,' said Morley.

'I'm sure. An ancient fuel. A safe fuel. And yet in Colchester alone we've already replaced most of the old oil lamps that used to light the town – and we've no more than maybe a dozen or so lamplighters left. One day soon if we're not careful there'll be none.'

'So you're thinking of local employment and safety, rather than your own business interests?' said Morley.

'*As well* as my own business interests, Mr Morley. That's right, yes. That's exactly right.'

'So it's a big mistake then, the electrification of the town?'

'I think so, yes.'

'And now that Marden's gone?'

'It makes no difference, I'm afraid. You've seen what they're doing to the roads, Mr Morley. It's all under way now. The damage has been done.'

This rather low note concluded, thank goodness, our discussion of the electrification of Colchester. I thought we'd escaped.

'Now, while you're here I'm sure you'd like to see the process?' offered Mr Cowley.

'We should really—' I began.

'Of course,' said Morley. 'That would be fascinating.'

In fairness, it was mildly – but only mildly – interesting. Cowley took us down and showed us around the mill. Touring factories, foundries, mills and other places of work was one of the great privileges of working with Morley – like being in one's own never-ending *Pathé Gazette* – as well as one of the great disadvantages. I have no doubt that if society were to collapse tomorrow and everything had to be re-invented and redesigned and built and manufactured that Morley would have had all the skills and knowledge to be able to rebuild civilisation pretty much by himself and entirely from scratch. Alas, I seemed to forget how to make a rivet or a typewriter ribbon almost as soon as I was shown how.

'It's a simple process,' said Cowley; but that's what they all said, and it never was.

For future reference, the process of manufacturing oil for street lamps in Essex in 1937 went something like this.

The very rear of the building backs on to the river. This is where the barges come, and where sacks of seeds and nuts are unloaded onto a rattling conveyor belt that brings them into the mill, where they are then run through heavy metal rollers, and heated by steam in vast vats, which are covered with what I assumed was canvas but which Cowley assured us were in fact special woollen sheets, before being placed into a hydraulic press, where the oil begins to flow into the metal pipework that runs eventually into wooden barrels and steel vats.

'And there's your street lighting,' said Cowley, pointing to the barrels.

'And the residue?' asked Morley.

'Is made into oilseed cake which is cut into blocks and allowed to cool' – Cowley pointed over to racks where what looked like yellow blocks of fat were being stored – 'and which is then sold to farmers for cattle feed.'

'Pretty efficient, then?' said Morley.

'This business is all about efficiency, Mr Morley.'

'Excellent,' said Morley, 'excellent.'

Bear all this in mind, in case of catastrophe and the collapse of the pylons.

We left the mill with a couple of slabs of complimentary seedcake for Morley's animals back at St George's, but despite this generous gift, which Morley would normally have been delighted to receive – I'd known him to write letters of thanks to farmers for gifts of windfall, to children who sent him scribbles and drawings, and to lady admirers who sent him poems and monogrammed handkerchiefs – he seemed despondent.

'What do you think?' he asked.

'Think about what?'

'Cowley.'

'He seemed like a—'

'Decent enough sort of businessman, would you say, Sefton?'

I was going to say something else, but was keen to get away and so thought it better to agree.

'Yes,' I said. 'He seemed decent enough.'

'Yes. Did he strike you as the sort of chap likely to murder a rival?'

'You never can tell with these things, Mr Morley,' I said.

'No, of course. But on balance?'

'Probably not.'

'That's what I thought. Shame.'

'Why?'

'Because it means we're no closer to discovering Marden's fate.'

CHAPTER 25

IN THE TRENCHES

On our way back into Colchester we were once again held up in the town's grid-locked streets. Armed with forks, shovels and pickaxes, gangs of men were slowly trenching their way through the town. Policemen were on point duty at the top of North Hill and Headgate Corner.

'Come on, then,' said Morley. 'Let's get a couple of photographs of the excavations and then we'll pick up Miriam and bid the place farewell.'

We pulled over in the car, next to a trench where men were manhandling a rotten, rust-eaten pipe up out of the ground.

'Excuse me,' said Morley, clambering down into the trench, which could accommodate quite a crowd.

'Yes, sir?'

'I wonder if we might take a couple of photographs and ask you about your work?'

'I suppose,' said one of the men.

I clambered down into the trench also.

'Who are you?' asked Morley.

'We're the Gas,' said the man.

'And we're the Water,' said another, not a few yards away. 'And him down there' – he pointed a few feet further down the trench – 'they're the Electric.'

'The full complement!' said Morley. 'Working together in perfect harmony for a better Colchester!'

'That's one way of putting it,' said the Gas man.

'Trouble is, we hit one of theirs,' said the Water man, 'and then they hit one of ours, and we have to start all over again.'

'I see,' said Morley.

'The whole thing's taking months,' said the Gas man.

'It'll take years,' shouted the Electric man.

'And when are the works scheduled for completion?' asked Morley.

'No idea,' said the Water man. 'You can ask the foreman.'

'Who is?'

'Mr Campbell.'

'And where is Mr Campbell?'

'I don't know, mister, but you can be sure he'll find you before you find him.'

And sure enough, a ferocious-looking Mr Campbell was in fact bearing down upon us at that very moment.

'What do you think you're doing in my hole?' he shouted down at us.

Morley used his charms to placate Mr Campbell, explaining why we were in his hole and our purposes in writing a book about Essex – and

282

Mr Campbell proved to be as kind and helpful as anyone we'd met. 'The key to all human interaction,' Morley often advised me, 'is simply to ask others about themselves. Nothing else matters – and everything then follows.'

'How did you end up as foreman on the works?' asked Morley, taking his own advice, after having persuaded Mr Campbell to allow us to take as many photographs and as many notes as we liked.

'I'd been quarrying for years,' said Mr Campbell. 'And then I left and started working the roads.'

'Ah. And where were you quarrying, in Essex?'

'It was Marden's quarry, out on the Lexden Road.'

'Marden, as in Arthur Marden?'

'That's right.'

'It's still there?'

'Most of the land's been sold now.'

'And so you left.'

'I left before that.'

'Can I ask why?'

'It was a long time ago now, sir. Twenty or more years. We were working at the bottom of a pit, me and Harry Ball, beneath a big sloping bank of sand and gravel – thirty foot or more it must have been – and we were in this hole that was maybe six foot deep. And there was a sort of a crack and this wall of earth came down like, hit poor old Harry, trapped him up to his neck.'

'Oh dear,' said Morley.

'And so we were trying to get him out but we couldn't do it. He was choking, you see.'

'Choking?'

'On all the dirt and sand and gravel. He went blue in the face, and that was it.'

'Dear me.'

'I tell you what, sir, I was in the war with the Essex Regiment, but that was the worst thing that ever happened to me, God's honest truth.'

'That is *awful*,' said Morley.

'It was. And worst of it was, the borough coroner said he thought the pit was safe, and so poor Billy and his mother never got a penny but of course Marden went from strength to strength—'

'This is Arthur Marden?'

'That's right.'

'The mayor? Who died last week?'

'Indeed. Some people might say it was a sort of comeuppance, I suppose.'

'Did you say Billy Ball?' I asked. 'Was he the son of the man who died in the quarry?'

'That's right.'

'Who's Billy Ball?' said Morley.

'He works at the jeweller's,' I said. 'I met him at the Oyster Feast. Miriam's met him.'

'Miriam's met him?'

I didn't explain under what circumstances Miriam had met him.

'Harry's son,' said Mr Campbell. 'He's turned out all right.'

'Did you say you met him at the Oyster Feast, Sefton?'

'Yes. He was serving, and he helped me when

284

I cut my hand.' I held up my hand, in evidence. 'I was opening an oyster.'

'I see. And he helped you how?'

'He got a dressing for my hand.'

'When was this?'

'Just shortly before Marden died.'

Morley's eyes widened, his moustache twitched, his weskit throbbed from within. I'd seen it before. He suddenly sprang up out of the trench like a mountain goat ascending the Matterhorn.

'We need to go,' he said.

I clambered up out of the trench after him.

'Thank you, Mr Campbell,' said Morley. 'You have been most helpful.'

We got back in the Lagonda, drove as quickly as was possible under the circumstances and parked outside the George Hotel.

'I just need to check something,' said Morley.

'Right-o,' I said.

He went not to the hotel but to the Town Hall.

I smoked a cigarette.

'Excellent,' he said, when he returned.

'Where did you go?'

'To the toilets, Sefton, of course.'

'I see.'

'And now for your friend at the jeweller's.'

CHAPTER 26

JUMBO

As we arrived at Hopwood's jewellers and pawnbrokers it began to rain outside. (But of course it did. It could hardly rain inside. In one of his most famous and most frequently reprinted articles, 'The Rain Inside', first published in a short-lived little magazine called *Babel* in 1931, Morley corrects and disciplines a number of what he called 'lazy' idioms and phrases, including 'burning fires', 'safe havens' and 'wept tears' – rather ironically, since he was himself utterly devoted to all forms of redundancy and repetition in both his speech and in his writing. 'Hate the pleonasm, love the pleonast,' he sometimes liked to say in his defence.)

'I wonder if we could have a word with Mr Ball?' asked Morley of the man who had greeted me on Saturday, and who I assumed was Mr Hopwood himself.

'Mr Ball. Yes, of course, sir. Excellent timing.'

'Is it?' Morley consulted his watches.

'Just in out of the rain, I mean.'

'Ah, yes.'

'And indeed you're just in time to catch Billy.'

'Just in time?'

'I'm afraid he's leaving us.'

'Leaving?'

'Yes. Today's his last day. Going off on his travels. Taking off on his motorbike, apparently. You know what these young fellows are like! Full of dreams of adventure.'

'I see,' said Morley.

'But when you get to our age, of course! A different matter. Pipe and slippers.'

Morley looked utterly nonplussed. His life was one perpetual adventure. He was on a never-ending tour.

'We're going to miss him here, I have to say. A highly valued member of staff, our Mr Ball.'

'Is that right?'

'Indeed. Very popular. In fact, usually if an employee asks to leave we have to insist that they go immediately – for obvious reasons. You can't keep someone on in a jeweller's if you know they're intending to go!'

'Of course. And when did he decide to leave?'

'Oh, a few weeks ago. But he didn't decide until Friday that he'd be leaving us today.'

'I see.'

'He's been with us for so long and he's so popular with everyone, such a trusted member of staff. I really don't know what we're going to do without him.'

'I see. I wonder if we might have a word?'

'Of course.'

And so Mr Hopwood absented himself and Billy soon appeared from behind the curtain, as he had done before. He was looking surprisingly fresh and refreshed, dressed in shopwear and no longer done up in his dashing Wall of Death outfit.

'Mr Sefton,' he said, nodding to me with not a hint of shame.

'Billy.'

'How can I help you this morning?'

'Billy, this is Mr Swanton Morley,' I said.

They shook hands.

'Mr Morley is Miriam's father.'

Billy blanched. 'I see.'

'You've met my daughter, I understand,' said Morley.

'That's correct, sir,' said Billy hesitantly. 'Is everything all right?'

'Everything's fine. Yes, we didn't come to talk about Miriam!' said Morley.

'Of course not,' said Billy, cheering considerably.

'She can speak for herself,' said Morley.

'Yes,' agreed Billy. 'Well, how can I help you gents this morning? Do you need some more help with your valuation, Mr Sefton?'

'Your valuation, Sefton?' asked Morley.

'It was just something I was thinking of getting valued,' I said.

'Yes, a rather fine and rare lady's cigarette case,' said Billy.

'We'll leave that for another time,' I said.

'Indeed,' said Morley. 'We shall. Our visit this

morning concerns not so much how you might help us but more how we might be able to help *you.*'

'How so?'

'Well, I should perhaps start at the beginning. I was lucky enough to be a guest at the Oyster Feast last week. I understand from Sefton here that you were serving on the night?'

'That's right.'

'The night that Arthur Marden died.'

'Yes.'

'You'll have heard all the rumours that are flying around, of course.'

'I try not to take any notice of rumours, Mr Morley.'

'Quite right,' said Morley. 'In a small town. Unwise. And quite quite ludicrous, many of the rumours, as rumours so often are: "a pipe blown by surmises, jealousies, conjectures and of so easy and so plain a stop that the blunt monster with uncounted heads, the still-discordant wavering multitude, can play upon it."'

'Yes,' said Billy hesitantly.

'*Henry IV, part II,*' said Morley, in clarification. 'I certainly don't think Marden was murdered, for example,' he added.

'No?' said Billy, with great relief.

I wasn't quite sure where the conversation was going, so what Billy made of it goodness only knows.

'No,' said Morley. 'I think it was an entirely

natural death. I think Arthur Marden simply choked on an oyster.'

'Choked?'

'Yes, like a little bit of grit in the engine,' said Morley. 'Like in a car.'

Billy's face remained impassive.

'You see, when we saw Marden leaving the Moot Hall on the night of the Oyster Feast I think we all naturally assumed that he was . . . well, that he was going to use the toilet.'

'Yes?'

'But I don't think he was answering a call of nature, Mr Ball.'

'No?'

'Indeed not, sir. I think it was a matter of survival. Of self-preservation. I think he was dying. I think he was choking. I think he made his way to the toilets, panicking, in shock. I think perhaps an item of food the size of – let us say – a native no.2 oyster, had lodged at the top of his trachea, and his windpipe had closed around it and gripped it.' Morley mimicked what one might imagine to be the windpipe gripping at a native no.2 oyster. 'Swift action might have saved him, at that point. If someone was there. Someone who knew what was happening.'

'I see.'

'Yes. And I think you were that person, Billy.'

'Me?' He looked genuinely shocked and confused.

'Yes, you.'

'You think I was there when Marden was choking?'

'To death,' said Morley.

'What on earth makes you think that?'

'You were with my assistant here, Sefton, I understand, in the kitchens of the Town Hall, but at a certain point you excused yourself and left him.'

'I went to go and get a dressing for Sefton's hand.'

'Yes, that's right. From the first-aid kit, which is kept of course – as I've just discovered – in the gentlemen's toilets at the Town Hall.'

Billy no longer looked confused. He looked defiant.

'You can't prove that I did anything.'

'No, that's right. But I think we could prove that you did nothing, Billy.'

'What?'

'I think you watched Arthur Marden die, choking to death.'

'Why would I do that?'

'Why indeed? Perhaps because your own father had been suffocated all those years ago in Marden's quarry? Choked to death on dirt. Were you seeking to kill Marden that night, I wonder, or was it merely an opportunity that presented itself? An opportunity to do nothing, that you thought would solve everything?'

'That's ridiculous. I have never heard such nonsense in my life,' said Billy, having edged his way back towards the curtain behind the counter.

'"And Saul went in to cover his feet,"' said Morley.

'What?' said Billy.

'Sorry, Mr Morley?' I said.

'It's 1 Samuel 24:3, isn't it? David is hiding in a cave from Saul when Saul comes in to evacuate his bowels. And so God delivers Saul into David's hands.'

'Right,' I said.

'Similar situation here, in many ways.'

'Is it?'

'Sefton!'

But it was too late. Billy had taken the opportunity during Morley's moment of biblical exegesis to turn suddenly and disappear behind the curtain.

I followed him through the back of the shop, through the workshop, apologising to Mr Hopwood, through the storeroom and out onto the streets of Colchester, where the wind and rain had picked up and the sun was hidden by cloud: it could have been night-time and for half a moment I remember thinking, some places look better in the grey and the rain – almost as if they're varnished, or had been varnished a long time ago, in their heyday, and now were visible only through the blur. The rain, I thought, suited Colchester – a town no longer anything like a capital, a town of soldiers and civilians uneasily at peace. It was the perfect weather for a chase, and the perfect place.

Billy had mounted his motorbike. According to the police report, he headed through the town, onto Sir Isaac's Walk, and then onto Head Street, past Headgate Street, through the churchyard of St Mary's and around the old Roman wall towards the Balkerne Gate, which was by chance exactly where I was running towards. It was one of the only places in town I knew.

As I was running towards the gate, to my astonishment, Billy came riding towards me, swerved and came skidding to a halt at the bottom of Jumbo, the vast water tower that loomed over the town.

Jumbo – as readers of *The County Guides: Essex* will be aware – consists of a massive central tower and four supporting columns of red brick, of which more than a million were used in its construction, at a cost of £11,000 to build, to support a water tank with a capacity of over 200,000 gallons to supply the town with water, and that at its peak stands over 130 feet above ground level, and with a room at the top named Wicks' Folly, named after the councillor who saw through its construction. But readers will not know, perhaps, that there is a spiral staircase running up the central tower, or indeed what it feels like to run up that staircase, the rain coursing down the brick like flowing blood, and nothing but the sound of feet rattling on metal, and pigeons, and the sound of your heart hammering in your ears.

Wicks' Folly is a room with windows on all sides, affording a magnificent view of the whole of Colchester and far beyond, even in the thick varnishing rain. There were blankets neatly piled on the floor, tins of food stacked under the window, a few candles, a hurricane lamp, everything required for a little hideaway.

The three of us filled the space: me, Billy Ball and a young woman I recognised instantly from the newspaper at Edward Mountjoy's: Arthur Marden's daughter, Florence.

'Now, we haven't done anyone any harm here, Mr Sefton,' said Billy, gasping, standing between me and Florence, once we had both just about recovered our breath.

'I'm sorry but I think you have, Billy,' I gasped back.

'What are you doing here?' Florence asked. And then more panicked, 'What's he doing here, Billy?'

'It's OK, Florence,' he said.

'It's OK, Florence,' I said. 'I'm here to help.'

'Don't listen to him,' said Billy, pushing Florence further behind him.

'Have you told her about Arthur?' I asked.

'Father? What about Father?' said Florence.

'Have you told her, Billy?'

'Why? What?' Florence was becoming increasingly agitated. 'What's happened to Father?' She was pulling at Billy's arm from behind.

'Nothing,' said Billy. 'It's nothing.'

'Do you want to tell her, Billy, or shall I?'

'What's he talking about, Billy?'

'If you don't tell her, Billy, I will.'

Billy shook his head – at me, at Florence, at everything that had come to pass.

'He's dead,' I said.

'Dead?' said Florence.

'I'm so sorry,' I said.

'He's lying,' said Billy.

'Billy, Billy!' said Florence, violently tugging at Billy's arm. 'Who is this man? What's happening?'

'You really haven't told her, have you?'

'He's lying,' repeated Billy.

'It's not me that's lying, Florence,' I said. 'It's Billy. Has he even told you about his own father?'

'Billy's father's dead,' said Florence.

'I know,' I said. 'He died when Billy was a boy. And do you know how?' And then without waiting for an answer I added, 'He died in an accident.'

'Why are you telling me all this? Who are you?' asked Florence.

'Come on, why don't you tell her, Billy?'

Billy was silent for a moment.

'We just wanted to be together. He didn't think I was good enough for his daughter. I was working so hard to prove him wrong.'

'Billy!' cried Florence. 'What's happened?'

'We were just going to – I had all the money from the Wall of Death – Florence was safe here – and we . . .' You could see and hear all Billy's plans and dreams collapsing as he spoke.

'It was in a quarry, Florence,' I said quietly. 'Billy's father died in a quarry.'

'A quarry?'

'Your father's quarry.'

'What?'

'I'm afraid so, and a few days ago, at the Oyster Feast, Billy took the opportunity to—'

Which is when Billy lunged for me, his face suddenly contorted with rage. He gave out a roar as he leapt forward but fortunately I twitched back as he came and Florence still had a restraining hand on his arm, enough for him to hesitate as he grabbed for me and allowing me to swing with my bandaged hand – the hand he had bandaged – to hit him hard on the side of the head. I have no doubt that the punch hurt me more than it hurt him. But what happened next hurt us all.

Florence was pulling Billy back, I was pulling him towards me. We all tumbled towards the doorway and I dragged him with me as I began to fall down the short flight of steps that led down to the water tank; as we fell Florence remained and stood and locked the door of the room behind us.

Billy aimed a kick at my head but then he turned and leapt up the steps, rattling at the door handle.

'Florence!' he yelled. 'Florence! I can explain! I can explain!'

But there was no more explaining to be done.

He turned and leapt down the stairs. I thought he was coming back to finish me off but he ran across the dark, airless space above the water tank towards one of the narrow arched wall openings. I got up and followed, by which time he had

296

wrenched open a door that led outside onto a narrow parapet that ran around the edge of the tower. I remember the gust of cold air come rushing in like toxic gas, and the sudden flash of light and I realised what he was planning. He was going to climb up outside to rescue Florence. He had no fear of heights: he was used to the Wall of Death. As he pulled himself up onto the parapet I called his name and he turned and I reached out my hand towards him to pull him back in but he twisted around and leaned back as I did so, presumably thinking I was about to strike him again. I didn't touch him. I had no intention of striking him. And he fell. The moment before he fell I thought he somehow stood a little straighter, as if a sudden realisation of his own height and powers had surprised him, the recognition that everything below was so small and so insignificant, and he fell back and over the cast-iron guard rail that ran around the tower, his still, perfectly parted hair still perfectly parted, falling from the tower. At the sound of his scream – Florence had opened the door of Wicks' Folly and come flying down the steps – it was all I could do to stop her jumping after him. She was still screaming when PC Adkins arrived and we managed to get her down.

CHAPTER 27

PARADISE, NORFOLK

We returned to Norfolk in low spirits. Of all the books we wrote together, Essex was perhaps the most bitter: born in disagreement, compiled amid argument and confusion and completed in despair. As we pieced together our notes and photographs in the dull autumn days that followed our return, Miriam and I argued endlessly – ending in a terrible fight one evening after we had both been drinking heavily that I regret to say concluded with our coming to blows. She had accused me of causing Billy's death – and perhaps she was right. I tried to explain to her again what had happened and she had slapped me, and then slapped me again, and then began sobbing and when I tried to apologise and to comfort her she went to slap me again. I tried to restrain her and she screamed at me to go away and – well, the whole thing was just a mess.

Morley of course worked on despite all this, burning bright in his perpetual furnace of endless work and self-renewal. He'd been right all along: Marden had died of natural causes and human cruelty. For him the whole episode in Essex was certainly unfortunate but the books were the only things that really mattered, and the completion of the next book, which would allow us to begin another, enabling us to head out again and to start anew, in order to try to define the thing that is by its very nature indefinable, as if our next journey and discovery could possibly prove or solve anything about England or anywhere. *The County Guides*, I came to realise many years later, was not a quest: it was an illness.

We worked all together in the library at St George's, working through our meals and often through the night, plates on our knees – cold chicken and ham provided by the cook – with a fine log fire that Morley tended as one might tend a new-born baby. Late at night he would occasionally doze in his wide armchair, a bookrest before him set with his notebooks and papers ready for when he awoke. He slept, I noted, exactly as he was when awake: jaw firm, breathing calm and steady but his arms and legs restless, as though ready to leap up in amazement or astonishment at any moment.

As for Miriam, for years after, she would not speak to me about Billy Ball. For years she carried with her a signed photograph of him and eventually she persuaded Morley to buy her a motorbike, a Brough Superior SS100, the Rolls-Royce of motorbikes, set up to her exact specification, with a wide saddle and the controls on the left-hand side and within the handlebars, to resemble Billy's

Indian Scout, and so that she had one hand free, like a Chicago cop, to be able to shoot her revolver. She would often go out riding at night, on the coast road, up to Wells and to Holkham and far beyond, riding too fast and going too far.

As promised, Morley had arranged for a cottage in the grounds of St George's to be spruced up and to be put at my disposal and the day after my big argument with Miriam, not a day too soon, the cottage was miraculously ready. Or as near ready as it needed to be. Morley was not entirely oblivious to the arguments going on around him. Finally I had somewhere to live and somewhere to be alone.

The cottage was small and secluded, tucked away at the very edge of the estate, in a little thicket of laurel and rhododendron. If you didn't know it was there you would never have been able to find it. It had thick walls, part stone, part brick, four rooms, two up, two down, no kitchen, no running water and no electricity. The roof and floors had been rotten and had been replaced and in order to brighten things up Morley had had many windows punched in – square windows, round windows, portholes, whatever spares he could find around the estate – which gave a wonderful view of the trees: oak, birch, an ilex, firs. It also made it terribly cold: after rain the trees would drip great raindrops onto the roof and onto the glass for hours and even in the summer the place verged on the chilly rather than the pleasantly cool.

Inside it had been treated with some kind of anti-woodworm poisoning and so everything had been stripped out and stripped back, reducing it to its bare minimum, the bare bones of a building. Flagged stone floors downstairs, wooden boards upstairs, an ancient stone staircase connecting the two.

Downstairs was the storeroom, for firewood and for all Morley's old junk, everything that had been half discarded from St George's: a vast phonograph, and phonograph parts, bicycles and bicycle parts, an odd assortment of chairs and tools, blunt axes and mementoes from his travels. Beyond the storeroom was a tiny bathroom, filled with an enormous bath, big enough for two, which Morley had recovered from a public baths in London and which he had christened Hercules. The walls in the windowless bathroom he'd had covered in thick dark sheet cork, which gave the room the appearance of a cave. There was no sink – water had to be hand-pumped from the nearby stream, and carried to the cottage in buckets – and there was no toilet.

'Ah yes, you're probably wondering,' said Morley when he gave me the guided tour. 'Let me show you the toilet.' And with that he opened the door and pointed outside, beyond the cottage's rickety wooden fence to the wooded glade beyond. 'Rather well-appointed, don't you think?' He then handed me a spade. 'You'll be needing this.'

Upstairs was one small windowless room which

Morley referred to as the pantry, which he'd had fitted with shelves and lined with aluminium, to keep the room at a constant temperature, and one large room which became my bedroom, study and sitting room, with an open stone fireplace, more shelves and a wooden plank set into the wall under one of the windows for a desk. There was no bed as such; instead, in the middle of the room Morley had had a low raised platform built over some old steamer trunks, for storage, which slid out from underneath, on top of which was a solid mattress with a thick cow-hide covering, a sleeping bag, a shabby quilt, and enough horse-hair cushions to satisfy the most demanding of loungers – more a resting place than sleeping place, but which did me well.

Basically it was in this room for the remainder of my years with Morley that I lived my entire life: when we weren't travelling this was where I worked, ate, slept and played. Strange and spartan as it was, I loved it. It had everything I needed. If I wasn't eating in the main house with Morley and Miriam I could boil tea and eggs on the fire and listen to records on Morley's old phonograph. My home-cooked meals consisted solely of bread, butter, honey, jam, cold potted things and things in tins. For fire-lighting Morley gave me one of the strange black egg-type firelighters that he had picked up in America many years before, and which he so admired, made of some kind of asbestos-type material on a wire handle, which sat by the fire in a pint pot of paraffin oil, ready to be lit and set to logs at any moment. The whole cottage therefore forever smelled of paraffin, sardines, tobacco and damp.

'We call it the old cottage,' said Morley, having shown me round, 'but you may name it whatever you will.'

'I think I'll call it . . . Paradise,' I said.

And so Paradise it became.

On the day we finished *Essex* I walked up to the main house for dinner, a walk of perhaps a quarter of a mile. It was late October but already it felt as though everything was packing up for winter. Across the stream the rushes were withering and the reeds were turning yellow. In the hedgerows there were blackberries, elderberry, hawthorn and crabapples. The beech leaves were turning gold and the chestnuts crimson, and in among the rotting tree stumps spiders had made their homes.

As I approached the house, up through the passageway of box and red-berried yews, I reached into my jacket pocket. I had Amy Johnson's cigarette case, which I was intending to hand over to Morley that night to return to Miss Johnson. It was the right thing to do. It was a scorching reminder of my sins and failings and of all our misunderstandings in Essex. It might easily have paid off some of my debt to Delaney, but in the end it would only have cost me more. Also, what I didn't mention to Morley or to Miriam was that in my struggle with Billy at the top of Jumbo I had seized from him the ceremonial silver oyster that he had presumably stolen from the mayor while he lay dying – and which was worth much more than Amy Johnson's cigarette case.

With my few free days in between books I travelled down to London, where I was easily able to find a buyer for the silver oyster at Klein's Russian Turkish Baths, and thus to present Delaney with his money. I then happily spent my time in Soho catching up with friends, making new friends, and consoling myself in the only way I knew how.

When I eventually returned to St George's, reporting in again for our next assignment, I found Morley and Miriam in the kitchen, Morley at his typewriter, of course, and Miriam instructing the cook over a meal.

'Aha!' said Morley. 'In your honour, Sefton! We are dining tonight in your honour!'

'My honour?'

It was oysters.

'Well, we thought we might enjoy our own modest oyster feast. Help us all to put Essex behind us, eh? We must move forward, you see. Always moving forward. The world is our brine, Sefton, and we are oysters, extracting whatever nutriment we can from the ebb and flow!'

'Very good, Mr Morley,' I said. 'Very good.'

We ate and tried not to argue. Morley revealed that in recognition of his work in uncovering the truth about the death of Arthur Marden, Colchester Town Council had arranged for him to have the rare honour of having a rose named after him by the Essex rose growers Benjamin R. Cant & Sons, 'The Home of the Rose', according to Morley, who were based just outside Colchester and who produced, apparently, 'the finest and hardiest roses in the world'.

'Congratulations, Father,' said Miriam. 'Next time you might consider having a cocktail named after you.'

'The Morley,' said Morley. 'I suppose it does have a certain ring to it. What do you think, a weeping standard, a standard on a briar, a climber, or a rambler?'

Miriam looked at me and I looked at her. It was the only time during the whole meal she deigned even to exchange a glance.

'Oh, I think a rambler, don't you?'

'Definitely a rambler,' I agreed.

After the meal, as I was about to head down to the cottage, Morley drew me aside.

'We must all work together, Sefton, you understand?'

'Yes, Mr Morley.'

'Me, you and Miriam. *The County Guides* rely upon us. We must take care of one another.'

'Of course.'

'And you, young man, must take care yourself. Do you understand?'

'I think so, Mr Morley.'

'You must be careful, yes?'

'I'll certainly try, Mr Morley.'

'Good, good.'

When I made it back down to Paradise I found that Morley had deposited some of his old reading copies of Dickens; the first book on the top of the pile was *Great Expectations*, open at the page at which Magwitch remarks, 'I first became aware of myself down in Essex, thieving turnips.' In the margin, in Morley's hand, was a tiny pencilled asterix. I took it – as it was doubtless intended – as a reminder and as a warning.

ACKNOWLEDGEMENTS

For previous acknowledgements see *The Truth About Babies* (Granta Books, 2002), *Ring Road* (Fourth Estate, 2004), *The Mobile Library: The Case of the Missing Books* (Harper Perennial, 2006), *The Mobile Library: Mr Dixon Disappears* (Harper Perennial, 2007), *The Mobile Library: The Delegates' Choice* (Harper Perennial, 2008), *The Mobile Library: The Bad Book Affair* (Harper Perennial, 2010), *Paper: An Elegy* (Fourth Estate, 2012), *The Norfolk Mystery* (2013), *Death in Devon* (2015) and *Westmorland Alone* (2016). These stand, with exceptions. In addition I would like to thank the following. (The previous terms and conditions apply: some of them are dead; most of them are strangers; the famous are not friends; none of them bears any responsibility.)

Stig Abell, Roger Ashton-Griffiths, A-Wa, T.J. Binyon, Valerie Bistany, Susan J. Blackmore, Adrian Bliss, Ernest Bramah, Eoin Butler, Peter Buwalda, Cafe Zédel, Mark Campbell, Maria Alessandra Chessa, Pema Chödrön, Agatha Christie, Coey and Johnstone, John Curran, Gerald Dawe, Meaghan Delahunt, Dublin City Library

Service, Jean Echenoz, the English Library (Alassio), Scott Flannigan, Lettice Franklin, Pascal Garnier, Hugh Haughton, Margaret Hayes, Abraham Joshua Heschel, Hamid Ismailov, Darryl Jones, Anne-Marie Kelly, Herman Koch, Mark Lauren, Filippo Tommaso Marinetti, Vladimir Mayakovsky, Mike McCormack, Conor McGregor, Cathy McKenna, Duncan Minshall, Chris Morash, Scholastique Mukasonga, Jenny Offill, Judge Eugene O'Sullivan, Eve Patten, Mrs Peabody, Richard Powers, Hilary Putnam, Colin Sackett, Judith Schalansky, Yakob Shabtai, Akhil Sharma, Alessandro Silvestri, Nina Simone, Patti Smith, Gary Snyder, Rabbi Joseph B. Soloveitchik, Stormzy, Brendan Teeling, Yann Tiersen, Daniel Todman, Miriam Toews, Iglika Vassileva, Juan Pablo Villalobos.